A Gathering of Crows

A Meadowbank Mystery

Margaret Alty

Published 2013 by arima publishing

www.arimapublishing.com

ISBN 978 1 84549 594 7
© Margaret Alty 2013

Printed and bound in the United Kingdom

Typeset in Garamond

In this work of fiction, the characters, places and events are either the
product of the author's imagination or they are used entirely fictitiously.
The moral rights of the author have been asserted. Any resemblance to
actual persons, living or dead, is purely coincidental.

Swirl is an imprint of arima publishing.

arima publishing
ASK House, Northgate Avenue
Bury St Edmunds, Suffolk IP32 6BB
t: (+44) 01284 700321

www.arimapublishing.com

Chapter One

In a couple of days the clocks would be put back an hour and the people of Meadowbank would start preparing themselves for the winter ahead and many of the older generation were hoping it wouldn't prove to be as long and severe as the last one, but, more importantly, they wouldn't have to endure another spate of killings, accompanied as they had been by a steady influx of members of the press. Apart from the unwanted media attention, with each shocking incident, they had felt the whole structure of their town shaken to its core and it would take some time to re-establish what their lives had been like before.

The Market Inn would soon be closing for the afternoon, the only customers being the regulars; a handful of the town's pensioners, doing their utmost to eke out what was left of their beer, sitting on bar stools at the far end of the room and facing the front door. This, whether by design or not, gave them an immediate view of each customer as they came in. They weren't saying much, having exhausted their morning exchange of news. No doubt, Melissa Morrison thought, polishing the glasses she had unloaded from the dishwasher, they were saving up what other topics of mutual interest they had left until later on when they would meet up again at opening time. To them, without the familiar haven of their local, their days would have been lonely, especially during the winter months. This morning, they had spent most of it talking about the recent demise of one of Meadowbank's oldest residents, Catherine Miller-Croft. Melissa couldn't help picking up snippets of what they'd been saying each time she had passed them; some of it predictable, gleaned from around the town, but the rest was pure speculation and mostly, Melissa was sure, fabricated from their fertile imaginations, but the final consensus of opinion, and not before a great deal of deliberation, among the four stalwarts, was that the lady must have been at least ninety-five; this being put forward by one of them and, perhaps because none of them were yet approaching that age, they had been quick to nod their agreement. It didn't really matter if this assumption was correct; they now felt comfortably reassured; in their opinion they still had a long way to go!

'I expect young Roy will be looking forward to his walk this afternoon, Melissa.' another of them remarked and simultaneously they all looked over towards the Labrador who, upon hearing his name mentioned, followed by the magic word "walk", pricked up his ears in comical anticipation.

'Oh, yes, Stanley.' Melissa agreed, 'Alright, Roy, I won't be long now and once these gentlemen have finished their drinks we'll go.'

'Well,' Stanley said good-naturedly, wiping the last of the froth from his white moustache, 'we can take a hint, can't we? Come on lads, let's hit the road!'

After a drizzly start to the day, the sun was making its first appearance, but there was a chill in the air; she would need a jacket Melissa decided, taking her fleece down from one of the pegs at the back of the kitchen door and, clipping on Roy's lead, called up to Brian to tell him she was off. He'd gone upstairs to the flat earlier and she knew he would be firmly ensconced in front of the television and looking forward to watching the afternoon racing.

She turned left outside the pub as Roy had fully expected her to do, by this time impatient to get on with his regular afternoon walk and starting to pull on his lead as if to say: "Get a move on, Melissa; I've been stuck in that pub all morning!" Melissa smiled to herself; she enjoyed this time of day: fresh air on her face and the stillness of the town, once she was away from the market square and with precious time to think, something which was impossible in the pub. Life was pretty good, she thought for the umpteenth time, more so since she'd married Brian in the early summer. They were a good team and now they had Derek helping out in the evenings and weekends, it wasn't quite as hectic as it used to be. She knew Brian liked nothing better than being behind the bar; pouring pints and talking to his customers and she was happiest in the kitchen, preparing the meals and devising new menus for the lunches, and now, hearing at the beginning of the week she was pregnant, she felt their lives would really be complete. They hadn't told anyone else yet, wanting to keep the knowledge to themselves for a little while longer, but they had only agreed that morning before they opened up, they'd better not wait too long, given the eagle eyes of the regulars.

Walking past The Bridge Inn she noticed Isobel Gallier had already closed for the afternoon; no doubt having a siesta Melissa decided. Isobel had been on her own for a number of years since her husband had gone; she'd had to work hard and most of the time singlehandedly, but now she was with Terry and although he was working he was always there in the evenings to help out, she must feel a big difference.

There was a piece of waste ground further along Bridge Street where she could let Roy have a good run and work off some of his boundless puppy-dog energy. Also, she knew from experience, the return journey would take longer, with him reluctant to stop playing games only known to dogs and lagging dispiritedly behind her. She was wondering how he would react when the new baby arrived, hoping he wouldn't be jealous, but she didn't think so; he had a placid nature, but she'd have to watch him all the same.

At first, so engrossed in her thoughts, she hadn't noticed the sky ahead darkening, but as she came closer to the waste ground she discovered what she was seeing was not an impending rainstorm after all, but hundreds of crows spreading across the sky, completely obliterating the sun, their wing tips almost touching as they surged forward in one huge black mass and then, as though pulled by invisible wires, swooping down only yards away from where she and Roy were standing, and landing on the waste ground at the other side of the hedge which separated the overgrown area from the road. Roy began to whimper, pushing his body closer to her legs and staring up at her in what she could only describe as a look of pleading. She bent down, stroking him lightly to try and calm him and as she straightened up again more crows were arriving, so close she could easily make out every feature which distinguished the crow species from any other bird of prey. The scene was awesome and slightly scary at the same time, making up her mind it would be best if they didn't go any further, although judging the nervous state the Labrador was in it was unlikely she would be able to persuade him to walk to the far side of the waste ground.

She turned away, not wanting to think what could possibly be the attraction, but Melissa had been brought up in the country and she had a fairly good idea whatever it was concealed behind the hedge would not be a pleasant sight. She recognised the farm truck even before it drew up across the road from her and waited until Phil Nicholson jumped down from the cab and was striding towards her.

'Hello, Melissa,' he called out, 'have you any idea what these devils are up to?'

'No, Phil, it's something at the other side of the hedge; a dead rabbit, maybe.'

'I would say it's something a bit larger than a rabbit. Hello, old boy,' he added, giving Roy a pat on the head, 'you're not too happy, are you?' he added sympathetically.

'There must be hundreds of them, Phil!'

'Thousands, more likely. Quite frankly, Melissa, I don't like this.'

'What do you mean?' for the first time a feeling of unease swept through her. Up to now she had assumed it must be some wild animal, but the expression on Phil Nicholson's face told her something quite different.

'Look, Melissa, I think it would be better if you go back home for now. The last thing I want to do is alarm you, but this might not be pleasant.'

'What are you going to do?' she asked, 'You're not going over there?'

'No, that wouldn't achieve anything, so the only thing which will shift them, only temporarily mind you, is if I fire a couple of shots in the air.'

'And are you going to do that now?'

'Yes, I have my shotgun in the back of the truck; it will only take minutes, but as I said, I don't think you should be here. Also,' he added, 'the noise would be too much for this young chap.'

'Of course,' convinced he was right and she didn't want to stay; cowardly though she was being, she had a feeling it may be too much for her also. 'I'll get back, Phil. By the way, where on earth do all these crows come from?'

'I would say they're nesting in the disused quarry at the end of the road; I've often seen them when I've driven past, not as many, of course. It's about half a mile further along from the farm,' he added, pointing back up the road, 'on the left-hand side; I don't suppose you've ever been there?'

'No.' She shuddered at what that image conjured up in her mind; to actually witness masses of crows all living together, 'Ughh!'

'Quite,' he smiled grimly, 'but we farmers don't actually detest them, you know, Melissa; they happen to keep our crops free from the non-predators who can be a real pest.'

'Normal birds.' she commented, unable to hide her repugnance of those species who fed off dead animals and smaller defenceless birds.

She had reached the closed shutters of The Bridge Inn when she heard the shots being fired; the sound loud and sharp in the quietness of Bridge Street. A much-subdued Roy, who had up until then been walking obediently at her heels, gave a yelp and started to tug on his lead as if to urge her to quicken her step. Melissa looked back to see the crows disperse and scatter fanlike into the air, but not flying away, instead they were hovering above their prey with some of them taking up positions along the top of the hedge. As Phil had predicted, it was only a temporary lull; they would be back.

After giving Roy some water which he lapped up straight away, padding over to his basket next to the Aga, Melissa went upstairs to tell Brian what she'd seen and when she'd finished, asking him what he thought.

'It could be a farm animal, I suppose,' he suggested, a puzzled expression on his face, 'I don't know, Melissa. The only farm along that stretch of road is Phil Nicholson's place and I would imagine he would have known if any of his animals had managed to stray across to the waste ground.'

'I thought it might have been a rabbit, but Phil didn't think it was anything as small as that. Anyway, Brian,' she continued, 'I don't remember seeing any rabbits around that area; they prefer to stick to the woods off the Stockbridge Road.'

'He's probably right, love; it must be something much bigger to attract so many crows.'

'They gave me the creeps, they really did. Roy was terrified.' she added.

'I bet he was!'

'I'll make us some tea, shall I? But, what about your racing, Brian? I've interrupted you.'

'Doesn't matter and, my love, tea sounds an excellent idea.'

Melissa was at the kitchen window filling the kettle when she looked down into the square to see Ian Ash drive past, followed quickly by one of the easily recognisable dark blue police vans. It wasn't entirely curiosity which made her open the window and lean out, but as soon as she saw both vehicles turning left into Bridge Street the feeling of foreboding she'd had since she had spoken to Phil Nicholson returned. That was no animal behind the hedge out there. Tell me I'm wrong in what I'm thinking, she inwardly groaned, but she knew she wasn't and at that moment as she remained standing at the open window, oblivious to the cold air drifting into the kitchen, she felt physically sick at what her imagination was conjuring up.

'Brian!' she called out to him.

'What's wrong, love?' and within seconds he was beside her, his arms immediately going round her shoulders and holding her close.

'I think it must be a dead body.'

'Melissa,' he whispered her name softly, 'why do you say that?'

'I've just seen the police turn into Bridge Street. That's why, Brian. Phil must have phoned them when he found -'

'Come on, love, we mustn't jump to conclusions in this way. We'll find out soon enough whether it is or not. You're letting that imagination of yours run away with you.'

'I know I am, but I can't help it.'

'If you are right, there is nothing we can do about it and remember,

Bridge Street isn't a dead end; they could be going further on. Meanwhile,' he smiled at her, tilting her face up to his, 'where's the tea you promised me?'

'There are times, Brian Morrison,' she smiled weakly, 'you can be really chauvinistic.'

'But you love me, don't you? he grinned, kissing her.

'You know I do.'

*

Some hours earlier; around eight-thirty, members of the late-Catherine Miller-Croft's family met up for breakfast in The King's Arms Hotel in Market square, having arrived from London the previous evening with the sole purpose of attending her funeral later in the morning.

Oliver Croft, taking on the self-appointed role of their chief spokesman since they'd heard of her death, was giving the impression of actually enjoying the occasion. Probably thinks he's chairing one of his board meetings, Christine Mason thought sourly, looking across the table at her half-brother as he waved his knife about in the air in that ridiculously pompous way.

'Well,' he was going on and in her opinion speaking far too loudly. They weren't the only guests in the restaurant; he could at least try to moderate his voice. Her mother had been a well known figure around Meadowbank and it had been no secret she had been an extremely wealthy woman and Christine, who hadn't been back to the town for well over twenty years, had no doubt there would be quite a number of people curious to know how Catherine, at the end of her life, had decided to distribute that wealth. 'Christine,' Oliver interrupted her thoughts, 'you weren't listening to me; I've just asked you a question.' he said querulously, a deep frown furrowing his broad forehead and reminding her for a fleeting moment of their father, although he had died such a long time ago, she'd only been five and could scarcely remember him.

'Sorry, Oliver,' she apologised, 'I was miles away.'

'Obviously,' he snapped, 'I was talking about mother's property and wondering who she'd left it to.'

'Which one?'

'Both of them, actually. They must be worth a fair bit, especially the house in Swiss Cottage, even more than "The Gables", although it's probably double the size.'

'Well, I have no idea, but I expect all will be revealed when we see Arnold Brutton later.'

'I do realise, of course, you and she had not been on speaking terms for years, but I thought perhaps Muriel may have told you. You two meet quite often, don't you?'

'Not all that often, but when we do, we hardly ever discuss mother. Muriel knows what I thought of her. Besides,' she went on, 'it could be that Muriel doesn't know either. She's always maintained she is non-materialistic.'

'It's easy to be like that when you don't have to concern yourself with money!' he retorted, exactly as she had expected him to do.

'You could be right, Oliver. To be honest, I've never believed it myself.' she said mildly, in an attempt to diffuse his increasing irritation, glancing at her watch, 'I thought she would have been down for breakfast by now.'

'She's probably gone for a walk.' Sonia, Oliver's wife remarked, dabbing her mouth delicately with a corner of her table napkin, 'You know how fanatical Muriel is about keeping fit.' she added quietly.

'I couldn't see her car outside.' Jason Miller commented. 'Perhaps she drove up to the Downs earlier; there are some good walks there.'

'If she has,' Oliver grumbled, 'she's cutting it a bit fine. Probably wants to make a grand entrance when she arrives at Saint Stephen's.'

'That's rather unkind, dear.' Sonia gently admonished him, but Christine didn't miss the little smile hovering on her red-painted lips. She had always known Sonia had been jealous of Muriel. The two women had never got on and if it hadn't been for Oliver arranging for them all to meet occasionally out of, Christine was sure, some sense of family duty, she didn't think they would ever see each other.

'Perhaps,' Oliver shrugged, 'but then, Muriel has always been a law unto herself. Take last evening for instance; we had no sooner booked in here when she said she was going out again. No explanations either; she just went, muttering something about going up to The Royal Oak.'

'Don't forget,' Jason put in, 'Muriel often visited Meadowbank to see her mother, Oliver, also she's made a number of friends here over the years, so it's quite feasible she could have arranged to see them last night.'

'My goodness,' Christine said, 'how you do stick up for your cousin!'

'Christine,' her husband spoke for the first time since they had sat down for breakfast, 'this is not the time for bickering.'

'Don't nag, Godfrey.'

'I don't know about anyone else,' Oliver said, pushing his chair back and getting to his feet, 'but I'm going outside to stretch my legs. 'What about you, Sonia, are you coming?'

'No, dear, I think I'll stay here.'

'Perhaps you could arrange for them to prepare our bill, then. There's no need to come back inside the hotel, and once we've had this meeting with mother's lawyer we can go straight back to London.'

'I do think it's most inconsiderate of Arnold Brutton to expect us all to traipse over to Winchester.' Christine complained, 'He could have made the effort and come to Meadowbank.'

'We've already gone into all of this, Christine,' Oliver said sharply. 'He had another appointment this morning and one he couldn't alter, if you remember.'

'That's what he *said*,' she emphasised, 'but it is still a nuisance.'

'I thought you, of all people, would be interested to hear the contents of mother's will.'

'What is that supposed to mean?'

'I don't think I need to spell it out to you, Christine,' he said, 'but don't tell me it hasn't crossed your mind to wonder just how generous mother will have been towards a daughter she didn't even talk to!'

*

Saint Stephen's was packed, a considerable number of the congregation being friends of Catherine Miller-Croft and the remainder, people who scarcely knew her, but felt sufficiently moved to pay their last respects to someone who had become a legend in the Meadowbank community. Catherine had been a likeable woman, gregarious in her younger years and during the time her second husband, Trevor Croft, had been alive, throwing extravagant parties which would continue well on until the early hours. She'd had a serious side even back then and had always been willing to contribute to any local cause, although in recent years she had become something of a recluse, seldom venturing out beyond the high walls of her large rambling house at the top of Winchester Road before it joined the A390 into the city, with only a daily help to talk to and visits from those friends who were left and still fit enough, if they didn't have their own transport, to climb the steep hill leading up to the iron gates of "The Gables". Apart from Muriel, who usually came to see her at least once a month and the occasional visit from her nephew, Jason, she had seen very little of the rest of her family for a number of years. People in Meadowbank had long memories and there was hardly a person in the church that morning who wasn't reflecting and regretting the passing of a woman who had formed a strong part of their town for more years than most of them could remember.

The family had the front pew, the one empty seat reminding them of the fact that Muriel, Catherine's step-daughter, had not made an appearance. Jason realised sadly as he knelt for the last prayer that the others weren't all that concerned by her absence, but he was. It was totally out of character for her, but, although they had waited at the hotel right up until almost eleven before walking across to Saint Stephen's, they had continued to believe she would arrive. He had thought of a number of reasons, but none of them made much sense. If she had gone up to the Downs, it was possible she may have had an accident, but if she had, it must have been a pretty serious one for her not to have phoned back to the hotel. He had suggested to Oliver when they emerged from the church that they should call into The King's Arms and find out if they'd heard from her, but he immediately rejected the idea, reminding him they had an appointment with Arnold Brutton at two, also that he had to get back to London before his business closed for the day. On the drive over to Winchester, Jason had phoned the hotel on his mobile, only to be told she hadn't come back and that there had been no message from her. He had already decided the night before to stay on in Meadowbank for the weekend; at least, he concluded, if anything had happened to her he would be on the spot.

His aunt's lawyers, Brutton, Brutton & Brutton, were in the centre of Winchester, close to the cathedral. The meeting with the senior partner, Arnold Brutton, lasted an hour, although to Jason, that hour seemed interminable, due mainly, much to his acute embarrassment, to the angry responses of Christine and to a lesser degree, Oliver, as the contents of Catherine's last will and testament were painstakingly read out by the elderly lawyer. Judging by the tight-lipped expression on Oliver's face, it was apparent to Jason he was exercising considerable restraint, but Christine, her voluble nature making it impossible for her to react in any other way, immediately made it clear what she considered to be totally unacceptable to her. Not unsurprisingly perhaps, Catherine had left a major share of her estate to Muriel and relatively modest bequests to Christine and Oliver and nothing to their offspring. It hadn't gone down too well either when they learned he had been left considerably more than the pair of them, but what really threw them was Catherine's final bequest; this being to a daughter none of them had known had even existed.

Catherine had not over-elaborated, except to say that a year before her first marriage in 1959, she had given birth to an illegitimate child and had been forced due to the stigma and scandal this would have caused, to have her adopted. She had bequeathed to this first daughter of hers not only a vast amount of money, but her property in Meadowbank, including the entire contents which Jason could remember from past visits consisted of many fine pieces of furniture, including a number of Old Masters and an impressive silver collection.

'She cannot do this!' Christine had exploded, 'She must be about fifty by now.' stating the obvious, 'She has absolutely no right to inherit!'

'That's where you're wrong, Christine,' Arnold Brutton had replied and Jason, recognising the closed-in look on his face, one which had instantly replaced his normal benign expression, that Christine didn't stand a chance. She wasn't going to win this one, he thought, knowing in advance how her attempt at confrontation would end, 'you see,' Mr Brutton had continued slowly, deliberately, almost as though he wanted to further aggravate her wrath, 'your mother confided in me many years ago. She never revealed the name of the father of this child and as she'd arranged the adoption privately, she was able to find out where she was living, although she never got in touch with her.'

'That doesn't make any difference!' Christine had retorted, her cheeks by this time becoming unattractively flushed.

'But it does. The child's father was the man she married the following year, namely Howard Miller.'

'Who is she anyway?' Christine had demanded.

'The lady's name is Mrs Emily Craig, Christine.'

'She's married, then?' and to Jason, if to none of the others, sounding unpleasantly belligerent.

'Mrs Craig is a widow,' he said quietly, 'her husband died last year.'

'Rather like the prodigal daughter, isn't she?' Christine retorted, appearing oblivious to the shocked expression on the lawyer's face.

'I fully realise,' Arnold Brutton had said, looking round the table at each of them in turn, 'hearing about a relative none of you knew about must have come as something of a surprise, but I would suggest as Mrs Craig, who, incidentally, had no knowledge of the bequest, you could, if not actually welcome her into your family, accept Mrs Miller-Croft's last wishes.'

'This is all quite preposterous!' Oliver had exploded, shifting impatiently in his chair, 'You expect us to swallow this – this *story* of a daughter literally emerging from goodness knows where!'

'It may sound like that to you, Oliver,' Arnold Brutton had replied, 'but

I can assure you it's the truth.'

'But didn't she tell him?'

'No, she didn't. There was still the possibility of scandal, not only attached to her, but to her family. The Singletons were staunchly religious and would have been devastated. Life in those days, Oliver, was somewhat different from today; matters of that nature were considered something to be ashamed of and invariably covered up. Also, as your mother told me, she had made her decision; there was no going back to reclaim the child and therefore in her opinion, it wouldn't have achieved anything to have confessed to her new husband.'

There had been more, but as Jason had thought, the situation remained the same and thankfully Arnold Brutton had brought the meeting to a close.

The last Christine said to him as she waited for Godfrey to unlock the car door for her was she would be contesting the will. And as the two cars drove off, leaving him standing on the pavement beside his own vehicle, he found himself shaking his head in disbelief at her greed and crassness. It wasn't as though Godfrey and she were not well off, quite the contrary; Godfrey's consultancy business in London was firmly established and occupied a prestigious position off the Strand. Both their children attended one of the most expensive fee-paying schools in London, but still they weren't satisfied; they wanted more. And Oliver; he was the same, Jason thought bitterly, pulling away from the kerb and heading out of Winchester and back on to the A390, the bitter taste of such undisguised avarice staying with him for most of the journey.

It was well after four by the time he reached the outskirts of Meadowbank; being a Friday afternoon probably accounted for the heavy traffic with many hold-ups. He was able to find a parking space outside the front of The King's Arms and walked up the flight of steps into the hotel. As soon as he mentioned Muriel's name to the receptionist he could tell by the concerned look on the woman's face that Muriel hadn't returned.

'And, Mr Miller,' she said, 'her room wasn't slept in last night.'

'What about her clothes, her travel bag, for instance?'

'Oh, they're still in the room. I really haven't known what to do for the best. I did consider phoning the police, but I decided not to, thinking she may come back at any time and there would be a perfectly simple explanation.'

'I understand how you must be feeling, but I think I ought to speak to someone there. My cousin may have had an accident; they'll be able to advise me what I should be doing next.'

The Meadowbank police station was two buildings from the hotel and it took him only a matter of minutes before he was in the main entrance lobby and talking to the desk sergeant; a young man, no more than nineteen or twenty, Jason guessed.

He listened intently and without interrupting to what Jason had to say, all the time filling in the regulation report form.

'You mentioned the lady's car, sir. What make is it?'

'A white Renault, a Clio,' Jason added, 'but I don't know the registration number.'

'That's alright, sir. We can easily trace that if it becomes necessary.'

'Of course.'

'If you could just wait for a couple of minutes,' he said, 'I'd like to have a word with my Inspector.' coming round to the front of the desk and taking the report form with him, walked along the corridor to the left of the lobby. Within minutes he had returned, during which time Jason was beginning to get the strong impression something was wrong. Surely, he reasoned, reporting a missing person would be a routine procedure, but it would seem this wasn't so. Police inspectors didn't normally involve themselves at this stage when that person could turn up at any moment. He remembered reading once that the majority of people who were declared missing did in fact return, but unable to prevent the insidious thought creep into his brain that perhaps Muriel was in the minority.

'Would you come with me, sir,' the desk sergeant said, an uncertain smile on his face making him appear much younger, 'Inspector Ash would like to see you for a moment.'

Jason followed him to the end of the corridor which opened out into a large open-plan office, with glass-partitioned offices and work stations, and with every step bracing himself for the worst, his instincts telling him something was very wrong here.

Inspector Ash, a tall, slim man, young to be an inspector was Jason's first impression as he was shown into his office.

'We understand,' he said, once he'd introduced himself and gestured for Jason to sit down, 'you're concerned about Miss Miller.'

'That's right, I am.'

'What relation is she to you, sir; your sister?'

'No, she's my cousin, but perhaps I should explain,' Jason went on, 'it may help you to understand just why I am so worried about her.'

'I'd appreciate that; the more background we have to work on in a missing person case, the easier it is for us.'

'Right,' Jason nodded, 'first of all, I expect you'll have heard about the recent death of Mrs Catherine Miller-Croft?'

'Indeed, yes. Her funeral was this morning, I believe.'

'That's right and last evening members of her family arrived in Meadowbank, booking into The King's Arms. I was later than the others getting here and they had already booked in by then. I missed seeing Miss Miller because she'd gone out again, telling them she was going to The Royal Oak Hotel.'

'What relation is Miss Miller to Mrs Catherine Miller-Croft?'

'She's her step-daughter by her first marriage to Howard Miller.'

'And you, sir, you said you were her cousin?'

'My father was Howard Miller's brother.'

'I see,' he said, 'and the other members of your family?'

'There was Oliver Croft and his wife; he is Catherine's step-son from her second marriage to Trevor Croft,' Jason explained, 'and Christine Mason and her husband. Christine is her natural daughter. Rather convoluted, I'm afraid.' he added.

'A little,' he agreed, 'but I think I've got the picture. In respect to Miss Miller's car, sir,' he continued, 'we believe we may have located it.'

'Really?'

'Yes; we received a call from the proprietress of The Royal Oak Hotel telling us there had been a white Renault parked in their car park since last night. She had already checked with the hotel register of all the guests staying there and the car didn't belong to any of them, nor to any of the staff. She gave us the registration number and about half an hour ago we heard back from Swansea confirming that the car is registered in the name of your cousin.'

'As I've said, she did mention she was going there.'

'But this was before you arrived at the hotel?'

'That's right.'

'Mr Miller,' Inspector Ash said, moving slightly forward in his chair and looking directly at Jason, 'there is something else I have to tell you.'

'Yes?' dreading his next words.

'Shortly after three this afternoon, a body of a woman was discovered by one of our local farmers on a piece of waste ground outside the town. This may or may not be your cousin, and if this is not the case, it would go a long way to putting your mind at rest, therefore,' pausing and Jason, momentarily unable to say anything, merely sat there as the gist of what he'd said filtered into his brain. He wanted to ask him so many questions, but he was totally incapable, 'would you be prepared to accompany me to the mortuary?'

'Of course.'

Jason had no idea how long it took to walk down to the basement where the Station had their mortuary, but it couldn't have been more than five minutes. Time to him had lost all meaning and he knew with a dreadful certainty that what they were going to show him would be Muriel. The sheer weight of the inevitability of it all was dreadful, something he had never experienced in his life before. The pathologist pulled back the sheet and, taking a deep breath, Jason looked down at the dead woman on the marble slab. He nodded his head in the direction of the inspector and turned away from her; the woman he had known since they had both been children, no more than five or six; he couldn't remember much before then, although he had a clear memory of the earlier days before his uncle had died and they had still been living in London and then later, playing together in the gardens at "The Gables". Muriel had been a bit of a tomboy and perhaps that was why they had got on so well together, but now was not the moment to recall all of this stuff. Later, when he was on his own; that would be soon enough.

'Would you like some tea, sir?' Inspector Ash asked him once they had returned to his office. 'It might help.'

'Please.'

'I'm not going to keep you here for much longer, Mr Miller,' he said to him, having given him enough time to compose himself and he had been right; the tea, although too sweet, did help; the debilitating feelings of nausea had gone, 'but there are a few questions I would like to ask you, also the addresses of those relatives who were in Meadowbank. I take it they have left by now?'

'Yes,' Jason said, making a conscious effort to focus on what he was saying, 'after the funeral we had to go into Winchester to the lawyer's office, for the reading of the will, you understand, and afterwards they left for London.'

'And when do you plan to return, sir?'

'I'd already decided to stay on for the weekend and I see no reason to change my mind, Inspector. I dare say there will be various formalities I will need to attend to.'

'Was your cousin married?' Inspector Ash asked, 'We need to have the names of her next of kin.'

'No; she had been, but she'd been divorced for a number of years.'

'Any children?'

'No.'

'Any men friends?'

'I don't think she had anyone regular, Inspector.' Jason told him, 'She may have had, but she didn't tell me.'

'And last night, when she said she was going out, did she mention whether she was planning to meet anyone?'

'No, apparently not.'

'Finally, Mr Miller,' the inspector said, pulling a sheet of paper towards him, 'if you could give us the full names and addresses of those relatives, including their contact numbers, this would be helpful. Also,' he added, 'your cousin's address.'

When the inspector had written down the last details he asked Jason whether Muriel had been Howard Miller's only child from his marriage to Catherine.

'Perhaps she had a brother or sister?'

'No, she didn't. She was the only one.'

'These names you've given me, sir,' he went on, 'are they the only living relatives of your aunt?'

'Except for Oliver and Christine's children, there's only Oliver's brother,' deliberately not mentioning the daughter Arnold Brutton had sprung on them earlier and not pausing to consider the wisdom of what no doubt would be described as withholding important information from the police, 'but it's doubtful,' Jason added, 'whether he would have known my aunt had died.'

'The brothers don't keep in touch?'

'As far as I know, Inspector, I don't believe they do. Lawrence is some years older than Oliver and left home when he was still in his teens.'

'How well did Miss Miller know him?' the inspector asked.

'Hardly at all,' Jason answered, 'she knew of him, of course, but when Catherine married Trevor Croft, he was no longer living with his first wife and the two boys were brought up by their mother.'

'They never visited their father?'

'Oliver did and continued to keep in touch with Catherine after he died.'

'But not his brother?'

'No, I always got the impression he resented his father.'

'Do you have any idea when they last saw each other; the two brothers, I mean?'

'I think it was probably when their mother died; this was in 1991 sometime and I remember Oliver telling me around that time that Lawrence was no longer living in London, but had moved to Brighton. Inspector Ash,' Jason asked, 'why are you so interested in him?'

'Formalities, Mr Miller; in a murder enquiry we have to be extra thorough and until we're satisfied on the authenticity of each person we interview, we have to continue. It's how we operate.' he added.

'I understand.' realising with a jolt that he was probably under suspicion. The very thought made him feel physically ill. What an unpleasant world they live in, he thought, glad he had elected to work in the relatively stress-free environment of estimating for one of London's leading construction companies, where being employed as one of a team, he didn't have to concern himself with the undercurrents of people's lives.

'There is something I need to ask you, Inspector.'

'Yes?'

'How did my cousin die?'

'We haven't yet been able to establish the exact cause of death, Mr Miller, but once we receive the pathologist's report later on today, we should be in a better position to give you an answer.'

'Poor Muriel;' he muttered, 'what a terrible thing to happen to her.'

'Murder is indeed terrible, sir, and we will be doing our utmost to find the person responsible.'

Chapter Two

The letter arrived on Saturday morning. Puzzled, Emily Craig picked it up from the floor inside the front door, turning it over a couple of times before opening the envelope. She had only been in "The Old Schoolhouse" for no more than a couple of weeks and hadn't had time to give any of her friends her new address, but it was addressed to her alright: "Mrs Emily Craig, The Old Schoolhouse, Market Square, Meadowbank" and in the top left-hand corner, the word "Confidential".

She sat down at the kitchen table, pushing to one side her half-drunk coffee, and started to read:

"Dear Mrs Craig,

As the Chief Executor of the late-Catherine Miller-Croft's estate, I am writing to inform you that, in compliance with her last wishes, she has named you as a beneficiary of the said estate.

I would, therefore, be grateful if you would telephone my office in order to arrange a mutually convenient time when we can meet to discuss the aforementioned.

Yours respectfully,

Arnold Brutton

Brutton, Brutton & Brutton, Solicitors."

This is positively weird, she murmured to herself, reading it again. Who was this Catherine Miller-Croft? There must be some mistake, some mix-up, she decided; there has to be. Why on earth would anyone leave her anything?

'Are you okay, Mum?' Jessica asked, coming into the kitchen and leaning over to kiss her on the brow; her blonde hair still tousled from sleep and wearing an old "Boys' Own" tee-shirt.

'I'm fine, Jess.' she said, getting up to pour coffee into her mug; the one Jessica had had for years, ever since she had started drinking coffee, in fact, 'Here you are, love.' she said, bringing the coffee over to her.

'Mum!'

'Yes?'

'Don't keep me in the dark. You looked so – so, oh, I don't know, but when I saw you just now, I thought you'd had some bad news or something.'

'I wouldn't describe it as bad news, Jess,' she said, sitting back down again and taking a sip of her own coffee which, had by now, gone cold, 'quite the opposite – I suppose.'

'What do you mean, you suppose?'

'It's this letter,' she said, passing it to her, 'I don't understand it.' she added, watching Jess' expression as she began to read through the formal wording.

'It's from a firm of lawyers, Mum.' she remarked, glancing first to the top of the page, 'They don't usually make mistakes, do they?'

'They shouldn't,' Emily answered, 'but everyone is fallible, even those in the legal profession.' but Jess wasn't listening; her lips pursed as she read to the end.

'Wow!'

'Is that all you can say?' Emily asked, but unable to keep her face straight. There were times her daughter, when faced with something out of the ordinary, would react like this; one single word which said everything; to quote those in Jessica's generation, she was gobsmacked.

'And you think this letter wasn't meant for you?' Jess managed at last and as she herself had done, reading it once more.

'It can't be, Jess,' Emily insisted impatiently, 'How could it; I've never heard of a Catherine Miller-Croft.'

'I have, though.'

'What!'

'That surprised you; didn't it?' Jess laughed, picking up her coffee mug and taking a sip, 'Yuk! It's cold!'

'I'll make some fresh coffee; give it to me, love, and I'll rinse it out. So,' Emily went on, 'when did you hear of this lady?'

'The other evening, Monday it was, a few of us called into The Bridge for a drink after work and some of the customers were talking about her. She lived in Meadowbank, had done for years, and they were saying how sad they were to have heard she'd died only the day before. Although she was quite old, it was really sad because there had been nothing wrong with her, although she hardly ever came into town, but she had a bad fall at home, fell down some stairs, apparently, and while she was in hospital suffered a stroke.'

'That is sad,' Emily said, 'but why would she have named me as a beneficiary in her will, Jess?'

'Well, it looks as though she has, Mum,' she said prosaically, with an old-fashioned expression on her face, 'and there is only one way to find out, isn't there?'

'I'd better give the lawyer a ring, then,' Emily sighed, 'but they may not work on a Saturday morning.'

'Mum! Honestly, why are you prevaricating like this; it's not like you.'

'I know it isn't' she agreed, 'but I don't like mysteries, not like this anyway, or coincidences either, if it comes to that.'

'Now you're being mysterious!'

'If, and only if,' Emily said, 'the lawyers are correct, I believe I may know why I've received this.' she finished, pointing to the letter spread out on the table between them.

'You sound terribly serious.

'I can't help it, Jess. You see, you never knew this, but I was adopted and I never knew who my biological mother was or anything about her family.'

'Good Grief! Did dad know?'

'Oh, yes, I told him, but we didn't see any point in telling you.'

'And you didn't try to find her?'

'No, I never felt the need, Jess. I always knew, from a very young age, that I had been adopted, but I loved the woman I called mother; to me she was my real mother.'

'I understand.' Jess said quietly, her lovely blue eyes, so like her father's, bright with unshed tears.

'It's all in the past, love.'

'I know.'

'So, having told you that, I'm now going to do as you suggested and phone Mr Arnold Brutton and make an appointment to see him.'

*

"The Courier", Meadowbank's weekly newspaper, gave the murder full front-page coverage, although to many who found the choice of wording for the headline of "MURDER RETURNS TO MEADOWBANK" not only insensitive but slightly disturbing, reminding them of those other murders, a good proportion of the town's residents couldn't wait to read all about the latest disruption in their otherwise predictable lives, no doubt resulting in the newsagents in the square being sold out by midday. The reporter who wrote up the piece must have moved quickly in collecting sufficient information to fill the page, including a photograph of the late-Catherine Miller-Croft surrounded by friends and family with a circle drawn around the victim, Muriel Miller.

Ian Ash was already in the office when Brenda Masters arrived at the Station shortly before nine. She had, the evening before, read through his report on the interview he'd had with Jason Miller and, once she had worked out the complexities of Catherine Miller-Croft's family, further complicated by the fact that most of them weren't really relatives at all and only through her two marriages, she was able to form some sort of idea of what it must have been like when they had arrived in Meadowbank on the Thursday evening. Ian, in her opinion, had been quite right in following up on the one member of the family who hadn't made an appearance. The explanation could have been as Jason had suggested to him that Lawrence Miller hadn't been aware of his aunt's death, but nevertheless, it was a loose end and needed to be clarified. Rather like clearing the decks she was thinking as she walked into her own office, noticing that Ian had left her a copy of the pathologist's report, having placed it in the centre of her desk where he knew she wouldn't miss it.

Forensic now confirmed that Muriel Miller had been suffocated after being rendered unconscious by a chloroform pad pressed against her mouth and nostrils, shreds of the white lint remaining stuck to her face. They had, the evening before, brought in her handbag; a soft leather pouch, which they found on the floor beneath the passenger seat where, presumably, it must have fallen when she'd been attacked. The contents: a wallet containing a couple of credit cards and five ten-pound notes; a purse with some loose change; a staff pass to Barclays Bank in Regent Street and a small address book. None of it of any great significance, except perhaps for the address book with two of the entries she had made. It wasn't the name of the first one which caught Brenda's attention and one she'd never heard before, but the telephone number. While she could understand why Muriel Miller may have wanted to make a note of the The Royal Oak's number, as far as she was aware, they didn't employ anyone called Bradley Cartwright, although she could be wrong, but it was something which needed to be checked up on. The second name in the book was that of a firm of solicitors in London; now this, Brenda decided, could be useful and somebody else she would be able contact while she was up there, having already decided she would personally interview those relatives who had been in Meadowbank.

She had just finished reading the report when Ian arrived, standing in the open doorway of her office.

'Good morning, Ian.'

'Good morning, ma'am.'

'Well,' she said, gesturing for him to sit down, 'I think this report tells us something quite telling, don't you?'

'That the murder was premeditated?'

'I think so, yes. I suppose it is always possible, although farfetched, that someone might be going around the countryside carrying a chloroform pad on the off chance of finding a victim.'

'I saw her car,' Ian said, 'when they brought it in yesterday and the smell of chloroform was very strong; I would suggest, judging by the churned up grass and earth and the deep impressions on either side of the body, she was dragged from the car and then suffocated.'

'You're probably right, but why not finish off the job while she was still in there? I would have thought less obvious if anyone should have been passing.'

'I don't know, ma'am.'

'What did he use by the way; the report doesn't mention that?'

'A travelling rug which could have already been in there.'

'No fingerprints, I suppose?'

'There were none on the steering wheel or the dashboard; they must have been wiped off and as far as the other parts of the interior, only those of the victim.'

'Obviously she couldn't have been driving, so whoever had been with her, Muriel Miller would have known him – or her?'

'I would say so.' Ian agreed, 'I was planning to drive up to The Royal Oak this morning and have a word with Ted and anyone else who may have seen her on Thursday night.'

'That's a good idea and I don't need to remind you,' she said, giving him one of her rare smiles, 'to look out for the manageress. She will not be pleased to see us again.'

'I know; Mrs Sandra Watson is one formidable lady.'

'She certainly is, but we can't allow her to intimidate us, although no doubt she'll do her best to show her displeasure and how our continual presence is ruining her hotel's reputation. You'll just have to remind her, Ian, the old much-used explanation that we are conducting a murder enquiry, etc., etc.'

'Oh, I will, ma'am.'

'Incidentally, Ian, while you're there perhaps you could find out who this Bradley Cartwright is; whether he works there or, on the other hand, he could be a guest.'

'Right.'

'It looks very much as though this case is not only going to be confined to Meadowbank, which means we'll have to spend a fair bit of time in London.'

'Yes, that's what I was thinking.' Ian said, 'Do you want me to go up there, ma'am, or would you prefer it if I concentrated on the investigations at this end?'

'I think it's best if you remained here, Ian,' she answered, 'especially as you will have made a start with following up Muriel Miller's last movements, from when she left The King's Arms until she arrived at The Royal Oak, also you should, hopefully, be getting some feedback from the feelers you've put out to find Lawrence Croft. In fact, you're going to have your hands full in and around Meadowbank.'

'That's alright.' he agreed, 'Jason Miller told me yesterday he was going to phone his relatives and tell them about his cousin.'

'That's good; one duty we've been spared, although by now, as the news has already reached the nationals, they would have read about it anyway at breakfast this morning.'

'Have you seen a copy of "The Courier" yet, ma'am?'

'I have and I wonder how they were able to get hold of a photograph of her so quickly.'

'That's a good question,' Ian frowned, obviously the thought hadn't occurred to him before, 'there is one thing, though,' he added, 'that photograph isn't a recent one; it must have been taken at least ten years ago.'

'Really?'

'Yes, I'm sure of it. The body I saw yesterday had been that of a middle-aged woman.'

'I'll give "The Courier" a ring before I leave for London; I know their editor and if, as I suspect, that photograph has been extracted from their photo library, he should be able to tell me when it was taken. I'm not putting a great deal of importance on this,' she added, 'but it would be good to get at least one loose end tied up.'

'In what way, ma'am?'

'Well, apart from immediately recognising Catherine Miller-Croft and how they had highlighted Muriel Miller, nobody else in the photograph was named as no doubt they would have been if, in fact, it had been taken especially for "The Courier" If you remember that Catherine Miller-Croft was a key member of the community, Ian, there was a time when she was actively involved in the town when any function she attended was treated as newsworthy. They'd cropped the rest of the picture, so there's no way of knowing whether it had been taken locally or not, but it could very well have been a family celebration.'

'Jason Miller was there, ma'am, so perhaps you are right. Those other people in the forefront could have been Catherine Miller-Croft's immediate family; the ones who were in Meadowbank yesterday.'

'That's what I was thinking, Ian. If nothing else, it would give us an idea of what they looked like.'

'There's something which didn't occur to me yesterday when I was talking to Jason Miller,' he said, 'but since then I've been going over everything he told me.'

'Yes?'

'About his cousin having once been married; but although she'd divorced, she was still wearing a wedding ring.'

'That's interesting. Why go to the bother of reverting back to her maiden name? There would have been no point in continuing to wear it, would there?'

'Not if she wanted to give the impression of being single. It's the first thing a man notices, you know, ma'am, when he meets a woman for the first time.'

'Is it?' genuinely surprised; she hadn't known that. Ian Ash continued to surprise her with his percipiency. He had come a long way in the five years they'd been working together and well deserved the promotion to Inspector last year for the way he handled his part in the Tilsly case.

'So,' she asked him, 'what sort of connotations do you put on that, then?'

'That she may have remarried.'

'Although she didn't tell her family?'

'Well, according to Jason Miller, he didn't appear to know; in fact, he didn't seem to know much about her private life.'

'Secretive woman.' she commented dryly, 'Perhaps when I speak to the other relatives, they may be more forthcoming.'

'Do you think her cousin wasn't being entirely truthful, ma'am?'

'At this stage, Ian, who can tell? She may have told him she'd re-married and why he withheld the information, once again, we don't know. Also, perhaps you can have another word with him today; find out exactly what time he arrived at The King's Arms and whether he did have an early night.'

'I'll do that when I come back from The Royal Oak, shall I,' Ian asked, 'I'm hoping to be able to establish, that is if anyone noticed, when Muriel Miller left there.'

'Ted doesn't miss much,' Brenda remarked, recalling how useful the barman had been during their last enquiries at the hotel, 'he has a good memory for faces, but from what we've already learned, Muriel Miller must have been fairly familiar with Meadowbank and that, probably, would have included The Royal Oak.'

The editor of "The Courier" knew immediately about the photograph which had appeared in that week's issue of their paper, explaining to her the reporter had to pass it by him first before going to print, and within ten minutes he had emailed it through to the Station including the write-up. Ian had been right, Brenda thought, printing out a copy and looking at it closely; the photograph, with more detail than the one she'd seen earlier, had been taken ten years ago and the occasion had been Catherine Miller-Croft's seventieth birthday party which had been held at The Royal Oak, immediately recognising the decor of one of their main function rooms, resplendent with the dark wood panelling and crystal chandeliers. Prominently seated in the forefront was Catherine Miller-Croft flanked on either side by her relatives, their names printed along the bottom of the photograph: "reading from left to right; Oliver Croft and his wife, Sonia; Jason Miller and Muriel Miller." but no Christine Mason and her husband, Brenda noted and then remembered hearing she hadn't been on speaking terms with her mother for many years. Seeing them together in this way, although only in black and white, gave her a better idea of what they looked like, preparing her at least for when she met the step-son and his wife.

Before leaving the office, Brenda made two calls to London; one to the number Ian had given her for Oliver Croft and the other to Christine Mason. Oliver Croft answered immediately, his manner changing dramatically to one of indignation once she had introduced herself, asking her what she expected to learn by talking to him and yes, he had heard about the unfortunate murder of Muriel and yes, it had been a dreadful shock to both his wife and himself, finally agreeing with reluctance to seeing her later on in the afternoon, although unable to resist adding it could only be a brief meeting because they were in the throes of arranging a dinner party. The second call to Christine Mason was no more cordial, Christine Mason telling her it was absolutely impossible to find the time to see her today; it would have to be tomorrow although being extremely busy she had precious little time to spare over a matter that didn't really concern her.

Some family, Brenda thought, walking through the office and placing the photograph on Ian's desk, together with a note asking him to make an appointment to see Catherine Miller-Croft's lawyer; they needed to know the contents of her will.

*

Halfway along Thomas Street, one of the many side streets from the centre of Mayfair, she finally managed to find a parking space and by the time she rang the door bell of number seventeen, it was four-thirty. She recognised Oliver Croft from the photograph, although he'd put on a considerable amount of weight since then and noticing also his expression as he opened the door was far from welcoming.

'Good afternoon, Chief Inspector,' he said, opening the door wider and gesturing her inside, 'we expected you earlier. As I mentioned on the phone we are in the midst of preparing for this evening's dinner party.'

'Good afternoon, sir,' Brenda replied smoothly, refusing to make any apology for something which she couldn't be blamed for. The arrangement had been for late afternoon; either his memory was poor or he was making an attempt to provoke her, 'and I do appreciate how occupied you must be, but I hope I won't need to take up too much of your time. There are, however, a few questions I would like to ask you and your wife.'

'I can't possibly think how we can help you in your enquiry, Chief Inspector,' he said, leading her across the hall: highly polished parquet flooring, partially covered by what appeared to her an extremely expensive Persian rug, and opening a door on the right-hand side. The room; high ceilinged, oak panelled and two sash windows overlooking the street, was sumptuously furnished, giving her the impression it was seldom used. A blonde-haired woman, who'd been standing at one of the windows, turned round as they came in and walked towards them.

'This is my wife, Chief Inspector.' he said, 'Sonia,' possessively placing an arm around her shoulders, 'Chief Inspector Masters is from Meadowbank.' he added in a poor attempt to imply her presence in their home was totally unexpected.

'Good afternoon, Mrs Croft.' Brenda said, unable to rid herself of the bizarre idea of being caught up in a stage setting. These people, she decided, were not for real. 'As I've already explained to your husband I apologise for disturbing you at the weekend, but in a murder -'

'- Oh, please.' she interrupted, her hands fluttering in front of her face, 'that word! Awful!'

'As you can see, Chief Inspector,' Oliver Croft explained, 'my wife is quite distraught over Muriel's death.'

'That's understandable.' Brenda replied, trying to move the conversation forward, away from what she felt were contrived expressions of regret for a woman who wasn't even related to them. 'However,' she continued, 'there are a few points which I need to have clarified; namely,' she said quickly, giving neither of them the chance to interrupt, 'on Thursday evening when you arrived at The King's Arms, I understand from Mr Jason Miller you reached there at the same time as Miss Miller and Mr and Mrs Mason. Is this correct?'

'If that's what Jason told you,' he said sharply, 'then it must be.'

'Mr Croft, I require a straight answer, if you don't mind. Apparently, he came later and learned you had all arrived more or less at the same time. Is this correct?' she repeated, deciding it was time to take a firmer line with him.

'Yes, it's correct.' a surly expression now appearing, 'Within minutes as a matter of fact. Muriel was already there when my wife and I walked into the hotel; this was about 6.30; Muriel had just finished booking in and shortly after that, Christine and Godfrey arrived.'

'How soon after, sir?' she asked him, 'Five or ten minutes?'

'It was quarter to seven and before you ask me why I can be so exact is because the clock in reception was striking the quarter hour as they came up the steps to the front door.'

'Thank you. Again, Mr Miller informed us that his cousin told you she was going out again, mentioning she planned to visit The Royal Oak Hotel.'

'Yes, that's right. She didn't even stop long enough to have a drink with us in the lounge bar.'

'Do you know whether she went to her room first?'

'What do you mean?'

'It's a matter of timing.' Brenda explained to him, 'We need to know, as accurately as possible, when she left the hotel.'

'Why is that so important?'

'Because, sir, once we've established when she reached The Royal Oak we will then know whether she drove there directly or called somewhere else first.'

'Well, all I can say is I have no idea. Muriel certainly gave the impression she was eager to get away, but come to think of it, I suppose she must have gone up to her room before she left, unless she took her travel bag with her.'

'Did you actually see her drive away from the hotel?'

'No, and how could we? The windows of the bar face the rear of the building, as I'm sure you are already aware.'

'Alright,' Brenda accepted, 'but did she mention whether she had arranged to meet anyone?'

'No, she didn't.'

'And did none of you think to ask her?'

'Why should we have done? We all knew Muriel; she was a very secretive woman, Chief Inspector and I think we realised she wouldn't have enlightened us in any case. She was like that.'

'I see. And how did you spend the rest of the evening?'

'What's that got to do with all of this?' verging on rudeness, but Brenda ignored the rapid change in his attitude, feeling at last she was beginning to get through to him; this was exactly the sort of re-action she wanted.

'For instance,' she explained calmly, 'did you wait for Mr Miller to join you before having your evening meal either in the hotel restaurant or one of the other restaurants in the town?'

'You've lost me, Chief Inspector.'

'We were still having our drink when Jason arrived,' Sonia Croft said, coming to his rescue, 'weren't we, dear?' a tentative smile appearing on her otherwise vacuous features, 'and that's where he found us.'

'Did you all eat in the hotel restaurant?' Brenda persisted. Honestly, she thought to herself, it would be easier getting blood from a stone than trying to extract information from these two.

'We all did, except Jason.' taking his time to answer.

'Perhaps he went out to eat.'

'Probably; I've no idea.'

'But Jason said he was tired, dear; don't you remember? He told us he was going up to his room and would have an early night.'

'Well,' Oliver Croft muttered, 'that's what he said, so I suppose that's what he did. I don't know.'

'You sound doubtful, sir. Did you have any reason for thinking he may have gone out again?'

'I've no idea. In many respects, Jason, although he wasn't related to Muriel, is very like her; no doubt because they practically grew up together.'

'Possibly.' Brenda nodded, but not entirely convinced. She was getting strong vibes that he didn't like Jason Miller; certainly he was going out of his way to be unhelpful. 'What time did you and your wife retire for the night, sir?'

'After our meal we went back to the bar for a nightcap; it was around ten-thirty when we went up to our room. That would be about right, wouldn't it, Sonia?'

'I think so, dear.'

'And Mr and Mrs Mason?' Brenda asked.

'As to that we can't say; they were both there when we left; you'd better ask them.'

'I will, sir.'

'Have you finished your questioning, Chief Inspector? We still have a great deal to do before our guests start to arrive.'

'Almost, sir.' she answered, 'Was your room at the front or the rear of the hotel?'

'Why on earth do you want to know that?' another quick flash of annoyance; here was someone she thought who was on a very tight fuse indeed. It wouldn't take much for him to lose his temper. No wonder his wife appeared so subdued.

'The reason I'm asking is to know whether by chance either of you heard Miss Miller's car. If your room had been at the front, you would have been facing the parking spaces especially allocated for guests' vehicles.'

'But Muriel didn't return to the hotel.' Sonia said quickly, looking up at her husband for corroboration.

'That's our understanding, yes,' Brenda said mildly, watching his expression closely, but it didn't alter. Instead, he remained standing in exactly the same position he had taken up when they had come into the room. 'But what I would like to know, Mrs Croft,' she went on, this time focusing on Sonia Croft, 'what makes you so certain Miss Miller didn't return to the hotel?'

'Because – well, because,' flustered and probably wishing she hadn't said anything in the first place, 'because,' she repeated lamely, 'her car wasn't out there the next morning; was it, Oliver?'

'No, Sonia,' he gave an exaggerated sigh, 'it wasn't there, so, naturally, Chief Inspector, rightly or wrongly, after we heard what had happened to Muriel, we assumed she hadn't returned that night.'

'Did Mr Miller tell you we had located her car?' Brenda asked him.

'No, as a matter of fact, he didn't. Did he know, then?'

'Yes, he did, Mr Croft.'

'Well, that's typical of Jason. Isn't it, Sonia? Just as damned secretive as Muriel. Where was her car anyway?'

'In The Royal Oak's car park.'

'You do surprise me.'

'Do I, sir?'

'Of course you do, when you consider she was found in Bridge Street and that's some distance away from The Royal Oak.'

'There are a number of possibilities how that could have happened.' Brenda said quietly.

'Well, Chief Inspector,' making no attempt to disguise his belligerence towards her, 'you may be able to think of them, but I'm damn sure I can't!'

'I only have a couple more questions to ask.' Brenda said, ignoring his outburst.

'Good.' and by his hostility, not making it easy for her, but she was used to such a reception. Over the years she had built up a mental barrier against overcoming such open animosity; his whole manner, whether contrived especially or not, was wasted on her.

'It's a small point, but –'

'– If it's such a small point, Chief Inspector,' he butted in, 'why do you feel it necessary to mention?'

'It's a small point, but,' Brenda repeated slowly and turning to face his wife, 'Mrs Croft,' she continued, 'are you at home all day, or do you go out to work? This may sound irrelevant to you in an enquiry such as this one, but I can assure you everything we can put together about the people we interview is helpful to us.'

'I hope I'm wrong here,' Oliver Croft put in, his voice rising an octave, unable to contain his indignation, 'but it sounds to me as if you're treating us as *suspects*, Chief Inspector, because if you are -'

'- Mr Croft,' Brenda interrupted his flow, 'we are not treating you as suspects; in fact we have no suspects; that comes later. By talking to you and your wife today is a mere formality and one with which we have to comply, however distasteful you may find it. I shouldn't have to remind you, sir, but this is a murder enquiry and we have a substantial amount of work to do yet, therefore, I would appreciate if you could be more helpful and you can only do that by patiently answering my questions.'

'Well, to answer your last question, Chief Inspector, there is no need for my wife to work.'

'And, Mrs Croft,' turning once again to her, 'may I ask what your profession was?'

'Up until I was married I was a dental technician.'

'Thank you.' Brenda nodded, 'and you, sir?'

'I am a specialist in fine arts,' he answered smoothly, the expression in those cold grey eyes looking directly at her, making it clear he considered his line of business far superior to any other, 'I don't suppose you've heard of "Croft's Fine Arts" in Bond Street, established, in fact, since nineteen-twelve?'

'I have as a matter of fact, sir.'

'You said you had a couple more questions to ask.' he said quickly, for the first time showing discomfort.

'That's right, I did,' Brenda said, 'and I would like you to think carefully before answering, but did either of you hear a car pulling up in front of the hotel that night, the closing of a car door for instance, or did you hear one pull away? You may not have gone to sleep straight away and being a Thursday night, it would have been relatively quiet in the square; it is just possible either of you may have heard something which at the time had scarcely registered with you.'

'Can't say I did,' Oliver Croft replied, 'I heard vehicles, naturally; two or three perhaps, before I fell asleep, but they were on the road, not immediately outside the hotel.'

'Mrs Croft?' Brenda turned to her, but not before she saw the quick glance she gave her husband, 'No, Chief Inspector, I didn't hear anything. I think I must have fallen asleep straight away and knew nothing until I woke up the following morning.'

Brenda waited until she and Oliver Croft had left the lounge and were on their way to the front door before mentioning his brother to him and for the second time gratified to see another spontaneous flash of annoyance.

'Lawrence?'

'That is your brother's name, I understand, sir?'

'How did you find that out? Oh, you don't have to tell me; that damn Jason again.'

'He did mention him, yes, but only when he was asked if there were any more members of your step-mother's family.'

'I expect he was delighted to tell you none of us know where he is.'

'You have no current address for him, sir?' she asked, once more side-stepping his outrage.

'No, I have not. Surely, you're not adding him to your list of suspects, Chief Inspector?'

'That remains to be seen,' Brenda said smoothly, 'but once we locate him, we will, of course, need to interview him.'

'Why in this world would Lawrence want to murder a woman he didn't even know and, as far as I'm aware, had never met?'

'Mr Croft,' Brenda said, 'someone had sufficient motive for carrying out this crime. Also, that person must have hoped to benefit by her death. We are only in the early stages of our enquiry and once we have contacted a few more people we should be able to find some answers, and believe me, sir, with considerable hard work and diligence on our part, we will.'

*

Ian's visit to The Royal Oak was unproductive. Sandra Watson, her personal antenna well to the fore, had been in reception when he walked up the flight of steps to the front door of the hotel.

'Good morning, Inspector Ash.' she said in her pseudo southern counties accent which didn't disguise her Welsh origins, and totally lacking in any degree of welcome.

'Good morning, Mrs Watson,' equally as correct, 'I presume you have heard about Miss Miller's death?'

'I should say I have,' she replied, pursing her lips in what Ian read as displeasure at having to think about yet another murder in Meadowbank and one which, as before, meant her hotel was the focus of police attention, 'one would have to be either deaf or blind, Inspector,' she went on waspishly, 'not to have heard, but what I would like to know is why the Meadowbank Constabulary should feel it necessary to come here, disrupting the normally smooth running of my hotel.'

'As Miss Miller's car had been left in the hotel car park, Mrs Watson, would be a clear indication she had been in here on Thursday evening,' he said, feeling there was no need to respond to her tirade of complaints, which sounded to him like a carbon copy of what they'd had to put up with the last time they were there, 'and we need to find out, if we can, the time she arrived, whether she was with someone and when she finally left the hotel.'

'You're going to tell me next that these are routine questions?'

'They are, yes.' Ian said, 'We understand,' he continued, 'Miss Miller was not an infrequent visitor; it's possible she was on friendly terms with, for example, your receptionist or your barman. Admittedly, so far, we don't have a great deal to go on and it's for this reason we have to start right at the beginning which was, as far as we are aware, from the moment she drove into the car park and walked into the hotel.'

'I suppose that makes sense, but honestly, Inspector, this is such an imposition and not for the first time either. The reputation of my hotel is bound to suffer and when I think of what we can very shortly expect when those reporters and photographers from London arrive, I positively cringe!'

'We regret the inconvenience and we'll do our best to minimise it, but meanwhile, I would like to have a word with your barman, if that is possible.'

'Oh, feel free.' she said, waving her arm dismissively and, turning on her heels walked away from him.

'Mrs Watson isn't very happy, Inspector. She's hating every minute of this.' the woman behind the desk remarked, stating the obvious.

'We understand how she must be feeling,' he said to her, 'it's only understandable.'

'I haven't been in Meadowbank very long,' she explained, 'but I've heard about those other murders and I have to admit it has made me quite nervous.'

'Were you on duty on Thursday evening?' he asked.

'No, I wasn't. I finished at six and then I wasn't on again until eight the following morning.'

'And this evening, Susan,' he asked, seeing her name on the badge pinned to the lapel of her jacket, 'will it be the same receptionist when you come off duty?'

'Judith? That's right, Inspector.'

'Right,' he said, 'it looks as if I'll have to return later on, then. Incidentally, had you met Miss Miller?'

'Not actually met her, no, but I'd seen her couple of times. It was Judith who told me who she was.'

'I believe she visited Meadowbank fairly often?'

'I think she did, but when she came here, she always went straight through to the lounge bar.'

'On those occasions can you remember whether she was on her own?'

'I never saw her with anyone, it's true, but it doesn't mean she wasn't meeting someone in the bar.'

'Well, I'll have a word with the barman; perhaps he will remember seeing her on Thursday.'

Ted, as Brenda had mentioned earlier, did have a good memory, which made him a reliable witness and while it was obvious to Ian he was anxious to be of some help in what he described as a tragic death to such a nice lady, he told him that Muriel Miller hadn't been in there on

Thursday evening.

'I'm positive about that, Inspector Ash,' he had insisted, wiping along the top of the immaculate bar, 'you see, we weren't all that busy on Thursday. And, I would have remembered anyway. When she came in, she always sat up at the bar and if I wasn't too busy we would have a chat. I liked her. And to think somebody would have done that to her – well, it doesn't bear thinking about. It really doesn't.'

'When you did see her, Ted, was she always on her own?'

'Most of the time, she was, yes.'

'And the other times?' he prompted.

'She was friendly with one of our resident guests and when they had a drink together, they would sit over at one of the tables.' he said, pointing towards the tables beside the French windows.

'I see,' Ian nodded. 'A resident, you say?'

'That's right. He's a landscape designer, working on the Riverside development in Bridge Street; you know,' he added, 'they've almost completed building those luxury houses.'

'I know. Very nice.' Ian commented.

'They are; not that I'll ever be able to afford to buy one, unless I win the lottery and fat chance of that ever happening.'

'One can dream.'

'That's true, but,' looking serious, 'Inspector?'

'Yes?'

'I hope you find whoever did that to Miss Miller.'

'We will, Ted; we will.'

By a stroke of luck Ian didn't see any sign of Sandra Watson when he left the hotel, but knowing he would be back later, he wasn't holding his breath he'd be able to avoid a further encounter with the lady.

The forensic team was clearing away the sheets of plastic tarpaulin when Ian drove past. He didn't stop, but continued along Bridge Street, passing Phil Nicholson's place on the right-hand side, by now the road narrowing and in places not much more than a single track. He hadn't been along here for years and he didn't think it was much used, except by

Phil and anyone else going to Bridge Farm, but he wanted to make sure it was the same as he remembered. Most of the area was farmland and very unlikely any of it would have been sold for re-development and, being lowland, would never appeal to any prospective investor. He remembered how treacherous the road could be in winter with the wind blowing over unchecked from the Downs, also there was something bleak and soulless but that could be his imagination. He was now alongside the old quarry, recalling how, as boys, they used to cycle along here, spending hours attempting to climb up the hewn-out stony face, pretending they were mountaineers and never for a moment thinking they were in any danger of breaking a limb or worse. Young lads, he thought; they have no sense of self-preservation. He carried on to the end of the road until it reached the A30 and, deciding there was no point in going any further, reversed and went back towards Meadowbank. It would have been extremely unlikely anyone else would have been driving along this way on Thursday night, making that piece of waste ground a relatively secluded spot to pull in close to the hedge and drag Muriel Miller from the car. How long would it have taken? Ten, fifteen minutes? No longer, he reckoned, but he'd been taking a risk all the same. The time of death had now been established at ten twenty-five; too early for the pubs to be closing, reminding him he should have a word with Phil Nicholson. He knew he drank in The Market Inn, although he also knew, he usually didn't leave until last orders had been called, but he would talk to him all the same. Phil had a couple of sons; they might have been driving along and if a car had been parked there, even with its lights switched off, they couldn't have failed to miss it. Also, because the way the road curved sharply a hundred yards or so along from The Bridge, anyone arriving or leaving the pub around that time wouldn't have been able to see the waste ground. It would have also been obscured from the turn off on the right into Bridge Lane. Whoever the killer had been, he must have made himself familiar with the terrain which Ian thought resignedly didn't exactly rule out anyone who didn't live in and around Meadowbank.

He called into The King's Arms before going back to the Station and walking through to the bar, the first person he saw was Jason Miller. Surprisingly, he appeared reasonably friendly; at least he didn't ignore him, and taking advantage, Ian pulled out a bar stool and sat down next to him.

'Good morning, Inspector,' he said, making room for him, 'you work on a Saturday, I see.'

'Usually,' Ian shrugged; it's all part of the job.'

'I expect so; I think so many of us have become used to the five-day week, although when I first started working, it was the norm.'

'Changed times.' Ian commented, ordering a half lager from the barmaid.

'How is the enquiry going, Inspector?' he asked, changing the subject, which was exactly what Ian wanted him to do.

'Slowly,' he answered, 'but that's only to be expected. It's often like this; one hard slog, when you don't think you're getting anywhere, but somehow or other you do. How did your relatives take the news of your cousin's death; you mentioned you were going to contact them.'

'Oh, I did; yesterday and naturally they were shocked.'

'I suppose they would have been. They didn't offer to come back here to help you out with the various formalities?'

'No,' he gave a rueful smile, 'you see, as I explained to you, we are a strangely put-together sort of family when the only blood relatives are Oliver and Christine, but even then they didn't have the same mother, not forgetting Oliver's brother, of course.'

'Difficult to get one's head round.'

'I should say so, but what I'm trying to say is that none of us are all that close, also not over-friendly towards each other.'

'Except for you and Muriel?'

'That's right; except for us. When we were young she was more like a sister than a cousin, actually, but as often happens, the big world takes over and that bond slackens.'

'How often did you see her?'

'In recent years, hardly at all, which of course I'm now regretting.'

'Could we just go back to Thursday evening, Mr Miller,' Ian suggested, expecting him to object, but he didn't.

'Sure.'

'My superior, Chief Inspector Brenda Masters, will be meeting the other four members of your family over the weekend and one of her questions will be that of time.'

'Time?'

'Yes, the time they arrived at the hotel; in fact, when you all arrived and when Miss Miller left for The Royal Oak and, of course, they must tally.'

'I see.' he said, 'Well, I don't really know what time they arrived, but not long before me.'

'After you had booked into the hotel, Mr Miller, did you go straight through to the bar?'

'I did, yes.'

'And as you've mentioned, Miss Miller had already left?'

'That's right; she had.'

'I can't help wondering,' Ian said, selecting each word carefully; he didn't want to raise any suspicions in Jason Miller's mind, 'whether you may have seen her drive away from the King's Arms.'

'Why should I have?'

'Because of the timing, that's why. I don't know whether your cousin went up to her room before she went out again; she may have done, but if she didn't I would have thought the time of your arrival, in fact the time you pulled up, presumably in front of the hotel, would have coincided with when she drove off.'

'She must have gone up to her room first, then,' he said, a look of wariness in his expression, 'because I can assure you, Inspector, I didn't see her.'

'How did you spend the rest of the evening?' Ian asked him.

'I had a drink with the family, and then I had an early night. I was tired,' he explained, 'I'd been late finishing work and then having to drive down to Meadowbank, I wasn't all that hungry and quite honestly, Inspector, I was in no mood for socialising. I had,' he added, 'been extremely fond of my aunt and I wasn't looking forward to attending her funeral on the Friday. Perhaps if Muriel had been there, I would have stayed and we could have indulged in a little nostalgia, but I don't know.'

'You didn't leave the hotel?'

'Only for an hour.' Jason said, 'I wanted to get some air, so I went outside but it started to rain, and instead of going back to the hotel, I walked along to The Market Inn and had a couple of beers in there.'

'What time did you finally get back to the hotel?'

'Oh, it couldn't have been much later than nine-thirty.'

'Was there anyone on duty at the front desk when you came in?'

'No, the receptionist had left by then and as all the guests are given a pass number for the front door, it wasn't a problem.'

'What about the bar and restaurant customers?'

'Last orders are taken at nine,' Jason explained, 'although the bar is open until eleven, but mainly for residents, unless of course any of the non-residents who had come into the hotel before nine.

'And you went straight to your room?'

'Yes.'

'Did you notice whether the other members of your family were still up?'

'I didn't as it happens and by then I was ready to get my head down.'

'And did you sleep soundly?'

'I think so.' he answered, looking surprised at the question, 'At least, I don't remember waking up at any time, not until my alarm went off at eight the next morning.'

'The reason I'm asking you is because if you hadn't, or perhaps had difficulty getting off to sleep, you may have heard cars pulling up outside the hotel, or if it comes to that, driving away.'

'No, I don't believe I did.'

'You see, sir,' Ian explained, 'your cousin may have returned here and it's possible someone may have seen or heard her.'

'But –' he faltered, 'but that doesn't make sense; her car was found still at The Royal Oak, and yet -'

'- I believe I know what you're thinking,' Ian put in, 'but we have to look at all the possibilities, no matter how unlikely they may appear.'

Ian didn't have another lager and buying a ham and cheese roll at the bakers next door to the hotel took it with him back to the office, intending to spend the remainder of the afternoon catching up on paperwork which had accumulated since they had begun this enquiry.

It was almost six when the call from Jennifer Stevens was put through to his office. He hadn't seen her for a while and this was the first time she had ever phoned him at work and hearing her voice on the other end of the line gave him the much-needed fillip he needed after the last two gruelling days.

'Hello, Ian,' she said, 'I hope it's alright phoning you?'

'Of course it is, and it's good to hear from you. I had been meaning to call you, but each time there's been one crisis or another to prevent me, especially these last couple of days.'

'I can well imagine,' and he heard the sympathy in her voice, reminding him what a nice girl she was, 'but are you free this evening? Please say you are.'

'I am, actually. I've only got one more call to make and that will be that until, hopefully, Monday.'

'That's great. Would you like to accompany me to a party?'

'Yes.' he laughed out loud, realising this was probably the first time he'd laughed for days. How very serious I've become, he thought.

'It's Penny and Paul's engagement party,' she explained, 'and they're holding it at The Bridge, also,' she continued, 'Penny told me she would love it if you could come.'

'I'd like that.'

'Fantastic.'

'Would you like me to pick you up?'

'Well, there really isn't any need, is there? As you know, I live only a stone's throw away from the pub. I tell you what, though, why don't we meet for a quick drink in The Market Inn first and then we can walk along to The Bridge together? It should be a good evening, Ian; all the usual crowd will be there.' she added.

They arranged to meet at seven-thirty, Ian telling her he should be finished by then and as he rang off he couldn't remember when he had last felt so happy, almost euphoric, in fact. It really was time he started to live and not be so embroiled in his career, realising there was a danger of him becoming, not only old before his time, but an exceedingly dull person.

His luck was holding: Sandra Watson was not in evidence, although he had to wait several minutes until the receptionist dealt with a family of four who had arrived at the hotel shortly before him.

'Hello, Inspector,' she said to him, 'Susan told me you'd been in earlier.'

'I don't want to delay you;' he said, 'I've just seen a coach pull up outside, so it looks as though you have some more guests.'

'That's alright,' she smiled at him; a pretty blonde-haired girl he hadn't seen before, then he remembered she must be Alison Moore's replacement, 'it normally takes them a while to get their baggage sorted out and they always have so much of it!' she added. She certainly had the right kind of disposition, he thought, to work for someone as strong-willed as the indomitable Sandra.

'On Thursday evening, Judith,' he said, 'I believe you were on duty?'

'Yes,' she answered, 'It's about what happened to poor Miss Miller, isn't it Inspector; that's why you're here?'

'It is,' he nodded, 'do you remember seeing her that evening; apparently she'd told people she was coming here.'

'I do, actually,' she said, 'it was shortly after seven when she came in.'

'On her own?'

'Yes, although I think she must have arranged to meet someone.'

'Why do you think that?'

'Because she didn't go into the lounge bar, that's why. Instead, she went through the other door into the restaurant. Also,' she went on, she hadn't made any reservation for dinner as she had done previously.'

'Were there many bookings for Thursday?'

'Quite a number, but none of them for so early in the evening; the first ones were for eight and they were mostly guests, preferring to eat later.'

'Did you happen to notice when Miss Miller left the hotel?'

'I can't be sure about the exact time,' she said, 'but I think it must have been around ten. I'd just come back from my break as they were coming out of the restaurant.'

'Would this have been the person she'd had dinner with, do you think?'

'I would say it was very likely; I'd often seen her with him before.'

'And they both left the hotel at the same time?' Ian asked, scarcely believing what she was saying. Was this case going to be as easy as this to crack, he wondered, but he knew better than to think like that; he had learned from when he had joined the force never to accept what appeared to be an obvious solution.

'They did, Inspector, but Mr Cartwright didn't stay outside for long, he was back within five or six minutes.' she said, her words immediately confirming exactly what he'd been thinking. Who was it, he wondered, trying to remember, who said there was no such thing as a free lunch.

'Is Mr Cartwright a frequent visitor?'

'He's one of our regular guests, Inspector; he's a landscape designer and is working on the new riverside development in Bridge Street.'

'I see; well, you've been very helpful, Judith, thank you.'

'Not at all,' she smiled sadly at him, 'I only hope whoever did such a wicked thing is caught, Inspector.'

'We're doing our best,' he told her, 'and speaking to people like yourself helps us a great deal, you know, and we have come to depend on any feedback we can get. Now,' he went on, 'if it's possible, I would like to have a few words with Miss Miller's friend. Would you check for me please, Judith and see if he's in the hotel?'

'Oh, he won't be,' she said quickly. 'I know that already because he's in London this weekend, something to do with the people he's working for on the landscaping project, and won't be back until late tomorrow afternoon.'

'That's too bad; I'll have to wait until then. Meanwhile,' he asked, 'do you know the name of these people, also Mr Cartwright's Christian name?'

'It's Bradley, Inspector, but I'm afraid I don't know the name of the firm he's contracted to; he's never mentioned it.'

Chapter Three

'This is lovely, Mike,' Brenda said over her shoulder to him as their waiter showed them to an alcove table, 'and what a great atmosphere.'

'You approve?' he smiled, sitting down beside her on the white leather banquette.

'Very much.'

He had brought her to "El Cid's", a relatively new Spanish restaurant in the heart of London's theatre land and one Brenda had not been to before. Immediately she had stepped over the threshold she had felt transported to the Mediterranean where the sun always seemed to be shining and when each evening would stretch out for hours over tapas and deliciously cool white wine and meanwhile being serenaded by the guitarists weaving their way around the tables, exactly as they were doing tonight; the hauntingly and infinitely romantic gypsy flamenco music adding to the ambience; a thousand miles away from Meadowbank.

'What sort of an afternoon have you had?' Mike asked, opening the wine menu.

'As far as work went, not productive, I'm afraid.' she admitted, 'It looks as though I'll have to stay on until Monday when the offices will be open.'

'I'm not complaining, Brenda.' he said softly, placing a hand on her arm.

'I know.' she smiled. It had been the right decision for them to get back together again, she thought. Perhaps this time, being older and, hopefully, wiser, they would be able to make a go of their relationship. There remained the problem of them living and working apart, although she knew she could change that. Mike had suggested earlier in the year she should apply for a transfer to London and while she realised she would do this eventually, she continued to hold back on making such a radical change to her life. She had lived in Meadowbank for so long and however stymied she had begun to feel, she was still nervous about the idea of moving away. It wasn't as though she didn't know London; she did and she also knew once she finally made the decision she wouldn't have any real difficulty in adapting.

'You know, Mike,' she said, after he had ordered their meal, 'coming in here this evening has reminded me I haven't had a proper holiday for at least three years. That's awful, isn't it?'

'I think we're all rather guilty of that,' he answered, 'it's the nature of our work, I suppose. And,' he added, 'you're right, it isn't good, pretty unhealthy actually. We should try and get away this winter, Brenda, even if it's only for a week; it would do us good.' he added.

'What a lovely idea, but as usual and something which has been happening all too often in recent months, Meadowbank, or I should say, events in Meadowbank, have quite literally taken over, making it practically impossible to plan something as simple as that.'

'I understand; you know that, don't you?'

'I know.' she said, 'But, this afternoon for instance; I did something I haven't done for ages.'

'What was that?' a quizzical smile hovering, reminding her for a moment of how he used to look at her when they had first met; a younger Mike and one she had been passionately in love with and had truly believed would last forever, but of course it hadn't. Now, she realised, feeling unusually philosophical and blaming it on the strength of the wine, what they had rediscovered in recent months, was far more important. There was a depth to their feelings which had never been there in those early days.

'I went shopping.' she said, trying to shrug off such pathetically mental ramblings.

'You went shopping.' he repeated, grinning.

'I hope you're not making fun of me, Mike Harper.'

'No, I'm not, but it was the way you said that; well, it was funny, although in a way rather sad.'

'Why sad?'

'It has reminded me, not that I really needed reminding, that you've been working too hard, Brenda. For far too long.'

'I suppose I have, but I'm finding it extremely difficult to change; to jump off that particular treadmill. Going back to this afternoon, Mike,' she said, 'although I enjoyed in a little retail therapy all the time I felt guilty.'

'Guilty?'

'Yes; there I was in Oxford Street while back in Meadowbank Ian Ash was probably slogging away making inroads into solving this latest case.'

'There's no point in me telling you to feel any differently, because I do know how you feel.'

'I'm like the proverbial mother hen.' she smiled, watching as he refilled her glass.

'Perhaps, but a particularly lovely mother hen.' and leaning over to kiss her on the cheek, 'Incidentally, although I didn't really want us to talk shop this evening, I have been thinking about this Muriel Miller case.'

'Yes?'

'In particular, the missing relative.'

'Lawrence Croft?'

'Yes, as soon as you mentioned his name to me earlier, I knew I'd heard it before.'

'And you had?'

'Yes, I had. Suffice to say, Brenda, I'll be most surprised if you find him, not under that name anyway.'

'Why?' she asked, her professionalism coming to the fore, in spite of wanting to keep this evening free; free from any interventions and a reminder of work.

'Well,' he started to explain, 'and I don't want us to spend too long talking about this; I don't want it to spoil our evening, but Lawrence Croft has a police record and before leaving the Yard this evening I ran a check on his background.'

'This doesn't augur too well for him, does it?'

'Perhaps not, but he served a twelve-month sentence for a rather daring and spectacular jewellery robbery in Bond Street, one of many as we later learned; this was during the eighties, but he wasn't actually caught until nineteen eighty-nine.'

'What happened to him after that?'

'He had been living in Lambeth, but moved to Brighton on his release from prison; we did have his address in Brighton, but not any longer. We thought at the Yard he'd probably gone overseas, so as far as our records go, Lawrence Croft ceased to exist.'

'He possibly changed his name, then; that is if he came back to this country?'

'I would think so.'

'I admit,' Brenda said, 'it is an added complication, but we should be able to trace him. The problem is, Mike, as you know, this will all take time and my supervisor is an extremely impatient man and if it turned out once we did find him he had nothing to do with this murder, my head will definitely be on that block; wasting police time and all that.'

'Bill Simms has always been an impatient man, Brenda. It's in his nature; he can't help it.'

'I know that, but it's as though he thrives on other people's inadequacies. Normally, I let this ride over me, but there are times when I've thought he could be a little bit more – well, -'

'Understanding?' he suggested.

'Perhaps; I don't know, but it's like having a large black monster hovering and waiting to pounce.'

'If it's any consolation, I know exactly what you mean, but don't let him get to you.'

'I'll try.'

'Anyway,' he smiled, 'I see our tapas are on their way to our table. Let's talk about something more conducive to our evening, shall we?'

'I'll drink to that,' Brenda said, raising her glass, 'to -'

'- to us, darling Brenda.'

*

'Hi, Jennifer! And Ian; great you were able to make it!' Penny called out to them as soon as they arrived at The Bridge.

'Hi, Penny,' Jennifer said, 'you're looking fabulous. I bet you didn't buy that dress in Meadowbank.'

'You won't believe this,' she laughed, 'but I've actually had it for years. And,' she added, 'you're right, I didn't buy it here; it was on one of my rare visits to London.'

'Oxford Street?'

'Where else? Anyway, a drink. Ian,' she said, turning to him, 'beer or champagne?'

'Champagne?'

'Yes, Jennifer,' Penny said, 'and why not? It's a gift from Paul's father.' she added.

'I'll have a glass please, Penny;' Ian said, 'it will make a change from my usual lager.'

'It will do you good, Ian. I bet you're up to your eyes at the moment with this latest business. But,' she wagged a finger at him, 'I promise not to talk about it, not tonight anyway.'

'I'm glad.' he smiled at her. For this evening at least he intended to forget about work and try to remember it was a Saturday night and he'd been invited to a party, also he was with Jennifer. He had only been five minutes late meeting her in The Market Inn and it had been good to spend a little time together, just the two of them. She'd always been in a crowd when he'd been in her company before, although realising he only had himself to blame; he could easily have altered that, but had never been sure how she felt about him, fearing rejection, but the fact she had been the one to take the initiative had given him confidence.

'I don't think you will have met Jessica Craig?' Penny said, introducing him to a dark-haired girl, elfin-featured and slanting grey-blue eyes, a little like a young Leslie Caron. Jessica told him that she and her mother had recently moved to Meadowbank and that she'd been fortunate enough to get a transfer to Lloyds Bank in the square.

'And what do you think of Meadowbank?' he asked her.

'It's okay; take a bit of getting used to after Manchester, but I think I'll survive!'

'You'll find us a friendly lot.'

'Oh, I do already.'

'Hi, Ian,' Paul said, coming up to them, two brimming glasses of champagne in each hand, 'good to see you.'

'Hello, Paul,' Ian answered, taking one of the glasses from him, 'and congratulations to you and Penny.'

'Thanks very much.' he said, 'My bachelor days are almost at an end!' he added with a wry grin.

'Congratulations, Paul.' Jennifer said, raising her glass.

'To the happy couple!' someone at the back of the pub called out and, in unison, everyone raised their glasses, Penny blushing as the toast was made and then everyone started talking at once.

'Hello, Ian; great evening, isn't it?' Jacqueline Wellings said to him, 'we haven't seen you in here for ages.'

'I know; I'm afraid I've allowed work to take over my life these last twelve months or so.'

'Not good.' she commented, 'Ian,' she continued, 'I'd like to introduce you to Adam Fry. Adam,' she said, linking arms with the man who had been standing slightly behind her, 'this is Ian Ash. Adam has recently taken over the "Meadowbank Pharmacy".'

'Hello, Ian.' he said, formally shaking hands: a serious looking man in his mid forties, Ian reckoned, some years older than the rest of them, but when he smiled as he was doing right now, his whole expression lightened and he could see why Jacqueline was attracted to him. Ian had known her for a long time and he'd always thought of her as an extremely shy woman and, although she'd had boyfriends over the years, for one reason or another, they never seemed to last long. Perhaps Adam Fry would prove to be different. He hoped so. She worked for Meadowbank's estate agents in Market Square and had done since leaving college. She was extremely good at her job, never putting any pressure on prospective clients and, somehow, having an inbuilt ability to find the right type of property they were looking for. He had thought with the demise of her manager earlier in the year she would have been promoted, but instead, the company had brought in Martin Frame from their Winchester office, who, from what he'd heard around the town, hadn't wasted much time in rubbing people up the wrong way until most of them now tried to avoid him if they could.

'Have you met Jessica?' Ian asked her.

'I have,' Jacqueline smiled at the girl, 'in fact, we arranged the leasing of "The Old Schoolhouse" to Jessica and her mother.'

'Terry Simpson's old house?' recalling it was now common knowledge that Paul's father, Terry, had moved in with Isobel Gallier.

'That's right. And how are you both settling in, Jessica?' Jacqueline asked her.

'Fine thanks. We love the house; lots of intriguing nooks and crannies. It's like going back in time and I wouldn't be surprised if there weren't secret passages behind all that marvellous wood panelling.'

'Perhaps.' Jacqueline laughed.

'What about you, Adam?' Ian asked, attempting to bring him into the conversation, 'has Jacqueline produced something equally as interesting for you from her books?'

'She has, actually,' he said, 'although it will be a couple of months before I can move in.'

'Adam is buying one of the new Riverside properties.' Jacqueline told him.

'That's the development across the road, isn't it?'

'It is, Jessica,' Adam answered, 'and I consider myself extremely lucky to get one, but thanks to Jacqueline as soon as she learned of the sort of place I was looking for, she was quick to point me in the right direction and from the moment I went along there, I knew it would be ideal.'

That is twice in one day he'd heard the development mentioned, remembering what Ted had said to him earlier. It would seem impossible, Ian thought with weary resignation, to switch off from work, however hard he tried.

'It's good to know the "Meadowbank Pharmacy" is back in business.' he remarked, forcing himself back into the present. 'It's a strange phenomenon but, although Meadowbank has three chemists, I really believe everyone has their own favourite and I have to say, I do.'

'It's odd you should say that,' Jacqueline put it, 'but you're absolutely right, Ian. I'm exactly the same, so, Adam,' turning to face him, 'you should feel honoured to know you've been instantly accepted into the community.'

'Oh, I am,' returning her smile and putting his arm around her shoulders, 'and at the moment,' he added, 'the only problem I seem to have is trying to find a new assistant.'

'But,' Jacqueline said, 'she's only been working for you for a couple of weeks.'

'I know, but apparently, she didn't realise she was pregnant when she took the job and her husband is insisting she gives up work.'

'Adam,' Jessica said, 'my mother will be looking for a job; she wanted to get all the unpacking and everything done first, but I really think she would be interested. You see,' she continued quickly, 'she was with Boots in Manchester before we moved here and had done for years and latterly she'd been working in the dispensary side of the business.' she added.

'Really?'

'Yes,' she nodded, 'I'm not usually as pushy as this, you know, and to be honest I do have an ulterior motive.'

'Yes?' and by the way his lips were twitching Ian could tell he was amused by her. Well, who wouldn't be, he thought; there was something wonderfully refreshing about the girl.

'We've only been in Meadowbank for such a short time, but already I've realised there aren't many vacancies in the town and I didn't want her having to drive into Stockbridge or Winchester every day. I know she wouldn't have minded all that much, so I suppose I'm being selfish really.'

'No, I don't think you are, Jessica,' Jacqueline said, 'it shows you care about her. And, Adam,' she went on, 'I've met Jessica's mother; she's a lovely lady and I'm sure you will like her.'

*

'What's wrong, Christine? You've been in a very strange mood ever since you got up this morning.'

'I'm surprised you need to ask me that, Godfrey. I really am.'

'I'm sorry for being so obtuse,' he said, 'but -'

'- Oh, for goodness sake, Godfrey, don't be so pedantic. I am extremely tired; I didn't get a wink of sleep last night. I kept thinking about mother. I just cannot believe what Arnold Brutton told us on Friday.'

'You mean this other daughter?'

'Yes, I do mean her, but that's only part of it; I also kept thinking of the will mother left. Do you know, Godfrey, I am honestly beginning to wonder whether she wasn't going senile!'

'Don't you think you're being a trifle extreme? Besides, I'm sure the lawyer would be the first to notice whether she had been.'

'Don't you believe it. Arnold Brutton must have received a fair bit of money from her; he'd been handling her affairs for years.'

'I'm afraid we're stuck with the situation, Christine, unacceptable though you find it.'

'I have no intention of merely sitting here and doing nothing. I meant what I said to Jason on Friday about contesting the will. When I think of what she left us, it makes me furious. And, what about everything mother left to Muriel? Have you considered that? Who will it all go to now, I ask you?'

'Presumably, as Muriel had no family of her own, there must be some sort of proviso in place. Your mother was a wily old bird, after all.'

'Don't I know it! Everything will probably go to *this woman*. And, what about mother's share in Croft's Fine Arts? Have you given that a thought? I don't suppose you have!' answering her own questions, 'By right, that should now belong to me, you know. After all, I am her *legitimate* daughter!'

'What percentage of shares are we talking about here, Christine?'

'Forty per cent, with, of course,' she added grudgingly, 'Oliver having the controlling interest.'

'Incidentally,' Godfrey said, 'according to the share index, Croft's are doing extremely well.'

'That, Godfrey,' she sighed, glaring at him, 'is absolutely no consolation to me and all the more reason to go ahead and contest mother's will; otherwise as I see it, this Emily Craig woman is going to get the whole damn lot!'

'Can't we just drop it; you'll make yourself ill otherwise and don't forget we have the visit from Meadowbank's Chief Inspector this morning.'

'As if I am likely to forget. All I can say is I'm glad the girls are staying with their friends this weekend. I don't want them to know about any of this, Godfrey. You know what the pair of them are like; inquisitiveness should have been their middle name!'

The pendulum clock in the hall was striking eleven and Christine, in her present frame of mind, was quick to complain that at the very least the Chief Inspector could have been punctual, when it occurred to Godfrey, at that moment hearing the Sunday newspapers falling on to the mat inside the front door an hour later than they normally did, what was wrong. This only made her more irritable and predictably blamed him for not putting the clocks back before they went to bed the night before. To Christine, it was his responsibility, definitely nothing to do with her and reminding him once more that she had quite enough to contend with.

A couple of cups of coffee later and at precisely eleven, the front door bell rang, Godfrey offering to answer it, giving her a couple of minutes to compose herself for the coming interview, not having much idea of what kind of questions they were likely to be asked and, for the first time, wondering whether Oliver and Sonia had received a visit from her. She should have phoned them last evening, but of course it was too late now, hearing voices in the hall.

Christine's first impression of the Chief Inspector when Godfrey brought her into the lounge was how young she was for such an elevated position in the police force. She couldn't be much more than thirty-five, also, she was extremely attractive; thick blonde hair, naturally curly, and startlingly blue eyes which were now appraising her, giving her the unnerving sensation of being able to see right through her.

'I appreciate you agreeing to see me, Mrs Mason,' she said, 'especially on a Sunday, but unfortunately, it is necessary as I need to move forward with our enquiries while certain events remain clear in people's memories.'

'I don't see how we can be any help to you, Chief Inspector.' Christine said.

'It's to be hoped you can be, Mrs Mason. However,' Brenda continued, 'can you remember what time you and your husband arrived at The King's Arms on Thursday evening?'

'I am quite sure,' Christine replied, 'you know that already.'

'Whether I know or not, Mrs Mason, is hardly relevant; I'd like to hear from you.'

'About seven; wasn't it, Godfrey?' she asked him and including her husband for the first time.

'I would say so.' he agreed, 'We weren't actually watching the clock, Chief Inspector.' he added glibly, making it obvious he didn't put much importance on what she was asking.

'I understand you were joined by Mr Jason Miller for a drink before your meal.'

'Yes, but he didn't stay long; said he was tired and would skip dinner.'

'Did he go up to his room early, then?'

'I'm sure he did.'

'Honestly, Godfrey,' Christine Mason snapped, 'how on earth can you be so certain? It wasn't even eight when Jason left the bar and I can't see him going to bed at that time of the evening.'

'Where do you think he went, Mrs Mason?' Brenda asked her, slightly taken aback by the purposeful way she had pulled him up.

'I have no idea, Chief Inspector; probably went somewhere else for a drink.'

'Why?'

'Why?'

'Yes,' Brenda said, curious as to how she was going to elaborate, 'if he wanted another drink, why didn't he stay with you all in the bar?'

'Chief Inspector,' she sighed in exasperation, 'it's obvious you don't know my late-mother's extended family, because,' she went on, 'the only time we were together was at weddings and funerals and sometimes not even then. To put it in plain language, we had very little in common and the others, if they were being honest, would admit we didn't even like each other all that much.'

'And yet,' Brenda pointed out, 'Mr Oliver Croft is your brother.'

'Half-brother.' she corrected. 'I hardly know him. My father was already divorced and living away from home before he married my mother and hardly ever saw Oliver after that.'

'According to the statement taken from Mr Jason Miller, he and his cousin were on friendly terms.'

'Well, I suppose they were.' she grudgingly admitted.

'Later that night,' Brenda asked her, 'did either you or Mr Mason hear Miss Miller return to the hotel?'

'How could we have?'

'Your room was at the front of the hotel, Mrs Mason.'

'I suppose Jason told you that as well!'

'I will re-phrase my question,' Brenda said, ignoring her scathing comment towards a man she so obviously didn't think a great deal of, 'but, first of all, what time did you and your husband go up to your room?'

'As to the exact time, I have no idea.'

'Approximately, then. After your meal in the restaurant, it is my understanding you returned to the lounge bar –'

'Do you know, Chief Inspector,' she interrupted, 'I see absolutely no point in asking us something you know already!'

'Please, Mrs Mason; this is a murder enquiry we are investigating and it is crucial we interview each person as thoroughly as we can and if we sound as though we're doubling up on our questions, it is the only way to reach a true picture of events. Now,' Brenda continued, 'if you can just confirm that you did in fact have a drink in the bar after your meal, I would appreciate it.'

'We did.'

'Fine, now, after Mr and Mrs Croft left the bar, how long did you stay there before retiring for the night?'

'No more than another five minutes or so. Do you agree, Godfrey?'

'Yes, that's right. It would have been shortly after ten-thirty.'

'Thank you. Did either of you hear any car pulling into the parking area which would have been more or less directly below your bedroom window?'

'I didn't hear a thing, Chief Inspector,' Godfrey Mason said, 'I think I must have gone to sleep the moment my head hit the pillow.'

'And you, Mrs Mason?' Brenda turned to her, 'Did you hear anything? If you were both in bed well before eleven it would have been too early for the pubs to be closing and it would have been relatively quiet at that time.'

'I heard nothing.'

'Where was Miss Miller's room in relation to the one you and your husband were in?'

'Why do you want to know that?'

'Mrs Mason, please; could you just answer the question?'

'It was next door.'

'And you didn't hear her return; a door closing, perhaps or even the sound of a television?'

'But she didn't come back to the hotel, so how could I have heard anything?'

'How do you know she didn't return, Mrs Mason?'

'Well, I don't of course, but she couldn't have, could she?'

'Why not?'

'Because of where she was found, that's why. She couldn't have been in two places at once, could she?'

'Finally, your professions;' ignoring the heavy sarcasm, 'I need this information for our records.' Brenda explained patiently, preparing herself for a further outburst of indignation.

'I'm in finance,' Godfrey Mason replied, 'and have my own consultancy firm in the Strand.'

'And the name of your firm, sir?'

'Mason & Thornton, Financial Advisory Service.'

'Thank you, and yourself, Mrs Mason.'

'I only work part-time now,' she explained, 'I'm a nurse at Guy's Hospital.'

*

Bradley Cartwright returned to The Royal Oak shortly after six on Sunday evening. He'd had a productive three days. Not only had he received a further stage payment from the Riverside developers, but he had also signed up as landscape consultant on a large twelve-month extension plan on a site south of the Thames; this, fortuitously, to start immediately after the completion of the Riverside contract.

Walking through reception towards the lounge bar he felt in the mood for celebrating and wished Muriel could have been with him. He had tried to phone her earlier in the day, but when there had been no answer either from her mobile or from the house in Swiss Cottage, he had assumed she must have been spending the remainder of the weekend with one of the family.

He had known Muriel for a number of years, having first met in Salisbury where he'd been living since moving there from Brighton in the early nineties. She had driven into Salisbury on that Saturday morning to do some shopping and had called into "Bruciano's", the Italian coffee shop in the centre of the town. The place had been packed, which was often the case back then before other less expensive cafes cropped up, and he'd asked her whether she would mind if he shared the table with her.

She had been easy to talk to, telling him she lived in London and worked for a branch of Barclays Bank in Regent Street and made a point of trying to come down to Hampshire once a month to spend the weekend with her step-mother. She had seemed genuinely interested in hearing about his work as a landscape designer and telling him he would find her step-mother's property in Meadowbank a real challenge. He'd had to confess he hadn't heard of Meadowbank before then and she had enjoyed describing the market town to him, amusing him by her portrayal of several of the locals who had lived there all their lives and, as she'd said, didn't take too kindly to 'foreigners', labelling them as newcomers even if they had been there for years. Apart from mentioning she had once been married, she said very little about anyone else in her family and, sensing her reticence, he had never pressed her, mainly because he was much the same. He had left home years earlier and had long lost touch with his own family and meeting her had been in many respects like finding a soul mate.

After that first Saturday, they continued to meet each time she came to Meadowbank; sometimes there, but more often she would come into Salisbury to see him. Occasionally, on those other weekends when they had both been free, he would drive up to London, staying with her in Swiss Cottage. Their relationship was an unusual one; neither of them making any demands on the other. While, what they shared could never be described as passionate, or even all that romantic, he felt comfortable with what had developed into a settled pattern. There was no other woman in his life and he very seldom thought too far ahead to a time when he may be ready to retire and, perhaps then to decide to make their arrangement a more permanent one, but he was as reasonably content as any man of his age could expect to be. He felt he had been fortunate to have achieved as much as he had after an extremely shaky start when he could have all too easily have spent the rest of his life ducking and diving from the law. Yes, he thought, Muriel was good for him, wishing once again she could be here and waiting for Ted to finish serving a couple who had come into the hotel minutes before.

'Sorry to keep you waiting, Mr Cartwright.'

'That's alright, Ted; I'm in no rush.' pulling out one of the stools and sitting down in front of the bar.

'You haven't heard have you, sir?' Ted asked him and for the first time

Bradley noticed the way he was looking at him; with an expression he'd never seen on his face in all the time he'd been coming in here and finding it difficult to interpret. The only explanation he could think of was that during the few days since he'd been away something had occurred to deeply trouble him.

'Heard what, Ted?'

'About your friend, Miss Miller.'

'Muriel?' completely thrown; her name being the last one he expected to hear, positive his heart had skipped a beat, 'Has something happened to her?'

'Oh, dear,' he sighed, looking more worried than ever, 'this is so difficult to say, Mr Cartwright, but -' floundering, as he struggled for the words he wanted, but Bradley was incapable of helping him out; he had momentarily lost the ability to say anything; he could only wait, a dull heavy ache in the pit of his stomach, '- but,' Ted repeated, 'she was found on that piece of waste ground in Bridge Street.'

'Found!' he gasped, 'Do you mean – she's dead?'

'She'd been murdered, sir.'

'But – but how, Ted? And when was this?'

'It happened late on Thursday night,' he answered quietly, 'but they didn't find her until the following afternoon.'

'My God! And I never knew!'

'Judith told me you were in London, sir, and may not have heard, unless of course you'd read about it in one of the nationals on Saturday; we've both realised what a terrible shock it would be for you.'

'I haven't seen a newspaper this weekend.' doing his utmost to control his emotions and wanting to order a scotch to deaden the ache, but immediately dismissed this as being a bad idea; he had no wish to go down that road, it would be too easy to end up wallowing in self-pity and that, in the end, would achieve nothing. He'd lost her and he had to learn to live with the sadness in another way.

More customers were arriving and, before moving along the bar to serve them, Ted offered to let him have a copy of the "Courier", although

Bradley could tell by his tentative expression he was doubtful whether his suggestion had been such a wise one. And, Bradley thought, taking the newspaper from him, he could be right, but he had to find out more, taking his lager with him over to one of the tables away from the bar.

A younger Muriel smiled out at him from the front page and the impact of looking at her again almost made him fold up the newspaper and take it straight back to Ted, but he didn't. Instead, taking a long sip of his beer, he read through the report, including the stark and, in his opinion, unnecessarily harsh headline.

"MURDER RETURNS TO MEADOWBANK

On Friday afternoon, the body of Muriel Miller was found by Philip Nicholson of Bridge Farm. He had become concerned by seeing what he described as thousands of crows flying and hovering over the waste ground in Bridge Street and on investigating made the grisly discovery.

The cause of death has yet to be established, but the police are treating the case as one of murder. Miss Miller had been a frequent visitor to Meadowbank for a number of years, spending weekends with her step-mother, the late-Catherine Miller-Croft.

Miss Miller had arrived the evening before to attend her step-mother's funeral the following day and, having booked into The King's Arms in Market Square, along with other members of the family, went out again to spend the rest of the evening at The Royal Oak. When she made no appearance at Saint Stephen's on Friday morning, nor had she returned to her hotel, her cousin, Mr Jason Miller, by then becoming increasingly worried about her absence, contacted the police."

It wasn't only reading where Muriel had been found and so soon after he'd watched her leave The Royal Oak on Thursday night which affected him, but the staggering fact that her step-mother, by some cruel twist of fate, had been Catherine Miller-Croft. This was something he really did not want to know.

'Excuse me; you're Mr Bradley Cartwright, aren't you?'

Bradley had been so deeply absorbed he hadn't noticed the young man approaching. Looking up at him now, he realised he had seen him before a number of times over the months since he'd been working in Meadowbank. It had been in The Bridge, opposite to the site, when he'd called in there for a drink after he'd finished for the day.

'Sorry?' Bradley said, 'You seem to know me, but I'm afraid, I don't know who you are.'

'I'm Inspector Ian Ash of the Meadowbank constabulary, sir,' he said, showing him his warrant card, 'do you mind if I sit down?'

'Not at all.'

'I'm involved in the investigation of Miss Muriel Miller's murder.' he explained and, as the sheer inevitability of it all gradually seeped into Bradley's brain, he tried to ignore the overwhelming sense of despair which was threatening to swamp him, 'You were a friend of hers, I believe?'

'That's right, Inspector. Muriel and I were very good friends and I've only just heard about her death and quite frankly, I'm shattered. I've been away since Friday and I simply had no idea, no idea at all.'

'When did you last see Miss Miller?'

'On Thursday evening; we had dinner together here.' as if you didn't already know, he added under his breath.

'What time did she leave the hotel?'

'About ten I think it must have been.'

'And what did you do next, sir?'

'What do you mean?'

'Well,' the inspector explained, 'did you go to your room or come in here for a drink?'

'I went straight up to my room, watched the tail-end of a movie and then went to bed. I had an early start the following morning;' Bradley told him, 'I had a breakfast meeting for nine o'clock in London with one of my business associates.'

'Where did you park your car overnight, sir?

'In front of the hotel; why do you ask?'

'Because, on Friday we had a telephone call from Mrs Watson to tell us your friend's car had been outside the front of the hotel all night.'

'Well, all I can say, it couldn't have been? Not all night, anyway.'

'Why?'

'After Muriel and I left the restaurant I went with her to where she'd left it, which was in the car park at the rear of the building and I saw her drive away, that's why.'

'And this was at ten o'clock?'

'Roughly, yes, but I can't be absolutely sure.'

'I understand,' the inspector nodded, 'and what time did you leave on Friday morning?'

'Shortly after seven-thirty.'

'And, of course, it would still have been dark?'

'Of course. Inspector, is all of this so important?'

'We believe it might be, sir. You've already mentioned Miss Miller had parked her car in the car park at the rear and that you saw her leave, but her car was driven back later and of course if it had been parked round the back you wouldn't have seen it when you left the following morning.'

'That's true.'

'I am somewhat surprised you didn't notice though.'

'Why should I have, Inspector?' Was he deliberating trying to confuse me, Bradley wondered, or was he suffering from a delayed reaction to what had happened, either way, he was finding the inspector's method of questioning off putting.

'Because Miss Miller's car had been left at the front of the hotel.'

'But, we'd already agreed that it would have been dark at the time I went out there.'

'Yes, but surely there would have been a light on above the main door?'

'Of course there was, but I still didn't notice her car. I was only interested in one thing and that was to get on to the motorway and reach London in time for my appointment.'

'How long had you known Miss Miller, sir?' confusing him further by his quick change in the direction of his questioning.

'Six, seven years.'

'It's our understanding you're a resident guest here?'

'Yes, I am and will be until the completion of the work I'm involved in with landscaping the Riverside development in Bridge Street.'

'And do you live in London?'

'No, I have a house in Salisbury, although for most of the time I do a considerable amount of travelling, but Salisbury is my base.'

'You say you knew Miss Miller for almost seven years; did you ever meet any of her family?'

'No, I didn't.'

'Did she ever talk about them?'

'Not really, except her step-mother. That was when we first met; she told me she drove down to Meadowbank each month to visit her, but she never talked about anyone else.'

'Did she mention her step-mother's name to you?'

'No, as a matter of fact she didn't, Inspector.' he said, 'I had no idea who she was until about five minutes ago, when I read the report in the "Courier", pointing to the newspaper on the table between them.

'I'm surprised she didn't introduce her to you, especially as you were actually living in the same town.'

'Are you?' Bradley asked, trying to fathom out where he was coming from. It was very much like being under a microscope. He may be young, Inspector Ian Ash, but he was sharp; there was no doubt about it.

'I am, sir.'

'I can't see why. It was Muriel I was interested in and she was the person I wanted to be with, not any member of her family, even although, unlike her step-mother, none of them were living here.'

'Did she ever mention her ex-husband?'

'Only once, when we first met.'

'Do you know whether they ever kept in touch?'

'I should very much doubt if they did, but as I've just said, she never discussed him.'

'Not even his name?'

'No.'

'Have you any idea why she continued to wear her wedding ring after the divorce?'

'I have absolutely no idea. Why shouldn't she, if that was what she wanted to do.'

'And yet,' he persisted, 'she had reverted to using her maiden name.'

'What exactly are you trying to say, Inspector,' Bradley asked, becoming increasingly irritated by his barrage of questions which didn't appear to be leading anywhere in particular, 'that Muriel and I were married? Because if you are, then that can be very quickly checked out, can't it?'

'Mr Cartwright,' he said, 'this is only the second day of our investigation and at this stage we are merely putting out feelers, all of which will be followed up in greater detail, but the more we can glean now, the quicker we will be able to find the person who was responsible for this crime.'

'Look, Inspector Ash,' and wishing he would bring all of this to a speedy conclusion, 'I'm tired and distraught and all I want is to try and relax, preferably on my own this evening, and do my best to adjust to what has happened to Muriel. I don't honestly think I have anything further to add which would be of any help to you.'

'Alright, sir,' he said, getting to his feet, 'I appreciate your feelings; this can't be easy for you. However,' he continued, 'it may be necessary to speak to you again, therefore I would be grateful if you would give me a contact number in case you may not still be in Meadowbank if and when that should occur.'

Chapter Four

Emily called into "The Boiling Kettle" for a coffee; a small quiet cafe around the corner from the lawyers' offices. Her head was still reeling from what Arnold Brutton had told her and she needed time on her own and in the tranquil setting of somewhere apparently untouched by the twenty-first century in order to think, without the background clamour in the more popular cafes in the centre of the city.

The amount of money Catherine Miller-Croft had left her was staggering. She had yet to see "The Gables"; Mr Brutton had assured her it was quite vast and had gone on to list the various items inside the house which had also been bequeathed to her. Although he had referred to Catherine Miller-Croft as her mother, Emily could not see her in that way. As she had told Jessica the other day, the woman who had lovingly and unsparingly brought her up for all those years had been her mother, not this stranger, someone she had never known. Not for the first time since she had died, only a matter of months before her husband, Emily wished she could have been here with her to share what she saw as a burden and one with which she seriously wondered whether she could handle. At least, she smiled to herself; her pragmatic daughter would soon bring her down to earth when she heard. Often, Emily had thought it was as if their roles had been reversed; Jessica, the practical one while she was the dreamer, always trying to analyse even the smallest of issues. Well, she sighed, stirring her coffee, the enormity of this bequest could hardly be described as such! Even Jessica, once she had fully absorbed the news and realised how it must change their lives, would be hard-pressed to come up with an easy solution of how she could best manage it all.

Arnold Brutton had offered to act for her and she had been quick to agree. The firm of lawyers she had used before were in Manchester and, up to now and since moving south, there had been no necessity to find another one. She had liked him; 'one of the old school' as her mother would have said. He had given her the keys to "The Gables", together with a copy of the contents of the house and they had made arrangements for another meeting when she could sign the various documents; she hadn't felt up to it this morning and he hadn't pressed her; in fact, he had been quite sympathetic, clearly realising she was finding everything a bit too much. Emily took the bunch of keys out of her bag, looking at each of them in turn. There were six of them altogether and he had already explained to her where the various locks were located in the property. She was about to replace them when her mobile rang and, as invariably happened, it was right at the bottom of her bag, scrabbling now to find it.

'Hi, Mum; it's me.'

'Jessica. Everything alright, love?'

'Of course,' she laughed, 'it's you I've been worrying about.'

'Oh, I'm fine,' Emily said, 'I'll tell you everything when you get home this evening, but I'm glad you phoned. I now know what people mean when they say they're 'punch drunk'!'

'I can't wait! Where are you?'

'In a rather quaint little cafe, not far from Winchester cathedral.'

'Is the coffee good?'

'Very good, actually.' already, merely by talking to her, trivial though their conversation was, helped. She felt her flagging spirits beginning to dissipate.

'I'd better go now,' Jessica said quickly, 'customers.' she added. 'By the way, Mum, good luck for your interview this afternoon.'

Slipping the mobile into one of the side pockets inside the bag, she realised she had completely forgotten about the meeting she had later with Adam Fry. Talking about work was exactly what she needed; something she knew about and wondering what he would be like.

The cafe was beginning to fill up, most of the customers, judging by their shopping baskets and carrier bags, taking a mid-morning break. Emily wasn't in the habit of listening in to other people's conversations, but when she heard Meadowbank being mentioned by a woman at the next table, she couldn't help it, also, it wasn't as though she was making any attempt to lower her voice; she could hear her quite plainly: 'Yes, as I was saying, Freda,' the woman was repeating without pausing to take another breath, 'Meadowbank is in the news again. *Another* murder! What I would like to know is what's going on in that town!'

'How was the woman killed, then?' her friend asked her, 'It never said in the paper.'

'It didn't, did it? I expect the police are keeping that quiet for *some* reason. They do that, you know,' she added, as though she was an authority on police procedure.

'I expect they have their reasons.'

'If you ask me, it's something to do with that Miller-Croft family.'

'You could be right, I suppose. After all, she was the old lady's daughter.'

'*Step*-daughter, Freda.' quickly correcting her.

'Do you think the police are hushing it up, then?'

'Could be.'

'You mean money talks?'

'Well, it does, doesn't it, Freda.'

Emily had heard enough. Without waiting to ask for her bill, she stood up and walked over to the counter to pay for her coffee, the words of the unpleasant snippet of conversation repeating themselves in her brain. Whether she liked it or not, she also was a member of the Miller-Croft family, although up to the time the contents of the will had been read out to them, Mr Brutton had been the only person with that knowledge. How long would it be, Emily wondered, before it would become known locally and when this did happen, which was inevitable, what sort of reception could both Jessica and she expect to receive. She had spent most of her life living in a city and had no experience of the way people behaved in smaller communities, but if what she had just overheard was any indication, she didn't need much imagination to work out what it could very well be like when there were those, like the two in the cafe, with too much time on their hands and an insatiable appetite for gossip. Perhaps it hadn't been such a bright idea to take the radical step of moving south and starting afresh in a town as small as Meadowbank, but after Adrian had died, the loss she had suffered had been so intense, when re-visiting places they had been to had been physically painful, she needed to get away and try something new. Through those dark months Jessica, although grieving deeply herself for the loss of her father, had been an enormous help and when she had first broached the idea of moving, had been all for it and had suggested she put in for a transfer at the bank she was working for in Manchester. It had been like pinning the tail on the donkey blind-fold; from that moment, events moved swiftly with Jessica being offered a position at Lloyd's bank in Meadowbank. In many respects, it had been Meadowbank choosing them, rather than the other way round. Jessica had adapted almost immediately and had already made friends as Emily knew she would, at the same time realising it would take her a little longer, but she liked the town and "The Old School House" was perfect for them both. But now, she continued to fret, walking back to where she had parked the car, was all this newly found equilibrium going to disappear?

*

Ian Ash was in the lawyers' waiting room, having arrived about ten minutes too soon for his meeting with Arnold Brutton, noticed his previous client leave and as she walked past the window he thought he had seen her somewhere before, although it wasn't until the secretary was showing him into Mr Brutton's office, he remembered. He hadn't seen the woman before at all, but her resemblance to Jessica Craig was too remarkable for her not to be related. It had been Jacqueline who had mentioned to him that Jessica and her mother had taken over the lease of "The Old School House". He could be totally wrong, but he didn't think so.

'Good morning, Inspector.' Arnold Brutton greeted him.

'Good morning, sir;' Ian said, 'it's good of you to spare some time for me this morning.'

'Not at all.' gesturing for him to sit down, 'You've already explained on the phone the purpose for your visit and, naturally, I must comply, although I feel I should point out to you that we have been handling the estate of Mrs Catherine Miller-Croft for a number of years, even before my time, in fact; my father was a personal friend of William Singleton and responsible for the Singleton estate.'

'I'm sorry, sir,' Ian said, interrupting the flow, 'but you've just mentioned William Singleton; who was he?'

'Mrs Miller-Croft's father, Inspector. Singleton was her maiden name.'

'But,' Ian said, trying to fathom out what appeared to be a further complication in what they had so far learned about the family, 'it's our understanding she only moved to Hampshire later in her life; when she married her second husband and that she originally came from London?'

'That's absolutely correct,' the lawyer said, nodding his head, 'The Singleton family came from London and that was where my father first met them. However,' he paused for a second, looking at Ian over the rim of his gold-rimmed spectacles, reminding him of Mr Pastry, 'I'm sure you're not here to receive a history lesson on the Singleton family.'

'Well, no, sir,' Ian answered, 'although I do find it interesting all the same.'

'Oh, it is, believe me. You see,' unstoppable now it would seem, 'Mrs Catherine Miller-Croft, or Catherine Singleton as she was before she married, was already an extremely wealthy woman. Catherine was an only child, you understand, and when her parents died, relatively young as it happened, she was, naturally enough, the chief beneficiary and this was,' he added, 'some years before she married Howard Miller.'

'I understand.' Ian said, wondering how he was going to be able to move him forward to get round to telling him why he'd made the appointment to see him. He only wanted to know the details of the woman's will after all.

'I have a reason for telling you this, Inspector Ash,' he said, 'but up until the death of Catherine, there was a member of the family who had remained unknown to them.'

'Yes?' was he, Ian wondered, deliberately trying to confuse him. He was finding it extremely difficult to keep up with his prevaricating way of talking.

'Before I convey to you the details of Mrs Miller-Croft's last will and testament,' Arnold Brutton said, 'I must tell you, that apart from her step-daughter, Muriel Miller, who tragically is no longer with us, she bequeathed the bulk of her estate to the daughter she had before she married Howard Miller.'

'And no-one knew?'

'No; surprising though that may sound to you in these modern times, nobody did. She confided in me; this was some years later, after the death of her husband and before she re-married and moved to Meadowbank.'

'And the daughter had no idea?'

'None whatsoever. Oh, she was aware she had been adopted, but she was never told the name of her mother, nor her father, if it comes to that.'

'This is an amazing story.'

'I suppose it is, but back then, Inspector Ash, it wasn't all that uncommon. Disgracing the family was taboo and avoided at all costs. However,' he went on, 'what I'm leading up to is this; I have this morning met with the lady and broken the news to her, which came as something of a surprise, shock even, if I may say so. Also, and this is the crux of the matter, as far as we are concerned, she has agreed to me acting for her and in this respect I intend to do so and this means I will do my utmost to protect not only her interests, but to make sure she receives no aggravation or negative intrusion to her private life.'

'Alright, Mr Brutton,' Ian said, 'I appreciate this is a sensitive matter, and we will treat what you're saying as confidential, but we will require to have the name of the lady.'

'I realise that, Inspector.'

He had then gone on to outline the contents of Catherine Miller-Croft's will and, although not giving Ian a copy, he was able to write down the salient points; namely, as the lawyer had mentioned, the bulk of the estate had been bequeathed to the daughter, including "The Gables", where Catherine Miller-Croft had lived up until the time of her death, a lesser proportion to her step-daughter, Muriel Miller and relatively modest bequests to her nephew, Jason Miller and her step-son, Oliver Croft and Christine Mason, the daughter she had from her second marriage. This was what he needed; a fairly straightforward will, but he couldn't help wondering how the family had reacted on Friday after they'd learned about the existence of another daughter. Not too well, he reckoned.

'Did Mrs Miller-Croft live alone, sir?' Ian asked him.

'May I ask you why you want to know, Inspector?' a speculative expression on his face.

'Well, as you've mentioned the contents of the house, in particular the paintings and the silver collection, I was wondering about security, especially if the property is now empty.'

'I see.' he nodded, removing his spectacles for a second, as though playing for time. It was fairly obvious to him the lawyer was reluctant to disclose much more about the family he had acted for over the years, 'The house is indeed unoccupied at present. Mrs Miller-Croft had lived on her own for many years, Inspector; ever since her step-daughter left to work in London and in recent years, apart from seeing Muriel when she would visit, she had few visitors and, apart from the woman from the town, who went in there six days out of the seven, she led an extremely quiet, even reclusive, life, but she had often reassured me that she preferred it that way. As for security,' he continued, clasping his hands in front of him and, once again, peering across at Ian above his spectacles, 'entry to the property can only be accessed by the front entrance and those gates are kept locked, I understand, for most of the time. The windows also, had security locks fitted; this was done about a year ago when there was a spate of robberies in the district, but,' shrugging, 'in these times, Inspector, how secure is secure? Naturally, she was insured.' he added.

Jason Miller hadn't been wrong, Ian thought, when he'd described the structure of his family as being convoluted. And, now, with the appearance of a daughter who had, apparently, been unknown to any of them, even further complicated the case. He only had Arnold Brutton's word for what he'd just told him. And what about Emily Craig? He'd said she had always been aware of being adopted; it was feasible she may have made a point of finding out who her biological mother was. Years ago, it would have been almost impossible, but not now with the relaxed laws which applied to adoption. Also, how did Ian know that Catherine Miller-Croft, in her later years, hadn't confided in her step-daughter? Again, this was possible. The enquiry, he stifled a sigh, was in danger of going round in ever diminishing circles. He needed to talk to Brenda, but would have to wait until the middle of the afternoon when she would be back in Meadowbank.

To work out why Muriel Miller had been murdered wasn't too difficult, the question being, because of so many likely suspects, which one.

'Thank you for your assistance, sir,' Ian said, standing up, 'but before I leave, could I have the lady's name, please?'

'It's Mrs Emily Craig, Inspector.'

*

Brenda Masters drove into Market Square at four in the afternoon to the accompaniment of the chimes from Saint Stephen's. It was a wintry scene which greeted her as she pulled up in front of the Station. She had only been away since Saturday, but it felt longer. Already, London, and its constant bustle seemed much more than an hour and a half's drive away. Here, winter had come early: the trees across the square and lining the pavement in front of "The Salmon's Rest" restaurant and the terrace houses on either side had, she was sure, changed colour dramatically over the last couple of days; the scattering of leaves swirling upwards in the cold north-easterly wind, only going to prove to her the harsh reality of living in such a quiet and exposed part of the country and comparing the town unfavourably with how London would be, with the brightly-lit shop frontages and the seemingly never-ending stream of scarlet buses weaving their way in and out of the late afternoon traffic. Yes, she decided, stepping out on to the pavement, shivering and pulling up the collar of her overcoat against the sudden chill, it's time I moved on, but first things first: the Muriel Miller case; that had to be successfully resolved before she could take the final plunge of officially applying for a transfer.

Ian was in the outer office when she walked through and saw her as soon as she pushed her way through the swing doors.

'Hello, Ian;' she said, going towards him and taking off her coat, 'any developments on the Muriel Miller case?'

'There have been, actually, ma'am.' he said, 'I've just this minute finished writing up my report.'

'Good; I'll get us some coffee and then we can compare notes, although I have to admit, I didn't make as much headway as I'd hoped in London, most of which we knew already, in fact.'

It didn't take her long to read through his latest report, the name of Bradley Cartwright immediately catching her attention. Perhaps, she thought, these past couple of days haven't been so unproductive after all.

'I had a meeting with Muriel Miller's lawyer this morning,' she told him, 'and apparently she had made Bradley Cartwright her beneficiary, the one and only one, I might add.'

'Unless he's a very good actor, he gave me no inkling he knew anything about this, but then he wouldn't because, apparently, he had only heard about her murder minutes before I met him yesterday.'

'How sound do you think his alibi is?'

'Well,' he answered slowly and she could tell he was sifting this latest piece of information to tie in with what he'd already learned about Bradley Cartwright, 'this does put a different light on things. Before, I couldn't come up with any motive; there just seemed to be no reason, but now -'

'- I know what you mean,' Brenda interrupted, looking again at the report, in particular to the section where he had itemised the amounts of the various bequests made by Mrs Catherine Miller-Croft. Muriel Miller would have inherited a very substantial sum and if she had told Bradley Cartwright she'd made out a will in his favour, this in itself could be sufficient grounds. 'and I must admit, from how you've described their friendship, it does strike me as being more of a platonic one. Wouldn't you have thought, Ian, that after a period of six or seven years they would have decided either to get married or live together on a permanent basis? They certainly didn't see each other all that often, did they?'

'No, you're right.' he agreed, 'And, we only have his word for it that he went straight to his room after she had driven off on Thursday night.'

'That's what I'm thinking,' she nodded, 'especially as you say her car had been parked at the back of the hotel; it would have been dark round there and he could have rendered her unconscious; it wouldn't have taken him long, and still be back in reception within the time the receptionist saw him. The only problem I can see is how was he able to leave the hotel and return later without being noticed?'

'There could have been a way; his main concern would be in case anyone would have seen him either in reception as he walked through or from the bar area.'

'That's true, but returning to your report, Ian,' Brenda said, 'and dismissing for the present any likelihood of Bradley Cartwright being responsible for her death, let's concentrate on those relations of Mrs Catherine Miller-Croft, the ones who were in Meadowbank on Thursday night. Assuming the murder was carried out by one person, their hardest task would be that final walk back to Meadowbank from The Royal Oak and not to be spotted when they returned to The King's Arms.'

'Getting into the hotel wouldn't have posed any real problem, ma'am,' he told her, 'they don't have a night porter and as each guest is provided with a pass number, they could return at any time they wished, possibly waiting until the pubs had closed and the town had quietened down.'

'Whoever killed Muriel Miller, presumably for gain, although we can't rule out any other motive there may have been, but for whatever reason it would seem the crime was premeditated. It's been mentioned a couple of times how secretive she was and even her cousin, Jason, wasn't sure whether she had a regular boyfriend or not. It is possible that if one of her relatives had known about the contents of Mrs Miller-Croft's will, they were taking a gamble that once Muriel was permanently off the scene, they would be in a stronger position to contest it, being so certain that, not only had she not made a will, she had no next of kin.'

'If that had been the case,' Ian suggested, a worried frown appearing, 'they must have had a shock when they learned about Mrs Miller-Croft's other daughter.'

'Exactly. Therefore, someone must be very angry indeed.'

'Emily Craig could be in some danger.'

'She could be, but that will is pretty well a *fait accompli* now although what does concern me about this case, and I've nothing positive to support what I'm going to say, but I feel we're dealing with a person who isn't quite sane here.'

'Is a murderer ever truly sane, ma'am?'

'A moot point, Ian; probably not, but no doubt the psychiatrists would argue there are different degrees of insanity, although I've always maintained there are no grey areas; either one is insane or not.'

'You mean, once they've chosen to go down that particular road of disposing of someone, they reach that irreversible point of no return?'

'Yes, I do mean that.' once again, surprised by his perception, 'And, when that happens, I believe their brains cease to function normally.'

'Arnold Brutton did mention to me he got the strong impression Mrs Craig wasn't exactly overjoyed about the bequest.'

'She probably wasn't. Come to think of it, I think I wouldn't have been either in her situation.'

'Why do you say that?'

'Because; here we have a woman, having made the decision to move away from what had been her home for a good part of her life, after losing her husband and trying to make a fresh start. I would say the last she wanted to hear was something which very likely was going to change her life for the second time.'

'And yet,' he pointed out, 'her inheritance means she won't have any financial worries, probably for the rest of her life.'

'Money isn't everything, Ian,' Brenda said, 'and I don't want to sound like your maiden aunt, but what I am trying to do is get under the skin of these people. It's not easy.' She added ruefully.

'What were your impressions,' Ian asked, 'of those relatives you talked to in London?'

'I'll put it this way,' she said, 'I've met more likeable people. They weren't exactly grieving over Muriel Miller's death; in fact, they didn't have one kind word to say about her and now you've told me that guests staying at The King's Arms could gain access to the hotel at any time during the night, it means we can't dismiss them as possible suspects.'

'I haven't had any further feedback on Lawrence Croft yet.' he said.

'I'll be surprised if you do, Ian, because according to New Scotland Yard, he has a police record; a twelve-month prison sentence for his part in a jewellery robbery; this was in nineteen eighty-nine when he was still living in London and, as Jason Miller told you, he did go to Brighton, but has since moved from the address he had there and from then onwards there's been no further trace of him. The consensus of opinion at the time was that he may have gone overseas.'

'Presumably, ma'am,' Ian suggested, 'as the brothers didn't keep in touch; he wouldn't have told his family?'

'I would say that was the case.' she agreed, 'When I asked Oliver Croft about him on Saturday, he confirmed what Jason Miller told you; namely, that none of them know where he is, so it looks very much it will be up to us to locate him. Whichever way you look at it,' she continued, 'Lawrence Croft wanted to disappear, create a new identity for himself, whether in this country or overseas. No, Ian, we'll find him, unless of course there are more sinister connotations, but I'm reluctant to pursue that line, not at the moment anyway.'

'He may turn up,' Ian said, 'what I mean is, if and when he learns about his step-mother's death.'

'That's always a possibility. He wouldn't know how she'd bequeathed her estate, but he would be aware of the extent of her wealth. The temptation to return and see for himself whether she'd left anything to him may prove too tempting.'

'I'll arrange for a routine check to be carried out with passport control, shall I, and if we draw a blank there, we can then focus our energies on this country.'

'That's fine, Ian. He could be an important cog in all of this and, as I felt as soon as we learned of his existence, we should make every effort to discover where he is now, also what he's doing.'

'We appear to have quite a number of suspects, don't we?'

'How right you are,' she agreed, 'it's rather like trying to peer into a muddy fish pond! But, you know, I believe someone is going to slip up and when that happens we'll be ready for them. I find it hard to accept that no-one noticed anything that night. We've agreed that whoever it was had taken an enormous risk, more than one, in fact, and I think that's what we should be concentrating on.'

'I called into The Market Inn last night to check up on what Jason Miller had told me and Brian was able to confirm, not the exact time he arrived in the pub, but when he left, which was as Jason had said, around nine-thirty, but unfortunately for him, no-one was around the reception area when he returned to his hotel.'

'Wouldn't you think, Ian,' Brenda commented, 'that in a town the size of Meadowbank, people would be more observant? You would expect it in cities where there are so many people and the majority of them with little or no interest in anyone else, even if they passed them in the street every day they wouldn't even know their names.' she added.

'That's true,' Ian said, 'I'd always thought people here were a bit too interested in what others were doing. However, when I was talking to Brian, Phil Nicholson came into the bar and was able to confirm he was in there on Thursday night and didn't leave until after they'd called last orders and that it must have been after eleven when he drove along Bridge Street. He said there'd been no car parked by the waste ground, although by that time, presumably it would have gone, also he didn't pass any vehicle on the way back to the farm.'

'What about his sons, Ian? Were they out that evening?'

'Steve, the younger one, had been away all week on a course, but Gary had gone out. Neither he nor his wife knew when he returned home, but

Phil thought it must have been some time in the early hours of Friday morning.'

'Where was he; did Phil say?'

'He didn't know, but apparently, although Gary had still been at home when he left to go to The Market Inn, his wife told him that he'd had gone out later telling her he was meeting his girlfriend.'

'Well,' Brenda sighed, 'it looks as if that part of the evening was fairly risk-free, which means we will have to pay another visit to The Royal Oak, but going back to Muriel Miller, Ian,' she went on, 'something, while not exactly strange, did turn up. It would seem she hadn't been divorced after all; London's central registry office has no record of any divorce.'

'So,' Ian suggested, 'somewhere out there, she still had a husband?'

'Yes,' she agreed, 'and this is someone else we have to find. If he should happen to hear about her death, how long will it take him to learn also about the inheritance, and if and when that happens, he'll also find out about the boyfriend, Bradley Cartwright, therefore, the sooner we locate him the better.'

'I can put someone on to that straight away.'

'If you would; it's time we started eliminating some of these people from our list which is in danger of getting out of hand.'

'Right, I'll do that,' Ian said, turning over to a fresh page in his notepad, 'what's the husband called, ma'am?'

'Adam Fry, but unfortunately that's all I can give you.'

'Adam Fry?'

'Yes, that's what I said. What's wrong; do you know him?'

'I met him for the first time on Saturday evening,' he told her, 'he was with Jacqueline Wellings from the estate agents and she introduced him to me.'

'Well, well, even I have to admit that must be a coincidence! Where was this, Ian? In Meadowbank?'

'Yes, in The Bridge; he's recently taken over the pharmacy in the square.'

'This enquiry,' she said, shaking her head, 'is really stretching credibility!

First, Muriel Miller's boyfriend is working here and now, presumably her estranged husband is also and don't forget Emily Craig, who has decided to come to live in Meadowbank. Don't you think, Ian, all of this is just rather too much to swallow?'

Chapter Five

Gary Nicholson waited until late in the afternoon on Monday to make his telephone call, but not from his mobile; he'd watched enough police thrillers on television to learn calls could easily be traced. Instead, in his infinite wisdom, he decided to use the public telephone box in Market Square. There was more than one reason why it had taken him so long to do this; mainly, he'd needed the time to work out in his devious mind how he, personally, could profit from what he'd seen on Thursday night and it hadn't been until the following day as he'd been outside The Market Inn, waiting for the pub to open, when he'd spotted the person who had driven away at great speed from the waste ground in Bridge Street, the idea came to him of how he could achieve this. He couldn't believe his luck. He had at first thought it must have been a hit and run accident and certainly he never expected to see the driver again, but there was no doubt in his mind now; it was the same person alright. And by Monday, he'd convinced himself that victims of hit and run weren't usually hidden out of sight behind hedges.

Gary had been on his Vespa 90 scooter and on his way into Meadowbank to spend the evening with his girlfriend when he'd seen the car parked up on the verge with its headlamps dipped and by the time he had almost drawn level, although it had been a dark night, he had been able to make out the figure who, dashing out from the waste ground and flinging open the car door had, with a grinding of gears, reversed and accelerated away, back towards the town. He had waited until the car had turned the bend at The Bridge, making sure there were no other vehicles on the road and, leaving the bike where it was, walked across the road. It was raining quite heavily by then, but it didn't take him long to find what at first he'd mistaken for a bundle of discarded clothing dumped in the overgrown grass and weeds. He could have stopped there; gone back to his bike and continued on into Meadowbank, but for some reason he didn't and was never to know whether it had been curiosity or not which had drawn him to move closer and to go so far as to pull back a corner of what he could now make out was a tartan travelling rug.

Even with his limited knowledge, Gary realised the woman hadn't died naturally. Although he had no idea how it must have happened, he could tell by the distorted expression on her face that her death had been a sudden and a violent one.

And now, dialling the number he'd looked up earlier, he waited to hear the voice he'd heard on Friday and one he knew he would instantly recognise.

'Hello?' in that upper-class tone of voice which instantly grated on him and only strengthening his resolve to continue. 'You're not trying to sell me anything, are you?' not giving him a chance to answer, 'Because, if you are -'

' – no,' managing to interrupt what he guessed was likely to be one long indignant tirade, no doubt resulting in the phone being put down on him, 'I'm not trying to sell you anything, but I am in possession of something which you may find interesting.'

'What *are* you talking about? And, who are you, anyway?'

'Does the name Muriel Miller mean anything to you?' and hearing the sharp intake of breath at the other end of the line.

'No; why should it?'

'Her body was found in Bridge Street on Friday afternoon; she'd been murdered.' and encouraged by the lack of any response, continuing: 'I happened to be there the night before and I saw you -'

' – Look here! I really do not know what you're talking about. Why don't you report this to the police, unless of course, it's all a figment of your imagination?'

'I've no intention of going to the police; there's nothing to be gained by me doing that.'

'Ah, so it's money you want?'

'What else?'

'Well, you're not going to get any. You have no proof, none whatsoever, to substantiate any of – of this rubbish!'

'I have sufficient proof if I decide to report what I'd seen and I'm fairly sure it would be enough for you to be pulled in for questioning and,' he added, 'I wonder how you would cope with that. You *were* there that night; you had parked up on the verge and you came out from behind the hedge and drove back towards Meadowbank. It only took minutes for me to find her, so, try and talk yourself out of that!'

It had been simple after that; they made arrangements to meet the following day in London and after an agreement had been made on the amount of cash to be handed over to him, he brought the call to a close.

Brian Morrison was behind the bar when he walked into The Market Inn and, apart from his usual group of regulars, he was the only other customer.

'Hello, Gary,' he greeted him, 'you're usual?' and anticipating his reply, reaching up to take down a pint glass.

'Please.'

'Do you want me to put your name down for the darts' match tomorrow evening?' he asked.

'I won't be here; I'll be in London and I'm not sure what time I'll get back.'

'Are you working up there, then?'

'No, nothing to do with work. I'm meeting a couple of friends, that's all.' wondering whether Brian could detect how he'd hesitated as he had tried to come up with a plausible excuse on the spur of the moment. Brian Morrison had know him since he was a young lad and probably knew of the various scrapes he'd been in, some of them pretty hairy, but this was the first time he'd ever tried to blackmail anyone but just as quickly dismissing any reservations he may have. This, he reasoned, was too good an opportunity to miss. It wasn't as though he was asking for a fortune, only five grand; it would be enough to enable him to get out of this hick town and set himself up somewhere else, anything to escape the continual nagging from his father. Hardly a day went by when he wasn't being asked if he'd found a job yet and reminding him what he thought of people dependent on handouts from Social Security. Gary had no interest in the farm, having, from an early age, taken an active dislike to working out of doors and, knowing he was a disappointment, only increased the level of pressure his father was putting on him to get down to some hard, honest graft. Well, he'd show him. Show them all, in fact; given time, that is and the necessary readies to make it possible.

*

'I've never known Phil Nicholson to miss a dart match before.' one of Brian's customers commented on Tuesday evening, 'He's not sick, is he, Brian?'

'Not as far as I know,' Brian said, 'he seemed alright when I saw him this morning at the bank.'

'Odd that. Perhaps he's been held up or something.'

'Could have been.'

Nothing more was said about Phil not turning up, the dart match getting underway, once Brian had rearranged the teams. There was never any problem in finding enough players to make up the numbers; Tuesday evenings always being popular with the locals. It wasn't until much later, around ten, when one of the drivers from Meadowbank's taxi firm came in at the end of his shift, they all learned the reason for Phil Nicholson's absence. For a second, after the man had broken the news to them, there was a stunned silence around the bar. He'd told them he'd taken Phil to Winchester station earlier to catch the seven-fifteen train to Waterloo as he'd received a call to say his son, Gary, had been shot.

'Shot!' Fred Smith, another of Brian's regulars, gasped and speaking for the rest of them, 'You mean the lad's dead?'

'Afraid so. As you can imagine, Phil was in a pretty bad way.'

'Gary told me he was going up to London today,' Brian said quietly, recalling how vague he had been and not elaborating on the people he was meeting, 'so how did it happen? Did Phil say?'

'He didn't know much; only that Gary was at Waterloo this afternoon, waiting he thought for a train back to Winchester and that was about all. I didn't like to press him.'

'No, of course not. And Phil was on his own?'

'Yes, he told me his wife had wanted to go with him, but he thought it best she didn't, especially as he would have to identify the body.'

The dart match wrapped up earlier than usual, none of them having the heart to carry on as though nothing had happened. One or two customers remained at the bar having a final drink before leaving, but the tone of conversation was sombre and, although no-one actually mentioned it, it was clear by their expressions each of them was remembering recent events in the town, not only the murder of Muriel Miller, who hadn't been a resident of Meadowbank, but of those other murders earlier in the year.

'What do you think, Brian?' Melissa asked him when he had locked the front door behind the last of them.

'I don't know what to think, love,' he sighed, 'but all I can say is, that it looks very much as if the problems surrounding our town haven't gone away.'

'You think there's a connection between Gary's death and Muriel Miller's?'

'You know me, Melissa,' he smiled sadly, 'I'm always the last to jump to conclusions, but I can't help thinking there must be. Mind you,' he went on, giving the top of the bar a final wipe, 'we still know next to nothing about what happened to Gary. He was always a bit of an oddball and Phil was far from happy about him. More than once he mentioned how he wished Gary would make an effort to get a job, but he never did.'

'Poor Phil.'

'Yes, it must be hell for him tonight, but there's nothing we can do, love.'

'Honestly, Brian,' Melissa said, 'it really has been one thing after another, hasn't it? There was a time when Meadowbank was a quiet market town with the main highlight being the summer carnival, nothing else. Most people outside had probably never even heard of Meadowbank, but now. Well,' she sighed, 'you know what this means, don't you?'

'The press.'

'Yes, and once again the place will not be our own. It's really horrible.'

'It's not pleasant, but I dare say we will weather the inevitable disruption, just as we have done before. Have you noticed, Melissa,' he added, a quirky grin on his face, 'how thirsty people become when they've something different to talk about?'

*

Brenda was still in the office when the call came through from New Scotland Yard. She hadn't expected to hear from Mike so soon, but immediately she heard his voice she realised this wasn't entirely a social call.

'Everything alright, Brenda?' he asked her.

'I'm fine; you sound as if you've something to tell me.'

'How well you know me;' he chuckled, 'but, yes, you're quite right. I've just had a call from the Met to tell me a young man was shot late this afternoon at Waterloo station. Normally, of course, I wouldn't have been informed, but the officer who arrived on the scene happened to be the same one who gave me the background on Lawrence Croft the other day and when he learned, not so much the identity of the victim, but that he came from Meadowbank, he immediately put the proverbial two and two together.'

'Who was he, Mike?'

'Gary Nicholson.'

'Phil Nicholson's son,' she said, experiencing that small flicker of excitement to indicate the case was beginning to open up, 'Phil Nicholson was the person who discovered the body of Muriel Miller.'

'Interesting.'

'I think it could be.'

'Did you know his son?'

'I didn't actually know him,' she explained, 'although I do know his father. He owns the farm in Bridge Street, not all that far from where Muriel Miller was found. It's quiet along there and the only building after The Bridge Inn is his farm. Ian asked Phil whether he had driven along there on Thursday night which he had, but it wasn't until fairly late and after the time she was killed. Apparently, Gary had told him he hadn't seen anything untoward when he drove past the same spot that night.'

'Perhaps he did.'

'You sound positive.'

'Well,' Mike answered, 'he had a rather significant amount of cash on him; not in his wallet, where one would expect it to be, but in an envelope, tucked into the inside pocket of his anorak.'

'You say significant; how much?'

'Five thousand pounds.'

'Good Grief! That is a lot, especially for someone like him.'

'Why?'

'Because Gary Nicholson has never had a job in his life. From what I've heard, he always refused to have anything to do with the farm and has been on social security practically since the day he left school, which must be at least eight or nine years ago.'

'It sounds as if he may have been blackmailing someone. Unless he was a gambler.'

'I wouldn't say he had sufficient knowledge or intelligence to be much of a gambler, but he could have seen someone that night, recognised whoever it was and made a stab at profiting from it.'

'If that was the case,' he said soberly, 'although he got the cash, it didn't get him very far.'

'It would seem not.' she agreed, 'So, what happens now; with the Met's enquiry, I mean?'

'They are running through the normal routine, but it would appear, although there were a fair amount of people around that area at the time, those who remained and didn't move away, none of them reported seeing anything suspicious, most of them saying the first thing they noticed was when he fell to the ground.'

'Presumably a silencer was used.'

'I would say so, but whoever fired the shot had experience in the use of fire-arms, in other words, he or she was no novice. It always surprises me,

Brenda,' he continued, 'how, in a situation like this, when there are so many potential witnesses around, not one single person noticed anything unusual.'

'I know. I suppose this is why so many shootings do occur in crowded places when most people are only intent on, as probably they were this time, in reaching their destinations and no doubt worrying whether they would be able to find a seat on the train or not.'

'That's right, but to get back to what you were saying, the Met will be reporting directly back to you, Brenda, and this will include faxing through the forensic report tomorrow morning. They all know you're conducting the Muriel Miller enquiry and the general feeling is that as Gary Nicholson came from Meadowbank wasn't a coincidence and, of course, the fact he had so much cash on him, further supports this theory.'

'I feel the same way. Although the method of killing their victims differ, there are similarities in that both crimes give every indication of having been planned, also, each time, they were taking enormous risks which I have to admit strikes me as irrational.'

'They were, weren't they?' he said, 'And, if we are right, and he was blackmailing the person who murdered Muriel Miller, the reason for his demise does make some sort of sense, but I don't think we can say the same for what happened to her. All I *will* say,' he emphasised, 'there must have been a pretty strong motive for wanting her out of the way and whoever carried it out must have been sufficiently confident the risk would be worthwhile.'

'There is another aspect.'

'Yes?'

'It is possible we could be up against an additional element here and one which has been concerning me right from the beginning. What I'm trying to say is, I can't help thinking this person, while perhaps not certifiably insane, may not be normal.'

'A chilling thought.'

'It is; goodness knows, it is difficult enough trying to discover what makes any murderer tick, but when their behaviour is as erratic as this one, it starts to become a nightmare'.

'I couldn't agree more, Brenda. You've got a tough case here. It does seem to hinge on that original will, doesn't it; the one made out by Catherine Miller-Croft?'

'I think so.' and going on to tell him about the other daughter Catherine had given birth to and who, presumably by chance, had recently come to live in Meadowbank.

'And this daughter didn't know who her biological mother was?'

'Apparently not. Catherine Miller-Croft's lawyer was quite adamant about that.'

'I see.'

'I believe we will need to go back to the period before Muriel Miller's death, Mike; perhaps to the time leading up to when Catherine Miller-Croft was admitted to hospital.'

'You could be right, especially when you consider the extent of the woman's wealth. That could be the root cause.'

*

Adam Fry didn't see a copy of "The Courier" until Monday morning, and although he had heard people in The Bridge talking about a woman's body being found, he hadn't heard anyone mention her name. He recognised Muriel immediately from the group photograph, but it was the picture of one of the other women which instantly caught his attention, transporting him back to a time in his life he would much rather forget, surprised to see them together at the same function, considering what had happened.

She had been the one who had introduced Muriel to him and from that first moment it was as if Muriel had cast a spell over him. Twenty years ago; he had been twenty-six, Muriel had been four years older, but that hadn't made any difference to him. Even now, so many years later, he was unable to explain or understand what he had found so compellingly attractive about her; she hadn't been particularly pretty, in some respects she was quite plain, but the super-confidence she exuded more than compensated for any lack of beauty. To him, she represented a different world; a privileged background where money was never a problem, she had wanted for nothing and to him, a grammar school boy coming from a working-class family and managing to gain a scholarship into university, she had been glamour personified. Gullible young fool that he'd been. The girl he had thought he was in love with no longer existed as far as he was concerned; Muriel became the focal of his very existence. It hadn't taken him long to find out how wrong and misguided he had been; almost from the early days of their marriage. Her outward display of affection had been a sham and as for passion, there was none. She just wasn't interested. She made it abundantly clear to him that mostly she preferred her own company, that was, when it suited her. It had been a short learning curve for him and long after they had split up he continued to feel the bitterness of what he had always described to himself as her deliberate attempt to convey a false image of herself, but in retrospect, and with maturity, he had come to the realisation Muriel hadn't been entirely to blame; he was equally culpable. She had never mentioned a divorce but this hadn't altogether surprised him. She had been a rare breed of woman, having little interest in being married, although perversely, once she had acquired a husband she had never shown any wish to change her status. Muriel had been accustomed from an early age in obtaining anything which appealed to her and had developed extraordinary skills in acquiring them, whether they were inanimate or, in his case, a man who had been more than willing to metaphorically fall at her feet and commit himself to the ultimate commitment of marrying her. She had been a collector and now, someone had taken it upon themselves to bring her life to a premature and abrupt end.

Up until now, the fact he was still married hadn't unduly concerned him; Adam was a one-woman man and had been nervous about making another disastrous mistake, but his attitude had changed since he had met Jacqueline. It had taken him until well into his forties to find a lady with whom he felt at ease. Jacqueline, the opposite to Muriel, was utterly feminine. He hadn't known her long, only two or three months, but already he wanted to put their relationship on a more permanent footing. Ironically, and without saying anything to her, he had been on the point of filing for a divorce. He hadn't known Muriel's address, but he thought it likely she was still with the bank in London, but if not, he'd planned to leave it to his lawyers to sort out and now, there was no need. As he re-read the report of her death, he didn't know what his true feelings were; shocked naturally, but not sad. Perhaps he should have been, but he was incapable of conjuring up an emotion he didn't feel. The second irony was that he was living in the town where it had happened and this placed him in an insidious position. Should he speak to the authorities and tell him she'd been his wife, albeit an estranged one? And, if he didn't and they were to find out during the course of their investigations, wouldn't that place him in an even more awkward position?

By Wednesday, he was no further forward in making up his mind what he should do, but when Ian Ash came into the pharmacy, that decision was made for him. He had only been open an hour and his assistant was dealing with a customer, making it possible for him to suggest to the inspector they use the privacy of the dispensary. Although in plain clothes; a dark blue roll-neck sweater and cords, Adam didn't need to be told he was on duty and hadn't called in to make a purchase.

'I should be addressing you as Inspector, shouldn't I?' Adam asked, finding the present situation slightly disconcerting, so different from when he was in his company on Saturday night.

'This meeting is a purely informal one;' Ian told him, neatly sidestepping an answer, 'but we need to clarify a few points in the enquiry we're conducting into the death of Miss Miller.'

'I expect you've found out I was married to her?' anticipating his first question.

'We have, yes,' he said, 'this was when we were checking up on her personal records. Am I right in saying you never divorced?'

'Yes; I realise this must sound strange to you,' Adam explained, 'but unless you had known Muriel, known her personally, I mean, it's difficult to explain.'

'Try me.' Ian Ash smiled.

'Well,' Adam started, taking a deep breath, trying to put his thoughts in some chronological order and not to come over as a complete waffler, 'you'll know the year we got married?'

'1986.'

'That's right. Muriel and I weren't together for very long, less than two years, in fact. She made it clear to me she was no longer interested in having me around. She had ceased to care, although I have to say it is doubtful whether she ever had. She was an extremely independent woman, you understand. I don't honestly believe she enjoyed *being* married; it just didn't suit her. When we finally separated, she didn't mention a divorce, although I did, but the only answer I got was a shrug. As I've said, she didn't care one way or another.'

'Strange woman.'

'Indeed; unorthodox, anyway.'

'But, what about you, Adam,' using his name for the first time, 'didn't you meet anyone you wanted to marry?'

'Surprisingly, I didn't. Too apprehensive, I suppose. I'd lost my confidence in the marriage stakes, afraid I would make another mistake.'

'And did you ever meet her again in all of these years?'

'No, never.'

'What about her family?'

'She didn't tell me all that much about them. She had been close to her father, I believe, from the way she talked about him. He had been widowed when Muriel was only a baby and from the age of three when he re-married, it had been Catherine who brought her up.'

'Catherine Miller-Croft?'

'That's right.'

'Did you ever meet the lady?'

'No, I didn't. Muriel had already left home before we met and was living and working in London. She told me from when her step-mother married again shortly after her father died she was never really happy.'

'And this was Trevor Croft?'

'Yes; he already had two sons by his previous marriage and then her step-mother had a child and, again from how Muriel spoke about her growing family, I got the impression she didn't like the new situation one little bit. She told me, not long after we met, she had never wanted any siblings, preferring to be the only child; spoilt, I'm afraid.'

'Sounds like it.' Ian agreed, 'You were saying on Saturday you had recently moved here; did you already know that Muriel Miller's step-mother lived in Meadowbank?'

'No doubt you're going to find this surprising, but I had absolutely no idea.'

'Muriel never told you?'

'No, she didn't. She was inclined to keep a lot to herself, secretive I suppose you would have called her.'

'Just for the record, Adam,' Ian asked him, 'where were you last Thursday night?'

'Ah,' Adam sighed, but not unsurprised by the question; Ian Ash was only doing what he had been trained to do in any murder enquiry, but it did disturb him all the same to think he must fall into the category of one of their suspects, 'that was the night Muriel was killed, which, incidentally, I only found out on Monday when I read the report in the local paper. Although I had heard a woman's body had been found, I didn't know it was Muriel. Anyway,' Adam went on, 'on Thursday evening, I was with Jacqueline. We had a meal at The Salmon's Rest after work and then spent the remainder of the evening in The Bridge and didn't leave until closing time.'

'That's fine,' Ian nodded, 'and yesterday afternoon, Adam?'

'Yesterday afternoon?'

'Yes; where were you?'

'I was in here; Tuesday, as you probably know is our late-night closing and I spent all day working, except for a short break at lunchtime and then again, around six it would have been, but only for an hour. I went across to The Market Inn for a pint.' he added.

'That's okay, then.'

'Why are you asking about yesterday? Has something else happened?'

'Afraid so,' Ian said, 'a young man from Meadowbank was shot dead yesterday afternoon in London; at Waterloo Station as a matter of fact.'

'Good Lord! And you think this has something to do with what happened to Muriel?'

'We are considering that possibility, Adam.'

*

'Wow!' Jessica exclaimed as Emily drew up outside "The Gables", 'It really is like something out of Dickens, isn't it?'

'You could say that,' Emily agreed, 'terribly neglected and much bigger than I had imagined and not all that inviting either.' she added in dismay, not looking forward to venturing inside and wishing she had waited until the weekend to come here, although it wouldn't have been until Sunday. The interview with Adam Fry had gone well and she had been eager to agree to his suggestion to start tomorrow, giving her the opportunity to work alongside the young woman for the remainder of the week.

'Come on, Mum,' nudging her gently in the ribs, 'where's your sense of adventure?'

'I wish I could share your enthusiasm, love,' she said, switching off the engine and taking the keys Arnold Brutton had given her from her handbag, 'but, alright, I'll try to buck up. What would your dad have said, Jessica?'

'Best foot forward!' Jessica laughed, getting out of the car to unlock the wrought-iron gates for her.

"The Gables", a rambling two-storey brick-built building, had been built sometime in the nineteen twenties, although over the years extensions had been added, giving it a lop-sided appearance. Tall sash windows flanked the sturdy front door with, Emily noticed, a rather pretty stained-glass fanlight; the last rays of the afternoon light reflecting on the coloured glass. It would soon be dark, not the best time to visit a house for the first time and turning the key in the double lock and taking a deep breath she stepped into the hall, immediately struck by the understated opulence of everything which had been bequeathed to her. The interior of "The Gables" was a complete surprise; unlike the grounds which seriously needed some attention, she got the impression everything she was looking at had been lovingly looked after. An enormous fringed dark-red Persian rug, almost covering the highly polished wood-block floor, predominated. A Welsh dresser caught her eye, also a glass-fronted bookcase and the two high-backed oak chairs with ornately carved armrests, together with a settle, upholstered in red velvet, the same shade as the rug, all showing evidence of care, although she knew from what the lawyer had told her nobody had been in the house since the night Catherine Miller-Croft had been taken to hospital, except for Muriel, her step-daughter, but she had left during the Sunday, having posted the keys to "The Gables" through Brutton & Brutton's letterbox. He had gone on to tell her that the woman who had cleaned for Catherine had never been given any keys; the only set, apparently, being the one he'd handed over to her; all of which went a long way to illustrate to Emily the type of person Catherine must have been.

Double doors led from the hall into the dining-room: wood-panelled; a long oak table in the centre displaying some of the pieces of silver listed in the inventory: a five-branched candelabra holding tall, slim candles which appeared to have been in use, not merely as an ornament and, on either side, two fine filigree silver fruit dishes; more high-backed chairs, similar to the ones in the hall and on the walls, a few of Catherine's collection of paintings:

Monet's lily pond and his dramatic portrayal of the waters in the English Channel; a miniature Picasso and, above the Adam fireplace, a couple of Turners. Everything she had seen so far was quite old, some of which were probably, even to her uneducated eye, antique items.

'What do you think?' Jessica asked at last, her voice little more than a whisper.

'I don't know what to think, love,' she answered, 'except I had absolutely no idea it would be like this.'

'Do you feel up to seeing anymore, or have you had enough for today?' she asked, a look of concern on her face.

'I think I have,' Emily admitted, 'but we'll just have a quick look upstairs. I must admit I'm finding everything a bit too much to take in. I need time to think; to work out what we should do about this -' faltering and struggling with her confused thoughts. She knew one thing; she didn't feel comfortable here and she most certainly didn't belong. Talk about being a reluctant heiress, she sighed, wishing Adrian could have been here. Not for the first time since he'd died she missed her husband's unflappable approach to the unexpected and this 'out of the blue' bequest from a woman she had never known undoubtedly fell into that category.

The room adjoining the master bedroom looked as if Catherine must have used as her own private sitting room: a pale walnut writing desk had been positioned directly in front of the window, and although by now the light was fading fast, Emily realised why she had chosen somewhere on the first floor to spend what was likely to have been a good part of her time. The room was west-facing and the sky, above and beyond fields and a small copse, had now become streaked with blue, peach and grey from the final rays of the sinking sun making a magnificent backdrop. A bookcase, a twin of the one downstairs, ran along the length of one of the walls and a small oval coffee table next to a chintz-covered armchair were the only other pieces of furniture. There were few ornaments and only one picture on the wall: a watercolour of a young woman; violet-blue eyes and a peaches and cream complexion. Her dress, high-waisted and reaching to her ankles looked Edwardian to Emily. It was simply called: "Evelyn Singleton", but it was impossible to decipher the artist's name from the faded scrawl in the bottom right-hand corner of the canvas. Singleton had been Catherine's maiden name, remembering what Arnold Brutton had told her. Could she have been her grandmother, Emily wondered, moving closer to the painting.

'You look like her, Mum,' Jessica said, coming to stand next to her, 'you really do.'

'Do you think so?'

'Yes, I do.' Jessica smiled.

Emily looked again at the face of the woman in the painting, trying to find even the slightest hint of a resemblance, but she couldn't. Perhaps, she decided, the truth was she didn't want to. Up to the moment when she'd learned about Catherine, her life as she had always known it, had been relatively uneventful and she had never considered herself any different from anyone else she knew, but now, she was not so sure. She was still reeling from the news and, to her, the staggering wealth she had inherited and was loath to even consider how it may it change the way she had chosen to live and the last thing she wanted was to become embroiled in a family she didn't know. She realised she was probably being unreasonable, but she couldn't help it.

'Mum.'

'Yes?'

'Come back; you were somewhere else.' Jessica said gently, 'Let's go home.'

They had reached the front door when she remembered she hadn't switched off the light upstairs and had half-turned to go up again, but Jessica said she would do it and she was glad. She didn't want to go back into that room again; at least not today. Enough was enough and her wise daughter had been right; it was time to go.

Jessica didn't say much on the short drive back into Meadowbank and it wasn't until they were in the kitchen of "The Old School House", the thermostat of the central heating turned up and they had taken off their coats, that she looked at her closely realising her silence, unusual though it was, just wasn't natural. Something was on Jessica's mind and whatever it was hadn't been there fifteen, twenty minutes ago.

'What is it, love?'

'Well,' Jessica said, sitting down at the table, a small frown appearing on her forehead, 'I'm not sure whether there is a problem or not, but -'

'- yes?' prompting her.

'When I was coming back down the stairs, I happened to look down and I found this.' holding out her hand to show Emily what she was holding.

'Where was this, Jessica; just lying on the stairs?'

'Part of it was, but it was tied around one of the banisters and I suppose the light must have caught it, because otherwise I don't think I would have seen it, but when I gave it a tug, it came away in my hand. It looks like some kind of thread, doesn't it, she added, 'it's quite strong.'

'It isn't exactly thread,' Emily said, 'I would say it's similar to what's used for stitching wounds; suturing it's called.'

'Why do you think it was there?'

'I don't know for sure; I can only make a guess and quite frankly, Jessica, I don't like the way my mind is working.'

'You believe there's something sinister about it being there, don't you? What I mean is,' she went on, 'you think someone must have put it there deliberately as –' hesitating, 'as a kind of trap.' she finished quickly.

'I think so, yes.'

'You never said,' Jessica asked, 'but how did Catherine Miller-Croft die? Did Mr Brutton tell you?'

'He said she'd had a stroke after a bad fall.'

'And this happened when she was at home, at "The Gables"?'

'Yes.' and she could tell by Jessica's shocked expression she was thinking the same as her: Catherine's death had been no accident.

'Even if we are wrong, Mum,' she said, reading her mind, 'we have to do something.'

'I know. You said it was tied around one of the banisters; did you look across to the other one?'

'No, I didn't think to do that. I should have done, shouldn't I?'

'We're not detectives, love. We'll leave that to the authorities, but the fact it wasn't lying on the stairs perhaps having been dropped by someone means there must be something suspicious about it.'

'Should we go back there and take another look?

'No, I don't think so,' dreading the very idea of returning, 'I'll give the police a ring; they will know what to do. What was the name of the inspector you met the other night, Jessica? I'll see if I can speak to him.'

Chapter Six

Mavis Coleman had worked for Catherine Miller-Croft for over forty years, shortly after Christine was born and, although past retirement age, she had hoped to continue working for her a little longer. Hearing about the sudden death of her employer had shaken her, followed so soon after by what had happened to Muriel, had immediately filled her with a feeling of unease. She couldn't explain why she should have reacted this way; it wasn't as though she could ever be described as fanciful and didn't as a rule let her imagination take such a firm grip, but when she received a call from Inspector Ash on the Thursday morning, this impression intensified, looking up at him in bewilderment as he stood on her front door step and having no idea how she could possibly be any help to the police.

'I hope you don't mind me calling on you unannounced, Mrs Coleman,' he apologised, following her into the warmth of her kitchen.

'That's alright, Inspector,' she said, pulling a chair out for him at the table, 'although I have to say I am surprised. Muriel was a good woman, also a considerate step-daughter to Mrs Miller-Croft. I just cannot believe anyone could be so wicked. A terrible thing to happen. Terrible.' she repeated, sitting down across the table from him.

'The reason I'm here,' he began slowly and wondering how she would respond when he explained, 'isn't directly concerning Miss Miller's death.'

'Not Muriel?' she frowned, 'I don't understand.'

'I don't mean to alarm you in any way, Mrs Coleman,' Ian said, 'and I'll try to make this as easy as I can for you, but a few points have come to light regarding how Mrs Miller-Croft died and we hoped you would be able to assist us.'

'Of course, Inspector, I'll help in any way I can. I don't know whether you realise it, but I worked for Mrs Miller-Croft for many years and I was very fond of her.'

'I thought that might be the case,' he smiled sympathetically, doing his best to put the woman at her ease and not entirely convinced he was handling this conversation as carefully as he should be, 'and so, if you wouldn't mind, I'd like you to think back to the last day you saw her.'

'It was the day she had her accident,' she began, 'a week past Saturday. After finishing my chores in the morning, I prepared her lunch at midday as I always did and washed up before leaving.'

'And was Miss Miller with her, or had she already gone out?'

'Oh, Muriel was still there; she didn't want anything to eat, told me she would be having a meal later.'

'So, who left first, Mrs Coleman?' Ian asked her, 'You or Miss Miller?'

'Muriel did; this was around one-thirty and I was about half an hour later, in time to catch the bus back into Meadowbank. Actually,' she went on, 'I very nearly missed it because the phone rang just as I was putting on my coat.'

'Did you answer it?'

'No, Mrs Miller-Croft did. She was up in her sitting room by then and I waited until she'd finished before going upstairs to tell her I was going.'

'This may sound rather a personal question,' he said, 'but have you any idea who phoned her?'

'I do, yes; it was her step-son.'

'Oliver Croft.'

'That's right. He and his wife had been in Winchester that morning attending a friend's wedding and said they would call in and see her before going back to London.'

'And, of course, you wouldn't have seen them.'

'No, I'd gone by then.'

'How did Mrs Miller-Croft seem to you; was she pleased they were coming?'

'To be honest, Inspector,' she smiled gently, 'I don't think she was. You see, she was in the habit of taking a nap in the afternoons and I know she looked forward to this.'

'I understand. One more question, Mrs Coleman, and please don't take offence, but when did you last sweep the stairs?'

'What a strange thing to ask me, but no doubt you have a very good reason, Inspector.'

'I do, yes.'

'I clean them once a week, every Friday. Why?'

'Because,' Ian answered, taking the piece of thread from his coat pocket and placing it on the table in front of her, 'this was found near the top of the stairs yesterday. Have you seen it before?'

'No,' puzzled and picking it up, 'what is it, some kind of nylon thread?'

'Something like that.' not wanting to further alarm her.

'Well, it's not mine and I'm sure Mrs Miller-Croft wouldn't have dropped it, or Muriel either, if it comes to that.'

'How can you be sure it didn't belong to Miss Miller?'

'I can't, of course, but I'm sure I would have noticed it. I was up and down the stairs a few times that Saturday morning, but I didn't. Also,' she went on, 'when Muriel phoned me from the hospital the following morning and told me the sad news, she didn't ask me to go in and do any tidying up; she said she would be handing the keys into the lawyers' office when she left for London later in the day.'

'I understand what you're saying,' Ian said, 'and I don't want you to worry about this, Mrs Coleman, but it is important for us to try and discover how it found its way there.'

An idea was beginning to formulate at the back of his mind by the time he left, although he regretted the look of dismay on Mavis Coleman's face as she opened the front door for him, which left him in no doubt she had been shrewd enough to understand where he had been coming from, but it couldn't be helped. These had been questions he had had to ask and if he hadn't, he would not have learned about the phone call from Oliver Croft. They still had no proof who had placed the thread there, but someone had, and so far, there could only reasonably be one person who couldn't have done this and that was Catherine Miller-Croft.

Ian had fully appreciated Emily Craig's reluctance last night to return to the house, but nevertheless, he had driven up there and, as she had mentioned to him, he had found some more of the thread tied to one of the banisters on the other side of the staircase, which immediately confirmed it had been placed there deliberately. Even if Catherine Miller-Croft had survived the fall and the subsequent stroke, there was no guarantee it would have been discovered; presumably by the time the estate had been wound up and handed over to the new owner, all evidence would have been removed. He continued to think it would have been unlikely for Mavis Coleman to notice it, not until, perhaps, when she next cleaned the stairs the following week, but, then, she never returned to "The Gables". The thread was almost transparent and neither Emily Craig nor Jessica had spotted it when they had gone upstairs; it may have been pure chance Jessica did afterwards.

Before leaving for Winchester, Ian called Brenda on his mobile, wanting to give her an up-date of his talk with Mavis Coleman; in particular that Oliver Croft and his wife had called to arrange to see Catherine Miller-Croft on the day of the accident.

'And you say, Ian,' Brenda said, after he'd told her, 'Muriel Miller hadn't been there when the call came through; therefore, it's unlikely she would have known anything about their visit?'

'That's right.'

'Have you thought that it was possible the Crofts would have been aware of the likelihood of Muriel being at "The Gables" for the weekend?'

'No,' he admitted, 'it hadn't, but now you've mentioned it, I'm beginning to see the possible significance.'

'I thought you might.' she answered, 'I have been wondering why that piece of evidence hadn't been removed earlier; that has been bothering me.'

'I know,' he agreed, 'and once again, whoever did it, was taking a tremendous risk.'

'Unless the intention was to throw the blame on to Muriel Miller.' she suggested.

'That's an interesting point, ma'am and, within a week it would have been too late for her to defend herself in any case.'

'Quite.' she was quick to agree, 'It was a clumsily put-together trap, but it could have been considered by the killer to be the perfect crime, but as you and I know, Ian, that is a fallacy.'

'With this latest development,' he explained, 'I've decided to drive over to the hospital in Winchester and see if I can glean anything more about the accident. We don't know whether Catherine Miller-Croft was conscious or not when she was admitted; if she was she may have said something to indicate her doubts about what happened.'

'That's fine, Ian,' she said, 'meanwhile, I think it could be a good idea for me to go back to London and have another word with the Crofts, also, if I can, speak to Jason Miller, but I'll be back later on this afternoon. We should be in a position by then to collate what we've found so far and try to make a start in eliminating some of these suspects, all of which reminds me.'

'Yes, ma'am?'

'Bradley Cartwright. On the face of things, his motive does seem to be the most likely, when you consider, apart from Emily Craig, he did have the most to gain from both Catherine and Muriel's deaths. His alibis for both of those times are flimsy; it isn't improbable for him to have been in London when Gary Nicholson was shot. He could have finished work earlier on Tuesday and reached Waterloo in time. It isn't as though he will have to clock on and off on the Riverside development. So, Ian,' she continued, 'could you put out some feelers? This afternoon, if possible. I find it hard to accept he didn't know anything about Catherine Miller-Croft; somehow, that doesn't ring true. In other words, we know virtually nothing about his background and it's time we did.

*

The Royal Hampshire County Hospital was on the right-hand side of Romsey Road, leading directly down towards the centre of the city. Ian could hear eleven o'clock chiming in the distance as he pulled into the visitors' car park and walked up the steps to the main entrance.

It only took minutes for the girl in reception to give him the information he wanted, directing him to the ward where Catherine Miller-

Croft had been admitted almost two weeks previously, although telling him the doctor who had attended her wouldn't be on duty until the afternoon, but adding the ward sister would be able to help him.

'I was on night duty on October the twenty-first,' the ward sister told him once he had been directed to her office, 'and I remember when Mrs Miller-Croft was brought into the ward.'

'What I would like to know, Sister,' Ian explained, 'is not only the precise nature of her injuries, but whether she was fully conscious. It's our understanding she had been lying at the bottom of the stairs for some considerable time before her step-daughter returned to the house that night.'

'That's right,' she nodded, 'she had been. What I'm going to do is get the details up on the screen; it won't take long, Inspector.' she added, pulling her chair closer to the desk and pressing a couple of keys, scrolled back to the twenty-first until she came to the entry she wanted, 'Here we are,' she said, 'I'll let you have a print-out, but first, I'll run through those points which should answer your questions.'

'Thank you, that would be helpful.' he said, surprised as he always was when questioning medical staff how utterly professional they were, giving no hint of any curiosity of why he was there asking pertinent questions about what, as in this case, must have appeared a straightforward and not uncommon accident to an elderly lady.

'Mrs Miller-Croft was admitted to Casualty at twenty-three hundred hours. She had abrasions at the base of her spine and shoulders which bore out what she was able to tell us when she had tripped near the top of the stairs. X-rays were carried out, but there were no fractures or broken bones. She was then transferred to this ward, mainly for observation reasons; the patient's age being the prime consideration, although she was able to walk unaided.'

'Would you say she was fully conscious, Sister?'

'At that time, yes, but within twenty minutes in the ward she became slightly delirious.'

'Delayed reaction, perhaps?'

'That was our opinion and, once again taking her age into consideration, not altogether unexpected.'

'Was she able to tell you anything else about how she came to trip?'

'Not exactly,' she frowned, obviously trying to remember exactly what had been said; 'only that it must have been because of the carpeting which had probably become worn.'

Deciding to let that pass, Ian changed tack and asked her whether Muriel Miller had come into the ward with her.

'She did, yes, and stayed with her for most of the time.'

'You say for most of the time?' Ian prompted.

'Yes, because we suggested after a couple of hours she should take a short break and perhaps have a hot drink, because by then, the delirium had intensified and Mrs Miller-Croft was finding it difficult to recognise her daughter and, naturally enough, Miss Miller was finding this distressful.'

'I see.' Ian said, imagining what it must have been like. Although never having known Muriel Miller, he had once met Catherine Miller-Croft and from what he could remember she had struck him as an extremely forceful woman, also sharply intelligent. If she had suspected her accident had been deliberately arranged, he felt she would do her utmost to make this known, but it looked as though the shock had been too much for her. 'Latterly,' he asked, 'how coherent was she?'

'Part of the time; she was drifting in and out of consciousness. She was fretting about her accident. I think it must have been preying on her mind, if you understand what I mean.'

'In what way?'

'In that, and this was during the time Miss Miller was away, she kept repeating that she must warn Muriel.'

'About the carpeting?' he suggested, but not believing it. He had seen that stair carpet; it hadn't looked in the least bit worn to him, in fact, relatively new.

'That was our opinion.'

'And when Miss Miller returned to the ward, was Mrs Miller-Croft able to mention this to her?'

'I'm afraid not, Inspector. At three forty-five on Sunday morning,' she said, consulting the screen, 'Mrs Miller-Croft suffered a cardiac arrest. It was considered resuscitation, while being unadvisable, would not have been successful.'

*

Brenda phoned Jason Miller on the mobile number he had given Ian as soon as she arrived in London. He didn't sound surprised when she introduced herself or even when she said she would like to see him and, reckoning he could well be having his lunch break, suggested they meet in The Lord Moon of the Mall in Whitehall, knowing it was close to where he worked.

Ian had already given her a brief description of him and she had no difficulty in recognising him when he walked into the pub: tall, about the same height as Ian, thick brown hair, greying at the temples and rimless spectacles. Fairly typical of many of the businessmen around the same age and working in the centre of London, but she was certain it was him alright and the diffident way he looked around, finally convinced her. She waved over to him, not missing the way his eyebrows raised slightly in surprise. Of course, she thought amused; he would have had no idea what she looked like. Brenda had no illusions of the initial effect she had on people when they learned of her profession. She wasn't a vain woman and often wondered why, in a society where it wasn't such a rarity for a female to be taking on what was once considered to be the male's role in the professional world, many people reacted in this way.

'Mr Miller?'

'That's right.'

'Chief Inspector Brenda Masters.' she said, shaking hands and gesturing for him to sit down.

'I expect you want to ask me about Muriel?' he said, pulling out a chair.

'Not particularly,' Brenda said, 'but first, what would you like to drink?'

'No, please, Chief Inspector, 'I'll go up to the bar and get myself a beer.'

She waited until he returned; taking a sip of her coffee and regretting she couldn't have had a glass of wine, but she still had a lot to do, plus the drive back to Meadowbank later on that afternoon.

'There have been a few developments since you last spoke to Inspector Ash,' she began, 'which, while we are sure are connected with the death of your cousin, still require to be investigated separately.'

'Yes?'

'Did you hear about the shooting of a young man at Waterloo Station on Tuesday afternoon?'

'Only what I read in the 'London Evening Standard', but it didn't convey much, not even his name.'

'No, it wouldn't have; too soon, I expect. However,' she went on, 'he was Gary Nicholson and he came from Meadowbank.'

'Ah.' a look of enlightenment crossing his features for a moment, 'and you think his death had something to do with what happened to Muriel?'

'We don't have absolute proof, but there is a very strong indication that the person who murdered Miss Miller also killed Gary Nicholson.'

'Can I ask you why you're thinking along these lines, Chief Inspector?'

'First of all, let me tell you a little bit about Gary Nicholson;' she said, 'he was only twenty-three, but he had never worked in his life, also, and without going into too much detail, we have reason to believe he was blackmailing someone, namely Miss Miller's murderer –'

'– and that was why he was killed?' he interrupted.

'We believe so, yes.'

'And he actually lived in Meadowbank?'

'On the outskirts; his father owns a farm which is at the far end of Bridge Street.'

'So, he saw the – the person who –'

'– it is more than likely,' helping him out and sensing his discomfort, 'you see, his father has confirmed that Gary was out that evening and although he told him he didn't see anyone on the road, he may not have been telling the truth. He could have passed the area where Miss Miller's body was found around the same time as her killer was there and may have recognised him, either then or during the days leading up to when he was shot.'

'But,' obviously struggling to understand what she was telling him, 'he was killed in London. Not in Meadowbank.'

'I won't insult your intelligence, Mr Miller, by explaining any further. Besides, much of it would be guesswork and we deal with hard facts.'

'I know what you mean, Chief Inspector, but how can I help?'

'I'm not sure you can, but I'm trying to re-create, if possible, those last few days of Gary's life. For instance,' she continued, 'as I've explained, he didn't have a job and spent a fair bit of his time in either of the two pubs in Meadowbank. If he had recognised Miss Miller's killer, it may have been someone from the town and then very probably he would known him, but if whoever it was, didn't come from Meadowbank, it would have been unlikely for him to have done so, unless he happened to see them again, perhaps in a different context.'

'I see what you mean. You have a difficult job.'

'That's true,' she agreed, 'but I'm used to it. If we could go back to last Friday, the day of your aunt's funeral.'

'Yes.'

'I know, of course, that members of the family spent the previous night in the King's Arms Hotel and the following morning, with the exception of Miss Miller, you all had breakfast together.'

'That's right.'

'Afterwards, Mr Miller, before you went across to the church for the service, what did you do?'

'Well,' he said slowly, 'I don't know about the others, except that they went for a stroll around the town. We didn't finish breakfast until well after nine-thirty and the funeral was at eleven, so there wasn't a great deal of time until then. For instance,' he continued, 'I went out to buy a newspaper and took it back to the hotel and sat in the lounge reading it until it was time to leave for the church.'

'You say the others, Mr Miller, did they go out together?'

'As far as I know, except for Sonia. She said she was going to stay in the hotel.'

'She wasn't in the lounge when you went in there?'

'No, she wasn't, but she was probably in their room getting ready or at reception. Oliver had asked her to book them out to save them having to come back to the hotel, except to collect their cars before driving on to Winchester for the meeting with my aunt's lawyer.'

'I see. That appears to be clear enough and, presumably, you all left the church at the same time.'

'We did.'

'And went straight back to where you'd parked your vehicles?'

'Yes, but I've just remembered, Christine told us to wait for her; she'd forgotten to buy any cigarettes, so we waited while she went into the stationers for them and then we all walked back across the square together.'

'And only you returned to Meadowbank later; the others driving back to London?'

'Correct, Chief Inspector. Surely you're not suggesting that I was the person Gary Nicholson recognised?'

'I'm not suggesting that for one minute.'

'Because if you are,' he went on as though he hadn't heard her, 'you couldn't be more wrong. I'm no killer. I was extremely fond of my cousin and her death was a great blow to me and I'm still finding it difficult to come to terms with, far less understand, why she was murdered.'

'I understand,' Brenda said, 'we're not treating you as a suspect, Mr Miller.' which was true, but she had no intention of telling him that at this stage they didn't have any suspects.

'Good.'

'There is one last question.'

'Yes?'

'When did you last see Lawrence Croft?'

'Lawrence?' obviously not expecting that one, she thought.

'Yes,' she started to explain, 'I know you told Inspector Ash the family hadn't seen him for years, since his mother's funeral, in fact. As you weren't related to her, presumably you wouldn't have been there.'

'No, I wasn't and as to when I last saw Lawrence, well, it would have been around the same time, fifteen years ago. I bumped into him one evening in The Sherlock Holme**s** pub. I hardly recognised him at first, because the last time I'd been just a kid.'

'But he recognised you?'

'He did, as a matter of fact; from some family photographs.'

'Fifteen years is some time ago, but if you were to see him again, do you think you would recognise him?'

'I would say so. He'll be fifty-four now; Lawrence was a lot older than Oliver, eight years, I think, but perhaps he hasn't changed all that much. But, Chief Inspector, I asked the same question to Inspector Ash; why are you so interested in trying to trace a man who virtually cut himself off from his family several years ago?'

'Because, Mr Miller, Lawrence can be classified as a loose end, and quite frankly, we don't like loose ends, they need to be tidied up.'

*

Godfrey Mason recognised Brenda immediately, picking her out easily from the other pedestrians waiting at the traffic lights to cross the road. From his office window on the second floor he had an ideal vantage point, knowing that hardly anyone ever looked up, no doubt too intent on reaching their various offices before two o'clock. As the first time he saw her, he was struck once more by her appearance, which he realised was deceptive. She wasn't merely a pretty woman with nothing else on her mind but finishing work for the day and spending the evening with her boyfriend. He didn't need Christine standing beside him to remind him how chauvinistic he was, goodness knows, she'd told him often enough over the years. The lights had changed now and in one solid mass they all surged across to his side of the road and, instinctively, he knew the Chief Inspector would, within seconds, be ringing the bell to their suite of offices. And, on cue, he heard it, followed by Belinda's voice talking into the intercom.

Bracing himself for what he hoped wouldn't be another barrage of smart questions, all of which she would know the answers, he moved away from the window and returned to his desk.

'Good afternoon, Chief Inspector,' he said to her, once she was seated and Belinda had gone, closing the door behind her, 'I must say, I'm surprised to receive another visit from you. I was under the impression you had finished interviewing both my wife and myself.'

'In an ideal world, Mr Mason,' she said, a slight smile hovering for a second, 'yes, I would have, but invariably one question more often than not leads to others and each of them broadening the enquiry, but hopefully enabling us to fill in the gaps.'

'Well,' he said, making an effort to keep the exasperation from his voice, 'I can't think what else I can tell you about last Thursday night.'

'It's not Thursday I am particularly interested in at the moment, Mr Mason.'

'Really?'

'This murder enquiry is turning out to be considerably more complex than we had at first thought.'

'In what way?'

'Unfortunately,' she explained, 'there has been another one –'

'– another murder?' he interrupted quickly.

'Yes, a young man called Gary Nicholson, who came from Meadowbank, was shot dead on Tuesday afternoon at Waterloo Station; perhaps you heard about it?'

'Can't say I did, Chief Inspector. Shootings these days have, sadly, become the norm, especially in our cities. You say he came from Meadowbank, do you mean he lived there?'

'He did, yes. He lived at Bridge Farm which is further along Bridge Street and not too far away from where Miss Miller's body was found.'

'Are you telling me you're connecting the two deaths?'

'It is our belief they could be. He was on that road last Thursday night and it's possible he may have seen the assailant.'

'How can you be so certain?'

'Because we have strong evidence to support our theory that he was blackmailing the killer.'

'Good Lord!'

'Where were you on Tuesday afternoon, Mr Mason?'

'Here, in my office.'

'What time did you leave that afternoon?'

'The same time as I normally do; shortly after six.'

'And did you go straight home?'

'No, I didn't as a matter of fact. James, that's my partner, and I went round to The Sherlock Holmes for a drink.'

'And then you went home?'

'Yes, that's right.'

'And your wife; was she there when you arrived?'

'Of course she was. Look here, Chief Inspector, what are you implying? That I shot the man, a complete stranger. It's a ridiculous notion.'

'I'm not implying anything, sir,' she said, for once her voice sharp, 'but we have to conduct our murder enquiries in this way, how else would we be able to eliminate anyone even remotely connected with, as in this case, both victims?'

'I suppose so.' he muttered, but grudgingly; she really did have this disturbing ability of placing him on the defensive.

'How long have you been married, Mr Mason?'

'What on earth has that got to do with it?'

'Please, sir. I have a reason for asking you.'

'Since 1991.'

'Fifteen years ago.' she said, her voice thoughtful. 'That would have been the same year the family last saw Lawrence Croft, at his mother's funeral.'

'Was it? I never knew Lawrence, Chief Inspector.'

'Did your wife?'

'He was thirteen when Christine was born and I believe, according to Oliver, left home two or three years later and as you probably know,

Chief Inspector, both boys were brought up by their mother after their parents divorced.'

'I see.' she nodded, 'What I'm trying to do is build up a clearer picture of the family structure, sir.'

'Complicated, I know. It takes a bit of getting used to.'

'It does, I agree. You've told me you didn't know Lawrence Croft, but did you ever meet his step-mother, Catherine Miller-Croft? I am aware that she and your wife were estranged, but perhaps you met her at some time.'

What was she, this woman, Godfrey wondered; some kind of psychic. It was as if, uncannily, she could zoom into another aspect of her enquiry which to him appeared entirely at odds with what he was expecting. Quite formidable! He pitied any man who got latched on to her.

'No,' he said at last, 'I never met her.' hoping that would be the last of it.

'She didn't attend her daughter's wedding?'

'We didn't invite her, Chief Inspector. Christine and she had stopped communicating with each other a few years before we met.'

'And you have no idea why mother and daughter had fallen out?'

'Christine never elaborated, but I'd always thought it was a clash of personalities.'

'As simplistic as that?'

'Probably. It does happen in families, you know.'

'I realise that, of course, and yet you both attended her funeral last Friday and,' she added slowly, 'went with the other members of the family to the lawyers to hear the contents of Mrs Miller-Croft's will?'

'Well, yes,' he admitted, not having a clue where she was coming from, 'Christine was, after all, her natural daughter. We considered it only right and proper to be at the funeral service.' adroitly, he trusted, side-stepping why they should have expected to inherit anything from Catherine's estate, which of course that had been their sole reason for going along to Brutton's office on the Friday afternoon and a fat lot of good it did them. Christine was still harping on about what, in her opinion, had been a meagre bequest, although what really stuck in her gullet was the sudden appearance of Emily Craig.

'No doubt you, or I should say your wife, was somewhat surprised to hear about the additional and substantial bequest to Mrs Craig?' once again reading his mind.

'We both were. And that's all we know about her, Chief Inspector. We don't even know where the woman lives, but presumably she will eventually be moving into "The Gables", unless she decides to sell the property. Either way, no doubt she will show her face around Meadowbank, not that it matters to us I might add.'

'How often did you meet up with Miss Miller?' Brenda asked him.

'Hardly ever, except for weddings and funerals, those sort of family occasions. Christine and she did meet occasionally, but they didn't have a great deal in common. I think it was more out of a sense of family duty on Christine's part, if you understand? It wasn't as if they were actually related; different mothers and different fathers.' wondering whether she would swallow such a pathetic explanation. Part of what he'd said was true; Christine and Muriel did meet occasionally for coffee, but he knew damn well the only reason was for Christine to keep tabs on her. Ever since she had learned Muriel had started spending her weekends with Catherine, she had reached her own conclusions that Muriel had an ulterior motive for keeping in with Catherine and Christine, shrewd woman she was, had probably been quite correct. For all her outward appearances of not being materialistic, Muriel had been the opposite. She had been one of the most scheming women he had ever had the misfortune to meet and when, a couple of years ago, Jason had mentioned that Catherine was thinking of making a gift of her Swiss Cottage property to her, that was all Christine needed to finally convince her what Muriel was up to.

'Do I take it from what you've said, sir,' Brenda Masters was going on, 'that you have never visited "The Gables"?'

'No, I haven't.'

It was a relief when she left; probably realising there was nothing to be gained by bombarding him with more and more, in his opinion, pointless questions. Godfrey Mason did not like smart women. They had always intimidated him, going way back to his first days at university. Blue Stockings they used to call them and, as his mother would have described them, as she often had: "They're so sharp, Godfrey," she would say, "one day they will cut themselves." Well, he thought wryly, standing up and walking over to the window again, as far as Muriel was concerned, his mother would have been right. But, Chief Inspector Brenda Masters was smarter than smart, she was razor sharp!

As he stared unseeingly out into the street, he wrestled with his troubled thoughts. Perhaps he had been wrong to have lied to her. After all, he had nothing to hide. He hadn't been responsible for Muriel's death, or for the poor sod who had somehow become embroiled in the whole business, but part of him wanted to keep to himself, not even sharing it with Christine, the fact he had called in at "The Gables" with the proverbial begging bowl. As he remembered that evening, he still mentally cringed over the way Catherine had talked to him. It wasn't something he was exactly proud about and wanted, more than anything, to forget the whole unfortunate incident.

It had been a year ago; the second week in April, not long after Easter, and Christine had taken the two girls up to Norfolk to spend the school holidays with an old college friend. In retrospect, Godfrey was doubtful, if she hadn't been away, whether he would have decided, virtually on the spur of the moment to drive down to Meadowbank, but the business had been going through a rough patch and was sorely in need of a cash injection. They had managed to weather past global downturns, both James and he agreeing this had been largely because of a strong client base, but within a matter of weeks they had lost two of their major accounts, which, together with what was being rumoured in the city of the approach of another recession, coupled with soaring interest rates, had highlighted how weak they had become. With an immediate improvement in the financial structure of their firm, they would be in a better position to move forward and, hopefully, entice new clients on to their books. He was aware of James' concern, although he hadn't said as much to him, but both of them were realists and would, he knew, be prepared to face the unpalatable truth if and when it should happen and this was when he had first thought of how by approaching Catherine would go a long way in alleviating their immediate cash flow problem. To describe what he was about to do as begging wasn't entirely correct; it would be a loan and, if all went well, a short-term one and one from which she would receive a healthy return.

As he had parked outside "The Gables", Godfrey had no idea of what sort of reception he would receive from a mother-in-law he had never met, but if he had harboured any thoughts of appealing to the maternal side of her nature, one look at the hostile expression on her face as he introduced himself, rapidly shattered that illusion.

'Now you're here, Godfrey, you had better come in.' she had said, sounding for a fraction of a second like Christine, but apart from that, she didn't remotely resemble her. Catherine was a good head taller and where Christine's figure was pleasantly rounded, the woman who led him across the hall, was gaunt and he suspected always had been.

'I should have given you a ring first,' he started to apologise; already by her autocratic manner she was having that affect on him, 'but I didn't think you would agree to see me.' he finished lamely.

'Oh, I don't mind, Godfrey. I must admit I've always been somewhat intrigued to discover what sort of man my daughter had married.'

She offered him a drink once they were in the dining room, but he didn't accept, wanting to keep a clear head for what he was about to propose, realising it wouldn't be easy to convince her of his sincerity and deciding to cut out any unnecessary spiel, just give her the basic facts, although already suspecting in advance what her answer would be. She listened without interrupting until he had finished; sitting upright on the chair directly opposite to him, her head slightly tilted to one side and the intelligent grey-blue eyes unwavering as she heard him out.

'Well, Godfrey,' she said quietly, 'I won't prevaricate; that isn't my way, as no doubt you will have heard, but, frankly, I am not interested.'

'A pity.' was all he had said, making to stand up.

'For you and your partner, yes, I dare say it is and I'll put it like this, Godfrey; if you had been a friend, and one I had known for several years, I may have considered your proposition, but you don't fit into that category, the main reason being you are married to Christine, a daughter I haven't seen or spoken to for twenty years.'

'I thought that may have had something to do with it.'

'Are you aware of why this was?' she had asked, as though she hadn't heard him.

'Not really. Christine never said, only that you didn't talk to each other, she didn't tell me any more than that.'

'No, I don't suppose she would.'

'And I never pressed her.'

'I find that surprising. Weren't you interested? In my experience, I've found men eager to find out all they could about the women they intend to spend the rest of their lives with.'

'I reckon I must be the exception, then.'

'You must be. However, I think it's time you knew.'

At that point he had stood up from the table and had started to make his way back to the door, but before he reached the hall, she called out to him: 'My daughter, Godfrey, extracted money from one of my bank accounts without my knowledge.'

'I don't think I want to hear this.'

'It doesn't do to be an ostrich, Godfrey. You're a businessman; you should have realised that hard fact by this time.'

'I'm not, actually,' he protested, but only mildly, 'but I dislike talking about Christine in this way behind her back. It's dishonest. If she was here, at least she would be able to defend herself.'

'I doubt it.' she snapped. 'I doubt it very much. She forged my signature on half a dozen cheques, but fortunately I got wind of it before she depleted my account entirely. Of course I could have reported her to the authorities; after all, it was a criminal offence, but I didn't.'

'Why didn't you?'

'Too proud, Godfrey. It would have caused a scandal, but mostly because of the respect and love I had for her father and I was only glad he would never have known what she had done.'

'This all happened twenty years ago,' Godfrey said, 'and presumably you and Christine must have discussed it at the time. She would only have been twenty or twenty-one, very young.' he added.

'Perhaps,' she said, 'but old enough to know that what she had been doing was wrong.'

'What about forgiveness?' he found himself asking, partly in defence of Christine, but also because he was finding her attitude totally devoid of any compassion.

'The reason,' she explained, 'I could never forgive her was because she didn't ask me to.'

'What do you mean?'

'Christine refused to admit what she had done; in fact, she categorically denied it, that's why.'

'I'm sorry,' Godfrey said, wishing he could end this conversation, 'it does seem to me that perhaps Christine wasn't to blame after all. Have you considered that?'

'Of course she was! Who else?'

He had left then, no shaking of hands, realising it would be extremely unlikely they would ever meet again, also, he would never tell Christine. By the time he had reached the outskirts of London, he had rationalised his thoughts and impressions and had come to the most comfortable conclusion and, one he could live with, that it all happened a long time ago and he only had Catherine's side of the story, unpleasant though it was.

As he continued to stare out of his office window, seeing the diminishing figure of Brenda Masters rapidly being swallowed up in the crowds on the pavement below, he brought his mind back to the present, thankful now that Catherine hadn't agreed, especially as not long afterwards their business started to pick up with James, having sold a property he'd owned in Sardinia, providing the additional capital they needed and to a lesser degree, the recession rumours didn't come to fruition, resulting in an increasing confidence with companies taking advantage by widening and expanding their business interests. Meanwhile, Mason & Thornton began to show a healthy balance sheet which, should the current financial climate prove to be short-lived, enable them to be in the position to afford the terms on any future business loans. And now, Godfrey thought, Catherine, along with Christine's misdemeanour, had gone. He hoped Christine wouldn't pursue her idea of contesting the will, but he still wouldn't say anything to her. It must be her decision, but although Catherine hadn't informed the authorities, there was always the chance she may have mentioned it to Arnold Brutton, remembering how she had confessed to him all those years ago about the illegitimate child and concluded philosophically, everyone needs someone in whom they can confide.

*

It was three o'clock when Brenda finally reached New Bond Street, pausing for a moment to look in the window of Croft's Fine Arts, although the display of a couple of 'Constables' didn't particularly appeal to her. She had always found his work slightly depressing, which that afternoon, with still several hours to go before she would be finishing work for the day, more than usually oppressive with their darkening skies and sombre rural backgrounds and for some strange and unexplained reason reminding her of the meeting with Godfrey Mason. The man was probably still in his forties, but there was something dried up and pedantic about him which she had found at odds with his appearance. She supposed some women might describe him as fairly good-looking in a stereo-type of way, but there had been something about those slightly hooded eyes she had found disconcerting, also she didn't think he had been entirely honest when they had started to discuss Catherine Miller-Croft. Nothing she could actually pin-point; not yet, but given some time she would.

Pushing open the glass door, she braced herself for what she expected to be at least thirty minutes of blustering confrontation from another member of a family she was beginning to consider being somewhat different from the average, not only because of the tenuous link-ups through Catherine's two marriages, but by their rather incongruous, and difficult to understand, attitudes towards each other. She didn't think she had ever met a group of people who quite openly didn't like each other. Off-putting to say the least, she thought, looking around her, but not seeing any sign of the man himself and wondering when he would make his appearance.

'Can I help you, madam?' a short grey-haired woman asked, walking swiftly towards her. A no-nonsense type, Brenda immediately labelled her, noticing the way she was appraising her as she came closer, almost as if she was dismissing her dark blue overcoat, replacing it with the regulation police uniform. Fanciful, but that was the impression all the same.

'I was hoping to see Mr Croft.' Brenda said, waiting for the woman to ask her name, but she didn't.

'He's in the office, madam; if you'll wait a moment I'll go and see if he's free.'

'Ah, Chief Inspector Masters,' Oliver Croft said, emerging from one of the rooms at the far end of the shop, 'so, you've decided to make another visit to London.'

'I have yes, sir,' Brenda said, all too aware of the inquisitive stares from the woman who was standing behind him in the open doorway, 'I won't take up too much of your time; perhaps we can go into your office?'

'Of course. Of course.' his manner totally different to how it had been last Saturday. That earlier belligerence had gone, certainly for the time being, but she couldn't help wondering how long it would last. She had got the distinct impression the first time she had seen him that Oliver Croft operated on a very short fuse and she didn't think she was wrong. But, she reasoned, as she had discovered, husbands and wives often acted quite differently when interviewed separately; it was possible he felt more comfortable in his own environment without the inhibiting and hovering presence of his wife.

'So, Chief Inspector,' he asked, once they were in his office: a surprisingly small room and cluttered, not what she would have expected somehow and again, so different from his house in Mayfair, 'why are you here?'

'A number of reasons, sir,' Brenda answered, making up her mind it was time she changed tack here, otherwise she was in danger of going round and round in circles and getting absolutely nowhere towards furthering their investigation, 'first of all, the recent shooting of a young man from Meadowbank.'

'I read about someone from Meadowbank being shot on Tuesday afternoon; this was in the evening paper, although they didn't give any name,' he added, 'and if I may ask, are you putting the proverbial two and two together, tying his death with that of Muriel's?'

'We could be, Mr Croft.' she said, 'He was called Gary Nicholson and had been receiving what we believe was blackmail money, possibly from Miss Miller's assailant.' stretching the truth a little.

'Ah, very nasty. Silly man.'

'You could say that.'

'But, Chief Inspector, what can I tell you which is likely to help?'

'Perhaps not much, sir, as far as Gary Nicholson's murder is concerned,' Brenda said, 'but I would like to discuss another aspect of our enquiry, a further development which has forced us to extend our enquiries.'

'How cryptic you are.'

'It isn't my intention, sir. However,' she went on, 'for the record, would you mind telling me where you were on Tuesday afternoon around five.'

'I was here and didn't finish until six-thirty. A normal working day for me, I might add.'

'The lady I saw a few moments ago; was she here also until then?'

'Oh yes. Vera always locks up. She has been working for Croft's Fine Arts for a very long time; in fact as far back to when my father was still alive. She is,' he added, 'the absolute mainstay of the business.'

'I see. And when you finished work, did you go straight home?'

'I did, yes.'

'And your wife; was she there when you arrived?'

'Not on Tuesday, no she wasn't. Sonia attends Italian language classes every Tuesday afternoon and always goes for a glass of wine with her friends afterwards. It was probably around seven-thirty when she got home.'

'Could you tell me where the school is, sir?'

'It isn't a school as such, Chief Inspector. It's all very informal. Their tutor, an Italian woman, hires one of the conference rooms in the Royal National Hotel in Bloomsbury; that's where they meet.'

'When did you last see your step-mother, Mr Croft?' and as soon as she had asked him, she could tell by his startled expression, he hadn't expected her to come from that angle, but impossible to tell just how surprised he was. It could be another example of someone's immediate reaction to how she was in the habit of conducting her interviews, but there was no way of telling.

'Why in this world, Chief Inspector, do you want to know that?' he asked, the expression not budging.

'Because, sir,' she started to explain, 'there now appears to be an element of doubt of how Mrs Miller-Croft died.'

'What!'

'When did you last see her, sir?' Brenda persisted.

'On the day she died,' he answered, 'Sonia and I had been to a wedding in Winchester and we thought it would be a good idea to call in and see her.'

'You telephoned her beforehand?'

'It's obvious to me, Chief Inspector,' returning to his former blustering, 'you have found this out for yourself, so why ask?'

'We only have one person's word that Mrs Miller-Croft received a telephone call from you; we have to be certain of each fact. What time did you make the call, sir?'

'Good Grief, I can't remember the exact time. About quarter to two, I think.'

'Whose idea was it to visit Mrs Miller-Croft?'

'Whose idea?' he repeated indignantly.

'Yes, sir, was it yours or your wife's idea?'

'How am I meant to remember that?'

'Please, sir.'

'Oh, I think it was Sonia's,' making it seemed to Brenda a deliberate effort to remain calm, but obviously finding it difficult, 'Yes, she did suggest it, actually. We hadn't seen Catherine for a few months and she said as we were practically on the doorstep it would be a good idea.'

'How long did you stay?'

'Not long; no more than an hour. We had to get back to London before seven as we were meeting up with friends later that evening for a meal.'

'When you were with Mrs Miller-Croft, did you spend the time with her in her sitting room, which I understand is on the first floor or –'

'– in the dining room.' he interrupted, 'Sonia and I were never entertained in her private domain; Muriel most likely, but not us.'

'Did either of you go upstairs at any time?'

'No, we did not. I trust, Chief Inspector,' Oliver Croft demanded, any previous display of good nature no longer apparent, 'you are going to enlighten me. It has always been clear to us that my step-mother died as a direct result from a fall.'

'Theoretically, that is quite right, Mr Croft, but it would seem more than likely what everyone believed to have been an accident had, in fact, been contrived.'

'Contrived!' his voice going up an octave, 'What does that mean, for God's sake? She was an eighty year-old woman, Chief Inspector; she was not as steady on her feet as she used to be, but then she was stubborn. She would never take advice to slow down and continued to rattle around in that mausoleum of a place when she would have been far more comfortable living in an apartment in town. So,' he added, talking slower now, having obviously exhausted his personal diatribe, 'what do *you* think happened?'

'A length of thread has been discovered across one of the top stairs, each end having been secured to a banister at either side. It is our task now, sir, to find out who placed it there and when.'

'This is preposterous! Absolutely preposterous! What sort of thread was this, anyway, and who found it? That's what I would like to know!'

'The thread,' Brenda explained, 'is the type used by both the medical profession and veterinary surgeons for the purpose of securing wounds. Also, it is almost transparent and if your step-mother did trip over it, she would not have noticed it. The thread is also quite strong, but unlike nylon thread, it can break, as indeed it did in this instance. And,' she continued, 'to answer your last question, the thread was discovered by Mrs Craig and her daughter when they visited the house this week.'

'Mrs Craig?' frowning, 'Oh, you mean *Emily Craig*.' he emphasised, 'Has she moved in then?' he asked, a questioning expression on his face, the round dark-framed glasses giving him a donnish appearance.

'Not as far as we're aware, sir. Why do you ask?'

'No real reason, Chief Inspector; I suppose I'm merely curious about the woman. We were told very little about her when my step-mother's lawyer broke the news about her existence, except that she was a widow and now you say she has a daughter. "The Gables" is a rambling old place, also a bit out of the way; I can't see a woman and her daughter wanting to live there, somehow.'

'As to that, sir, I have no idea.'

'All of this is extremely hard to take in, you know. And, I suppose we can expect more media coverage; the press are going to have a field day. It's been grim enough with Muriel's death hitting the headlines without this.'

'So far, sir,' she told him quietly, 'this has not become common knowledge, although as I'm sure you are aware, if and when we make the decision to treat your step-mother's death as murder, it will be inevitable for the public to learn about it.'

'And, Chief Inspector,' pausing for a second, a deep frown creasing his forehead, 'are you going to treat this as a murder enquiry?'

'I have yet to consult with my superiors, sir, but I will be recommending that we do; the evidence in our opinion is too strong to ignore.'

Chapter Seven

The phone was ringing in the hall when Godfrey returned from work, and unbuttoning his coat, he picked up the receiver, surprised to hear Oliver's voice on the other end of the line.

'Hello, Godfrey,' he said, 'I wasn't sure whether you would be back home yet, but I'm glad you are. There's something I think you and Christine should know.'

'You sound a bit down, Oliver. What's up?'

'I had another visit from the Chief Inspector this afternoon -'

'- so did I, as a matter of fact.'

'You'll know then?'

'I suppose you mean about the shooting of the lad from Meadowbank and how she's connecting his death with Muriel's?'

'A bit more than that, actually,' Oliver went on quickly, 'it's about Catherine.'

'What about her?' puzzled now and reluctant to discuss the woman and be reminded of the one and only time he had met her.

'You may well ask, Godfrey,' Oliver said, 'because, apparently, the police are considering the possibility she may have been murdered.'

'My God! How on earth have they come up with that one? She must have given you some indication surely, Oliver?'

'Only that a length of thread has been found on the stairs, not ordinary thread exactly, but the kind the medical profession would use.'

'What do you mean by on the stairs; was it just lying there and who found it anyway?'

'Hold on, Godfrey; one question at a time! From what she told me it would seem as though it had been tied across one of the stairs near the top and had snapped, presumably when Catherine tripped over it.'

'But this is awful! Who on earth would do such a thing?'

'I've no idea, Godfrey, but if they are right, that will be their task to find out, not ours, but what does concern me more than anything is when this all leaks out, as it surely will.'

'The press, you mean?'

'Yes, but the inevitable aftermath, Godfrey. Not exactly good for business.'

'True, but I suppose we will just have to ride it out. We'll have no choice in the matter, Oliver.'

'I don't understand how you can be so – so matter of fact. We're talking about another murder, Godfrey. Another murder,' he repeated angrily, 'in the family!'

'I appreciate the implications, of course I do. Anyway,' Godfrey added, 'how did this thread come into the hands of the police? You haven't said.'

'I was coming to that,' his voice now tinged with impatience, 'we've got our new member of the family to thank.'

'New member of the family?' for a second confused until he realised who he meant, 'Oh, I suppose you mean Emily Craig?'

'Yes, she and her daughter found it when they made their visit to "The Gables" -'

'- and,' Godfrey interrupted, 'being public spirited immediately handed it over to the police?'

'I reckon that's more or less the way it was. Mind you,' he went on, 'obviously they considered it as suspicious and I suppose they couldn't have done anything else, but it's damnable all the same. Do you know, Godfrey, Chief Inspector Masters has an extremely devious way of questioning people. Talk about having a suspicious mind! Wanting to know when Sonia and I had last seen Catherine, that sort of thing. I'm probably her number one suspect!'

'Why should you think that?'

'Because Sonia and I were visiting Catherine on the day she died, that's why. And,' he went on, 'perhaps the last people, apart from Muriel, of course, when she returned to "The Gables" later that night, to have seen Catherine alive.'

'You don't know that for sure, Oliver.'

They didn't talk for much longer; both of them deciding to do so would be pointless; they had no option but to let events and whatever transpired from the police investigations take their course. Also, neither of them had pursued the question of who may have been responsible; it had taken Christine, within minutes of him relating the gist of the conversation, to put into words which perhaps Oliver and Godfrey had already been thinking.

'If,' she emphasised, hardly waiting until Godfrey had poured himself the stiff whisky he had been looking forward to from the moment Brenda Masters had left his office, 'the police can prove mother's death had been contrived, as far as I am concerned, Godfrey, it doesn't take two guesses who must have been responsible.' and, having delivered only what he had expected from her, waiting impatiently for some sort of response from him and watching him as he took his first deep and satisfying sip of his scotch, but he wasn't going to make it so easy for her. Why should he? Christine knew everything. She had always been the one in their marriage who somehow or another managed to orchestrate the pattern of their lives: where they would be spending their annual holiday; which school would be the best for the girls; when it was time, as she described it, to move up the property ladder and begin viewing other properties. They had been married for fifteen years and there had been a number of times, especially during the turbulent earlier years, when he had seriously wondered whether he had made a grave error in marrying her, but, in spite of her, at times, waspish bossiness, he did love her and, without her saying very much about her upbringing, he had managed to work out for himself, right to the core of her personality; namely, her mother's attitude towards her. Catherine, another strong character, had made it apparent to her she much preferred the more compliant and self-effacing Muriel.

'Alright, Godfrey,' she said, 'there's no need to stand there looking so po-faced. I know perfectly well what you're thinking.'

'Do you?'

'Of course.'

'Why don't you tell me, then, Christine?'

'As if you didn't know already. Alright, Godfrey, I'll put it on the line for you. Muriel. She would have had ample opportunity and, believe me, she would if she had thought it necessary, to arrange it and sufficiently clever to make the whole thing look like an accident.'

'Do you honestly believe she would have been capable of such an act?'

'Yes,' she answered quietly, 'I do actually.'

'And are you going to tell me why?'

'Muriel,' she started to explain, at the same time taking a bottle of wine from the fridge, 'for all her outward appearance of being non-materialistic, wasn't like that at all. She had to acquire anything which attracted her, especially if they were out of reach, and this trait extended beyond money, but to people also and by that, Godfrey, I mean men, and woe betide anyone who stood in her way.'

'Alright, I hear what you say,' realising the way she was describing Muriel as being overly materialistic was exactly how he'd been thinking of her earlier in the afternoon, and taking the wine from her, he opened the bottle and pouring out a full glass handed it to her, 'but why should she have gone to such lengths to dispose of Catherine? She had a good job, no doubt an excellent pension when she eventually retired, from what we've heard she had already been given Catherine's property in Swiss Cottage, therefore, she had no mortgage or rent to budget for each month. She had probably already had more than an inkling she would benefit financially eventually when Catherine died, so why the rush, Christine? Why couldn't she have waited?'

'But that's where you didn't know her, Godfrey. Muriel couldn't wait. When she wanted something, she had to grab it there and then; that was part of her character.'

'It seems pretty drastic to me, though. To contrive her step-mother's death; a woman she had known since she was a child and who had looked after her well.'

'You may think so,' Christine shrugged, raising her glass to him, 'but I think quite differently. You never knew Adam, did you?'

'Muriel's husband? No, I didn't, Christine; that marriage was over before I came on the scene.'

'Well,' Christine said, 'there was one evening in particular which I'll never forget; this was shortly before they were married. I had met up with Oliver in 'Annabels' and we were having a drink at the bar when he came in with his girlfriend and, by chance, Muriel was there as well. You don't know who the girlfriend was, do you?'

'Of course I don't.'

'It was Sonia. Apparently, Muriel and Sonia had been at the same school, although as you know, Muriel was a good five years older than her. Anyway, Sonia introduced Adam to her and I could tell immediately by the way Muriel looked at him, she wanted him for herself; she simply couldn't take her eyes away from his face. And, Godfrey, I was proved right, you know. Within a matter of months, weeks even, Adam and Sonia had broken up and he had moved in with Muriel.'

'Sonia couldn't have been very happy.'

'She was not. She was devastated! Haven't you wondered why Sonia disliked Muriel so much? Oh, she may come over as sweetness and light, but she absolutely detested her.'

'But then, she married Oliver?'

'Yes, that's right. They already knew each other, had been friends for years and, all in all, it appears to be a fairly good marriage. At least they are still together.' she added cynically.

'It sounds to me as though she may have married Oliver on the rebound?'

'You could say that I suppose. I don't know. However, Muriel's marriage lasted all of two years, if even that. Do you want to know my opinion, Godfrey?'

'Yes.' knowing she was going to tell him anyway.

'Muriel didn't really enjoy being married,' she started to explain, 'although what she did enjoy was the idea of *acquiring* a husband; she wanted the marital status. She was rather like a child, a selfish child who had never grown up. Once she had got what she wanted, she just as quickly grew tired of it and, perhaps fortunately, she never wanted children.'

'How did you learn this?'

'For the simple reason, Godfrey, she told me on one of the few times we ever met up in those early days. She'd only been married to Adam for a couple of months and, for once, she was in a confiding mood. I must admit I was surprised, because as you know she had this secrecy thing, kept things to herself to a ridiculous degree, but I put it down to having too many glasses of wine which loosened her tongue and I expect she regretted saying as much as she did when she woke up the next morning.'

'Alright, Christine,' he said refilling their glasses, 'I'm sure you're right in the way you've described her character, complex though it was, but just assume for a moment she did arrange Catherine's accident, why was it that she herself was murdered almost a week later?'

'How should I know?' she shrugged.

'So, what you're suggesting is that there are two murderers out there, not just one, assuming that the person who killed this chap, Gary Nicholson, was the same as the one who killed Muriel.'

'Again, I've no idea, Godfrey and as you said a few moments ago, this is for the police to sort out. But what's this Gary Nicholson to do with it all?

'That's the name of the man who was shot on Tuesday. You must have read about it, Christine.'

'I did, yes, but I don't understand the connection.'

'He came from Meadowbank, that's why.'

'Oh, I see.'

'Oliver is concerned how this additional development is going to affect his business, always assuming, of course, the police do decide to treat Catherine's death as murder.'

'Well, he would, wouldn't he? As far as Oliver has always been concerned, Croft's Fine Arts should remain as pure as the driven snow. Honestly, he really is the most blinkered and self-centred man I have ever known!'

*

The Market Inn was beginning to fill up although it was still early, not quite seven. At this rate, Brian thought, trying to serve two customers at once, he would be asking Derek to extend his working hours. Not that he was complaining, far from it, but wishing all the same it was a little less hectic. He couldn't help feeling concerned about Melissa; she shouldn't be working as hard as she was. Her pregnancy was hardly noticeable yet, but he was thinking ahead, to two or three months' time, perhaps when she wouldn't be as agile as she was now. He glanced along the bar to where she was serving another influx of customers, immediately recognising them as the three journalists from London, including the American woman who had been around a lot in recent months, much to the irritation of many of the residents, and remembering how pushy she was. They never stayed at the bar, but went as they usually did, over to one of the tables, from where Brian thought cynically they would be able to pick up snippets of conversation. What a bloody job! And glad he was just a simple landlord, his main task being to pull pints.

'Have you heard the latest, Brian?' Melissa asked him, walking along to where he was standing.

'Go on, tell me, love,' he answered, 'and judging by your expression this isn't going to be something good.'

'It's quite shocking actually, especially as there may not be any truth in it, but I overheard Stanley Coleman a few minutes ago telling his cronies that Mrs Miller-Croft's accident had been fixed.'

'What did he mean by fixed?'

'Somebody had, he said, tied some tape or thread or something across one of the stairs in her house and this had caused her to trip.'

'How,' Brian gasped, 'in this world, did he come up with that idea?'

'You probably didn't know, but Stanley's wife used to work for Mrs Miller-Croft and she told him that Ian Ash had been along to ask her if she had ever seen this thread thing before.'

'I just don't believe this! I really don't, Melissa. Surely it's stretching credibility too far?'

'I don't know,' Melissa said, moving away to replenish some more glasses, 'but,' she added, 'it's possible those journalists heard him. You know Stanley, Brian; he never bothers to lower his voice.'

'Silly man.' Brian muttered under his breath, looking across towards the three of them. They had heard alright and, as he watched, seeing the American take her mobile from her bag. A quick call to her paper, he thought, stifling a sigh, and the latest piece of Meadowbank scandal may be in time to catch tomorrow's headlines.

The journalists weren't the only people who heard what had been openly discussed at the other end of the bar. Emily, having completed her first day working for Meadowbank Pharmacy, had arranged earlier to meet up with Jessica for a drink, their table being next to where the journalists were sitting and, in particular, the American woman's voice, possibly because of the distinct New York accent, reached them both clearly. They looked at each other with raised eyebrows, but made no comment, when Catherine Miller-Croft's name was mentioned and the three of them had proceeded to discuss what they'd picked up at the bar:

'Mind you, Carol,' one of them said, 'I'm not trying to put a dampener on your enthusiasm for what could turn out to be a scoop for the paper but I can't help thinking it may have only been idle gossip among a handful of old-aged pensioners enjoying their nightly pint.'

'You could be right, Tom,' she answered, 'and I must admit if it hadn't been for Inspector Ash's name being mentioned, I may have agreed with you. Oh,' she went on, obviously warming to her theory, 'I realise what many people of that age are like, all with too much time on their hands with nothing better to do than compete for one-upmanship; it's exactly the same in the States, but I'm still inclined to believe what he was saying. It would certainly put more meat on the bones of an enquiry which is, quite frankly, going cold and that means uninteresting and will not sell newspapers.'

'Okay, okay,' the man called Tom said, 'I'll back you up, Carol, but we'll have to tread carefully; with the way we write up the piece I mean, otherwise we could end up with a slander case on our hands.'

'Gee, I know that. Trust me; I've had plenty of practice watching my back, but you both have to admit it would be crazy to ignore what we've heard just now. Don't you agree?'

'Okay,' he sighed, 'you win, Carol.'

'Come on then, let's drink up and get back to the hotel.' Carol said briskly, 'I'll give the office a quick ring to say our emailed report will be on its way within the next hour.'

Emily and Jessica remained silent until the three of them had finished their drinks and had left the pub before saying anything. Emily had lost count of the times over the last few days when she had seriously considered it had been a mistake moving to a town as small as Meadowbank, where it would seem that without too much difficulty everyone learned about everyone else's business.'

'Some woman!' Jessica said at last.

'She certainly is,' Emily agreed, 'and tough as well, I've no doubt. So, Jessica, it looks as though Ian Ash did take us seriously.'

'The police will have to follow it up.'

'I would say so; in the public's interest. Not that I know much about murder investigations. Jessica,' she added, 'are you happy living here?'

'I am, yes. Why do you ask, Mum?'

'I don't know, love,' she sighed, 'but it does feel claustrophobic in many respects, but then I expect all small towns are like this.'

'When all this business is sorted out,' Jessica said thoughtfully, 'I think the place will settle down, so why don't we give it another six months and see what we think then?'

'My practical daughter.'

'Someone has to be!'

'Cheeky!'

'But seriously, Mum, are you planning to tell Adam about being related to Catherine Miller-Croft?'

'I think I should. It seems a bit deceptive not to. Also,' she went on, 'I would say it's only a matter of time before news reaches the ears of the people of Meadowbank we are the new owners of "The Gables".'

'We won't live there, will we?'

'Never, Jessica. Therefore, the only alternative is to sell the property. I intend to get valuers in as soon as possible; they will be able to handle all the paintings and other valuables.'

'One step at a time, then?'

'I believe that's best, love. This inheritance has come as something of a shock and that's an understatement. I don't want "The Gables" or the contents, so I don't see any reason not to sell everything; it means nothing to me, Jessica. I hope you can understand that. I have absolutely no sense of belonging to Catherine's family.'

'I understand, Mum,' Jessica said gently, 'you don't have to explain.'

*

Brenda was later getting back to Meadowbank than she had expected. Traffic on the M3 had been smooth-flowing, there had been no problems, but once she had reached the last stretch of the M27, that's when the hold-ups began. At each junction, until she was finally on the A3057 Stockbridge Road, there was one bottleneck after another, with the result it was after seven by the time she drew up outside the Station in Market Square.

Ian was still in the office, although he wasn't the only one working at that time of the evening. Meadowbank may only be a relatively small town, but Brenda was well aware that many of the officers put in far more than the requisite hours each day.

'Alright, Ian?' she asked, walking over to his workstation.

'Fine thanks,' he said, 'I was finishing off my report from my findings today.'

'Did you make much headway?'

'A little; this case is proving to have a number of unexplained twists and turns.'

'Don't I know it. At times, it is just one long hard slog, but I'm confident we'll get there, Ian, although we do need a breakthrough and, hopefully, that will happen sooner rather than later. Anyhow,' she continued, 'I don't suppose you've eaten today?'

'A sandwich at lunchtime.'

'That's not enough, you know.' she said, aware she was no different. That was all she'd had herself in the middle of the afternoon which now seemed so long ago it was no more than a distant memory. 'Why don't we break our usual routine this evening and have a meal across the road in The Salmon's Rest; at the same time as having some well-deserved food, we can exchange notes.'

Barbara Wood, the new proprietress of The Salmon's Rest restaurant, showed them to their table. Brenda had only been in once since the Woods had taken over back in the summer and, as then, pleased to see they hadn't made any radical changes to the decor, still very much reminiscent to how Danielle Taylor had designed it; the clever mixture of Italian and French style, and although so very different from what Meadowbank was accustomed to, nevertheless pleasing to her.

'I haven't got very far in sussing out Bradley Cartwright's background;' Ian said, when the waitress had taken their order, 'which in some respects, I find odd.'

'Why?'

'Well,' he explained, 'without actually asking him, I've had to be discreet in the enquiries I was able to make, but those haven't taken me very far. Not even where he went to school for example or anything about his family and where he was brought up.'

'Perhaps,' Brenda suggested, 'we shall have to see him again.'

'I think that would probably be best. You see, he's only lived in Salisbury for eight years; that was when he bought his present house, after selling up in Brighton. This was at the time he qualified in landscaping design at the technical college there -'

'- just a minute, Ian,' she interrupted, immediately experiencing a small frisson of excitement, prepared to trust her instincts, rather than dismiss what he'd said as being of no consequence, 'Lawrence Croft moved to Brighton from London in 1990; how does that date fit in with what you have so far on Bradley Cartwright?'

'I thought of that, ma'am,' he said, 'and they could have both been living in Brighton at the same time. Bradley was there in 1998, although we don't know for how long -'

'- and if,' interrupting once more, 'by some fluke, they are one and the same person?'

'It is possible,' he said slowly, 'although the address I have for Bradley Cartwright is different from where we understand Lawrence Croft had been living, but perhaps it would be worthwhile doing a double check on that.'

'I think we should. We'll give him a ring first thing tomorrow morning and let's hope he'll be in Meadowbank over the weekend. One of my priorities is to have a meeting with Bill Simms. I believe it's time he was told about the question mark over Catherine Miller-Croft's death. He's not going to like it, I know, but we can hardly be blamed for not suspecting earlier.'

'I wonder how long it will be before the press get their hands on the story.'

'I trust not before my meeting with Bill Simms, but knowing the press are still around with nothing else to do at the moment but to listen-in to what the locals are saying, whether fabricated or not, I'm certainly not holding my breath.'

'Mavis Coleman is bound to tell someone about my visit yesterday; it would be unnatural for her not to.'

'It's inevitable,' Brenda agreed, 'I mentioned the likelihood of us treating Catherine Miller-Croft's death as murder to Oliver Croft when I saw him this afternoon and from his reaction I got the strong impression he would not want anything else to further taint the family name.'

Their meal arrived at that moment: they had chosen the same; lamb cutlets with mint sauce, sautéed potatoes and fresh vegetables, spending the next twenty minutes simply enjoying the food and agreeing the chef, who used to work for Danielle Taylor, had not lost any of his culinary skills.

'That was excellent,' Brenda said, 'coffee, Ian?'

'Please,' he replied, 'and you're right, it was good. We're lucky to have a restaurant like this in the town; it certainly makes a change from the

Chinese take-away.'

'Incidentally,' Brenda asked, 'did you get any feedback from passport control on Lawrence Croft?'

'I did, yes; it came through this afternoon. They apologised for taking so long, but it would appear they were conducting a thorough search and they found nothing to indicate that Lawrence left the country, in fact at any time during the last sixteen years.'

'So, as far as customs are concerned, Lawrence Croft is still in Britain?'

'That's right. Also, ma'am,' he added, 'his passport would have expired in 1998 and it hasn't been renewed.'

'I see. Perhaps you could ask Lambeth Met to email you a copy of the picture they'll have of him on their records. The reason I'm suggesting this is because I spoke to Jason Miller today and, although he hardly knew Lawrence, the last time he saw him being about fifteen years ago, he thought he would recognise him again.'

'You think he may have changed his name to Bradley Cartwright?'

'I do, yes. I realise it might sound as though we are clutching at straws and we could be totally wrong in what are, at this stage, only assumptions, but if we don't broaden our thinking on this case, I feel we will never move forward and reach a final conclusion.'

'I went up to The Royal Oak this afternoon,' Ian said, pausing for a moment as the waitress brought over their coffees, 'and learned that it would have been possible for Bradley Cartwright to have left the hotel without being seen that night.'

'Oh, yes?'

'His room is situated at the back of the building,' he explained, 'on the second floor and the window is within relatively easy reach of the fire escape. He looks in fairly good shape to me and I would say he could have managed it without a great deal of difficulty.'

'What about security, Ian,' she asked, 'do they have any cameras?'

'Surprisingly, they don't. In fact,' he went on, 'It must be quite dark at night round there; the only lights are at the front, two large ones on either side of the main door. They do have a night porter, but then he can only be in one place at a time.'

'That's true. I know the property looks secure,' Brenda said, visualising how it must be at night and, with very little traffic on the road, reasonably quiet, also remembering how high the hedge was at the rear of the hotel separating the grounds from the neighbouring fields, 'all the same, I wouldn't have thought it all that wise to be in such a vulnerable position especially when you consider the number of break-ins there have been in recent years. Still, Ian, that's not our job, is it? We're police officers and our brief is primarily to solve crimes. So, returning to what you've told me, Bradley Cartwright's alibi is far from foolproof. As we said before, he could have applied that chloroform pad over Muriel Miller's face when he accompanied her to where she had parked her car, returning to the hotel when the receptionist told you and then, with the help of the fire escape, leaving the hotel and driving to Bridge Street and after he had dragged her from the car and suffocating her, going back to The Royal Oak, returning to his room the same way he had left it, presumably unnoticed.'

'Difficult to prove though, ma'am.'

'I know, extremely difficult, but it could have happened like that. But, what we have to consider now, given our suspicions over Catherine Miller-Croft's death, is how he could have possibly rigged that length of thread on the staircase at "The Gables", especially when, according to him, he had been with Muriel.'

'We don't know what time they met each other.'

'A very good point, Ian; all the more reason to have another talk with him and, before we do, we should have that print from the Met. Even although you and I have never seen Lawrence Croft, his photograph may be sufficient for us to decide whether there is any likeness, however slight, and if there is, we'll ask for Jason Miller's assistance.'

*

'Who's the lady with Ian Ash?' Adam Fry asked Jacqueline, looking over her shoulder towards where Brenda and Ian were sitting.

'Of course,' she said, 'you won't have met her yet. She's Meadowbank's

Chief Inspector of Police, Brenda Masters.'

'My goodness,' Adam remarked, 'I would never have guessed; somehow, she doesn't look like a police officer.'

'Too feminine, I suppose you mean?' Jacqueline smiled at him.

'Well, yes, not that I'm in the least chauvinistic, at least I never thought I was. Do you remember that programme on television where a panel of celebrities had to work out the professions of selected members of the public?'

'Vaguely, it was some time ago.'

'It was and I don't think I was ever once able to guess. Anyway,' he asked, 'what is she like?'

'I've only spoken to her a few times, I've never seen her when she hasn't been working, but she always gave me the impression of being extremely astute and has, in fact, built up quite a reputation for herself over the years since she was promoted to chief inspector; this was about eight years ago.'

'They must have considered her worthy of the position,' Adam said, 'and she would have been fairly young then.'

'She's the same age as I am, Adam,' Jacqueline said, looking across the table at him, 'which is thirty-eight. There,' she laughed, 'I've told you how old I am.'

'I wasn't prying, you know,' he said, 'honestly, and I'd better come clean and tell you I'm forty-six, or I will be next week.'

'We must celebrate.'

'You don't mind the eight year age difference?' his expression becoming serious.

'Why on earth should I, Adam. I've no hang-ups about that sort of thing. I wouldn't care how old you were, although I must admit if you had been eight years younger, then I may have found it a bit difficult to handle!'

'I'm glad,' he said, 'I know we've only known each other for such a short time, although it feels I've known you for ages. I don't want to lose you, Jacqueline; you've become too important to me -'

'– I think I understand,' she said gently, 'and I feel the same way, Adam.'

'We've never talked about the past much, have we?'

'No, but does that really matter?'

'Well,' he started to explain, the fear of rejection if she didn't like what he was going to tell her paramount in his mind, but he really had no choice. She had to know before anyone else enlightened her; he wouldn't have been able to have coped if that happened. 'I was married, Jacqueline, and up until recently, although it had been many years since I had seen my wife, I had still remained married.'

'Yes?' wishing he hadn't brought the frown to her forehead.

'I don't think I'm putting this to you very well,' he apologised, 'but I'm finding it difficult to put it all into words.'

'It's alright, Adam,' she pressed his hand lightly and the instant warmth he felt was a help, enough to enable him to continue, 'I know you're struggling to tell me something, but I'm sure it can't be all that dire.'

'That depends on how you view what I'm going to say,' he answered, 'anyhow, I'll get to the point. My wife, Jacqueline, was Muriel Miller and,' he paused, trying to work out the expression on her face, 'before you say anything, or indeed ask me any questions, 'we were married in 1986, twenty years ago, but the marriage didn't last. I'm not going to bore or depress you with the details, but we decided to separate and, this probably is the difficult part to grasp, but I never saw or heard from her again in all that time. When people were talking the other night in The Bridge about a woman's body being found I had absolutely no idea it was her. No idea at all. You have my word for that. Believe me.'

'I believe you, Adam. You poor man; how awful this must have been for you,' dabbing at the corner of her eyes with a tissue, 'but you should have told me before. You've been keeping all of this to yourself, haven't you?'

'I have, it's true. Quite honestly, I didn't know what to do for the best. Whether to keep quiet or mention it to the police.'

'So, what did you do?'

'Well,' he smiled ruefully, 'as it happens, they had already learned I'd been married to her; they had discovered this when they were back-tracking through her personal records, and' he shrugged, 'Ian Ash came into the pharmacy on Wednesday to see me. He asked me a few questions,' Adam went on, 'he was somewhat surprised we had never divorced, but I think I explained well enough why we hadn't.'

'Adam,' she said, her hand remaining on his, 'I've no intention of asking you anything about your marriage. As far as I'm concerned, that is over and done with; the most important thing being now is for you to do your best to put that part of your life behind you.'

'Thank you.' he said, longing to take her in his arms, but that was something he hadn't done so far and in spite of what she had said and the obvious sympathy in her reaction, he wasn't sure it was the right time.'

'Adam,' she smiled and this time she didn't make any attempt to check the tears falling unchecked down her cheeks, 'I love you.'

It had been a long time since any woman had said those three words to him. Muriel never had, even in the early days of their relationship, whereas Sonia had never stopped telling him how madly in love she was with him, but somehow, and this could have had something to do with the way he had been quick to break up with her, although that was no excuse for the shabby way he had treated her. But, now, so many years later, he had come to the realisation that he had found Sonia's affection for him cloyingly claustrophobic. It was true they had been young, and perhaps too immature, to have acted any differently. Sonia had already told him about her unhappy childhood; her parents had already been in their forties when she was born, both of them lawyers with little time, or indeed much interest, in their daughter. Shortly before her seventh birthday she was sent off to school and although only a weekly boarder spent her weekends with an uncle and aunt who both left Sonia very much to her own devices. In retrospect, Adam realised now, when it was far too late, that the young Sonia had been almost totally deprived of any real affection and she had been trying to put all those pent-up frustrations into the relationship they never really made an effort to strengthen. Sad thoughts, but all in the past, and now he was with Jacqueline and unbelievably grateful for being given a second chance.

'I love you too, Jacqueline,' he said quietly, taking both her hands in his, 'and thank you for being so understanding.'

Chapter Eight

Sonia had truly believed that once Muriel had gone, she would be able to forget her, put the memory of her and what she had done, firmly to the far recesses of her mind, where it belonged, but she couldn't. Almost a week, but Muriel continued to live on. Even during the daytime now she would appear, not as she looked on the last day they all saw her before Catherine's funeral, but years earlier and sometimes as far back to when they had been at school. There had been a couple of times this week when Sonia had caught a puzzled expression on Oliver's face when he'd had to repeat something she hadn't heard the first time, but he didn't make any comment, but then Oliver wouldn't. He was, above all, a realist, and had known she had married him on the rebound and, although it was almost twenty years ago, Adam's name was never mentioned between them.

She never did have anything in common with Muriel, only in the fact they had both attended the same school in Berkshire as weekly boarders, the five-year gap in their ages meaning they seldom came into contact with each other, but this hadn't prevented Sonia, although only around ten or eleven at the time, to understand that Muriel had built up a reputation for herself, mainly in refusing to conform and comply with the rules and regulations like the rest of them had to. She had never shown an interest in being part of any group, and didn't appear to have a special friend. She would have been around sixteen then, mature for her age, and had developed a skill, to some an enviable one, of managing, always without detection as far as Sonia was aware, of sneaking out at night, usually on a Saturday, and returning to her dormitory long before the wake-up bell rang. Sonia never did learn where she went, or whom she met on those nocturnal excursions and later, after Muriel had left, she heard that no-one in her form had known either.

The next time Sonia saw her was at the school reunion in 1981 and, more out of curiosity than nostalgia, wanting to see what her ex-school friends and those she had lost touch with looked like now, she went along. Muriel had been there, which surprised her, looking older than her twenty-five years; expensively elegant in an ankle-length black velvet dress and strappy stilettos. She had brought her cousin with her as a sort of escort which had struck Sonia as somewhat out of character from how she had remembered her, especially in the now-enlightened times when young women were going all out to be independent. The swinging sixties had long gone, leaving in their wake a general acceptance of thinly veiled promiscuity when no questions were asked; girls and boys just got on with it.

The school had rather grandly hired the Banquet Suite in The Holiday Inn for the occasion and Sonia had been standing near the cocktail bar looking around to see if any of the girls who had been in her form were there and hadn't expected Muriel to come over, or even recognise her; she had still been a kid when Muriel had left school, not even in her teens. She had been slightly taken aback by the way Muriel greeted her; flinging her arms around her and kissing her on both cheeks, also she had been drinking; the strong smell of whisky practically masking the Chanel Number Five. Jason, the cousin, didn't say very much, looking, she thought, slightly uncomfortable, whether he wasn't accustomed to the impressive surroundings or it was because of Muriel's flamboyancy, she couldn't tell, and that had been the last time she had seen her until seven years later in 'Annabel's'.

Up until then, Sonia had no particular feelings about her; she neither liked nor disliked her, she had been entirely neutral, but that night her whole attitude towards Muriel changed. It had been a Friday and, as usual, she had been with Adam, whom she had known since their university days and, unlike many of her fellow students, they had continued to see each other after they had graduated. They had even been talking recently of her moving in with him; he'd a flat in Peckham in those days, only small, but she had been looking forward to turning it into a real home and being with him all the time, but Muriel, in a matter of weeks, changed all of that forever.

Muriel had been in Oliver's company that night in 'Annabel's'. Sonia had known him for a while, seeing him mostly at weekends when he would frequent the same night clubs and wine bars as Adam and herself. She had always liked him, although finding him a bit on the dull side, but no other man could ever have matched up to what she felt for Adam. Christine Miller-Croft, as she had been then before she married Godfrey, had also been there. Oliver told her later she was his half-sister, and although they shared the same father, Oliver had stayed with his mother when his parents divorced, this was a few years before Christine was born and he'd seen very little of her during the years they were growing up.

As soon as Muriel spotted her over the heads of the crowd milling around the bar, she hadn't hesitated, waving exuberantly to them. Even after eighteen years Sonia could remember every single detail of the evening which she continued to believe changed her life. Single-mindedly, from the moment Sonia had introduced them, Muriel proceeded to monopolise Adam. From those first couple of minutes Sonia felt she no longer existed; it had been Muriel he was focusing on and it was when she saw the open admiration in his eyes, an expression she had never seen before, she knew she had lost him. It was from that precise moment, the neutral attitude she'd had towards Muriel altered; hatred for her began to insinuate itself into her heart and there it had remained, refusing to go.

Everything had moved rapidly after that first meeting between Adam and Muriel, culminating two weeks later when Sonia had called round to see him on a Sunday morning to find Muriel there and, as she had been wearing his dressing gown, there was no way she could have talked herself out of what to any normally sensitive person would have been a compromising and embarrassing situation. Instead, she said nothing, an unpleasant smile distorting her lips and giving every indication she was enjoying her moment of victory, standing in the open doorway of Adam's flat, as Sonia's life crumbled painfully around her.

There had been times, especially since she had married Oliver and had been obliged to attend family functions, she had wondered if Muriel ever sensed the strength of this hatred, but Sonia didn't believe she had. Muriel had been for Muriel and that was the way she had been made. She had been impervious to animosity; a woman who, Sonia was sure, incapable of tuning into negatives vibes, but it was time she made a conscious effort to pull herself out of this quagmire of depression. She, Sonia Croft, was alive! She had a husband who provided a lavish lifestyle for them; a circle of friends to whom she could, when she felt in the mood, relate to; two growing sons, who up to now had not caused them any problems. What more could she possibly want?

As soon as Oliver arrived home on Thursday, later than he usually did, and told her about the Chief Inspector's visit, an idea began to formulate in her mind. The mention of Emily Craig had triggered it off. Up until then, she had only been the name of the woman, alright, the illegitimate daughter of Catherine, who had been bequeathed most of her fortune, they hadn't been able to put a face to her; she had been someone, completely unknown, hovering on the periphery of their lives and she knew Oliver probably felt the same way, although, being Oliver, he hadn't put it into words.

Oliver explained he had phoned Godfrey earlier, which surprised her, but perhaps what the Chief Inspector had to say about Catherine's accident had made more of an impact, upsetting his normal equilibrium and that meant his daily routine. And, to confirm this, he had gone on to say he'd called into The Moon, where he'd had a couple of beers, one more than he normally would have had, before driving home. He was such a creature of habit, and for some reason, this unprecedented deviation from his normal routine disturbed her and that was when she decided she must try and find Emily Craig, not for any rational reason, except she felt she had to do something. Whether this was out of curiosity or a genuine concern for her husband, she didn't know, but by the end of the evening, even before they had finished their meal, she had made up her mind. She would phone Arnold Brutton in the morning and ask him for the woman's address. She hadn't worked out what she would do after that, maybe nothing, but somebody in this extended family which she had married into must take a positive step, otherwise Emily Craig would remain a mystery and Sonia didn't like mysteries; she liked an orderly life, where everything was clear and understandable.

She waited until Oliver had left for work the following morning before telephoning the lawyer's office, asking the receptionist to put her through to Arnold Brutton, but she had neglected to take into account his intractable and unbending nature. He was polite as he always was, but she recognised the wariness in his voice after she asked him for Emily Craig's address. It wouldn't have made any difference how she had couched her words, she got the impression he could see through what was possibly not the most clever of explanations, namely that Oliver and she had decided it would be a friendly gesture to welcome her as a member of their family.

'What you're saying, Sonia,' he said when she had finished talking, 'is indeed heartening, especially after last Friday when I did feel a certain animosity among you towards the lady. However,' he continued in his laboriously pedantic way, 'as I don't know how Mrs Craig would feel if she should receive a visit from a member of the family about whom she has only recently learned, I won't give you her address, but I am prepared to let you have her telephone number and perhaps then you could give her a call; in this way,' he added, 'you would be able to introduce yourself without any face to face feelings of discomfort, and make an arrangement to meet.'

'Her telephone number, Mr Brutton?' wanting to yell at him; he really was the most infuriating of men. What was the matter with him? All she wanted was the woman's address; a simple request under the circumstances surely?

'Yes, Sonia, her telephone number,' he repeated, 'that would be best, I think.'

'I must say you are being very protective towards her.' she couldn't prevent herself from saying, doing her best to disguise her annoyance.

'In case I didn't make it clear on Friday, Mrs Craig is my client and I have to protect her interests at all times. It may not be convenient for her to receive visits from people she has never met before. I hope you can understand.'

'I believe I do.' Sonia said, knowing she had no choice but to accept his wishes and realising that after all the years she had known him, she didn't like him at all.

After jotting down the number, she rang off, trusting he couldn't detect the insincerity in her voice as she thanked him for his help. Not that it matters, she thought, replacing the receiver. Arnold Brutton was an old man and surely he wouldn't have many working years left.

The number he had given her told her considerably more than she had hoped. The prefix was a Winchester one, recognising it immediately. She had phoned it often enough in recent weeks prior to their friends' wedding. Also, having been blessed with a good memory for numbers, it reminded her of another one she had dialled only a week earlier when she had rung The King's Arms in Meadowbank to reserve their room. Could Emily Craig actually be living in Meadowbank? Was it possible, she wondered, slipping the piece of paper inside her wallet. She had no intention of using it, not yet anyway. Perhaps later.

Sonia had very little to do that morning, or indeed in the afternoon and Friday being the day in the week when Oliver would be having a drink after work with his usual crowd of cronies, meant it would be well after eight before he was home. In fact, she had the whole day to herself and the more she thought about Emily Craig, the more her brain tantalizingly insisted she could quite easily get into the car and drive down to Meadowbank. She didn't even stop to consider she had no idea where to start looking for her; she may not even be living in Meadowbank. So intent on following her instincts, she dismissed such an eventuality as insignificant.

*

Although not quite making front page news, far less an editorial scoop, the latest development, in what the press had initially labelled as 'The Muriel Miller Murder' had been allocated three columns half-way down on the second page of the newspaper. Brenda called into the stationers in the square as soon as she arrived in Meadowbank on Friday morning and bought a copy, taking it with her across the road to her office. Her immediate relief at not seeing the piece straight away was soon squashed when she turned the page to be confronted with a picture of "The Gables". Not taking time to take off her overcoat or even to sit down, she remained standing in front of her desk and read through to the end and not all that surprised to see Carol Cliff's name. As before, the American had done her homework:

"HAS MURDER RETURNED TO MEADOWBANK?" the headlines jumped provocatively out at her, "It can now be revealed that "The Gables" on the outskirts of Meadowbank, may have been the scene of another murder. Meadowbank, a market town on the edge of Hampshire's River Test, and up until recent months a reasonably tranquil town where nothing too spectacular ever took place, is once again making news. The recent death of the owner, Mrs Catherine Miller-Croft, aged eighty, of "The Gables", an elegant, although somewhat draconian eighteenth century mansion, had lived there for over forty years, was understood by the community of the town to have resulted from an accident in her home, but irrefutable evidence has come to light to indicate this could have been deliberately arranged.

"The deceased had been the step-mother of Muriel Miller; the body of Miss Miller having been found last Friday afternoon on waste ground in Meadowbank. The police, it is understood, are continuing with their enquiries, but so far no arrests have been made. Also, the authorities appear to be no nearer to finding the killer of Gary Nicholson, who came from Meadowbank, and was shot dead at Waterloo Station in London on Tuesday; the general consensus of opinion being there could be a possible connection with the three, still unexplained, deaths."

She certainly sailed pretty close to the wind, Brenda thought wryly. Somehow, the journalist had the knack of going just so far and no further. There was nothing incorrect in what she had written, also nothing libellous. Carol Cliff knew exactly what she was saying and Brenda had to, although grudgingly, admire her neatly controlled professionalism. Now, she sighed, folding up the newspaper, she had better get in touch with Bill

Simms before he summoned her to his office to face the proverbial music.

He also had a copy of the newspaper open at the same page, and one look at his grim expression as she walked into his office was sufficient. She had been warned; in other words, she should have seen him yesterday, but it was too late now.

'What is going on, Brenda?' he barked. 'How much substance is in all of this?' he added, pointing an index finger at the article.

'Basically, sir,' she began, 'what Carol Cliff has written, is theoretically correct.'

'I'm waiting for an explanation, Brenda.' and the tone of his voice leaving her in no doubt he hoped the explanation would be a satisfactory one. This is going to be tough, she thought with resignation.

'On Wednesday evening,' she explained, 'we received a call from Mrs Emily Craig; she's the new owner of "The Gables". She and her daughter had been up to view the house, this being their first visit and the daughter found a length of thread, the type used for medical purposes, tied on to one of the banisters. They considered this to be suspicious and promptly phoned the Station. Inspector Ash went up there, together with Constable Edmunds, and he found a second length of the same thread; it had snapped in two when someone had been coming down the stairs, namely Mrs Miller-Croft.'

'And you suspected foul play?'

'We began to seriously consider it could be, sir. Inspector Ash interviewed Mavis Coleman yesterday morning; she's the woman who cleaned for Mrs Miller-Croft. Mrs Coleman had been working there on the Saturday morning, the day of the accident and told him she had been up and down those stairs more than once during the morning, so when it had been positioned there must have been after she had finished work and gone home. Mrs Miller-Croft's niece, Muriel Miller, who had been spending the weekend with her step-mother had already left the house by this time and didn't return until later that night to find her step-mother lying in a semi-conscious state at the bottom of the stairs. However, Mrs

Coleman told the inspector that her employer was expecting a visit from her step-son and his wife some time during the afternoon; this promulgated me in deciding to go straight up to London and have a word with them. I was late getting back,' Brenda continued to explain, wondering how much more he would need to know when they were not even half-way through their investigation, 'and when Inspector Ash and I had finished our meeting, this being to confer and go over what we had both been doing that day, I considered it too late to phone you.'

'I see and, believe it or not, Brenda, I do understand. However, what I don't understand is how this woman, what's her name – ' he hesitated, glancing down at the newspaper article, '- Carol Cliff get hold of this information?'

'I don't know for sure, of course, but I think it's more than likely she overheard someone mentioning the doubts about Mrs Miller-Croft's death. She and her two colleagues from her paper have been in Meadowbank since last weekend trying to get as much information as they can glean about Muriel Miller' death; they're staying at The Royal Oak, but they spend a fair bit of time in both The Market Inn and The Bridge. As you know, sir, people talk and some of them like an audience. Perhaps it was unlucky that one of The Market Inn's regular customers happens to be married to Mavis Coleman.'

'Ah!' leaning back in his chair and folding his arms in front of his chest, his expression she was glad to see considerably less hostile. 'One of the ironies of our work, Brenda; the public can be helpful, but at times, they can be quite obstructive. However,' he continued, 'you've a lot on your plate; I appreciate that, although it's not good for the town, especially this shadow hanging over Catherine Miller-Croft's death. She was a valuable and much respected member of our community and I only hope there won't be any unpleasant repercussions. She came from one of the south of England's oldest and wealthiest families. I'm sure there are still Singletons out there, you probably know that was her maiden name,' he paused for a second, as though mulling over in his mind what form these repercussions would likely take, 'anyway, we're police officers, Brenda.

Our brief is to solve crimes as you are well aware and sometimes it does mean we have to step on a few influential toes, but, so be it!'

*

Twelve o'clock was chiming from Saint Stephen's as Sonia drove into Meadowbank and, carrying on through the square, she turned left into Bridge Street until she reached The Bridge Inn, pulling into the side of the kerb immediately in front of the pub. There were a few customers, most of them standing at the bar, and once she had ordered a glass of wine, took it with her over to one of the tables. This was the first time she had been in here. On the few occasions when she and Oliver had had a drink in the town they had either gone to The Market Inn or The Royal Oak hotel on the Stockbridge Road, but, today, even although it was unlikely she would see anyone she recognised, she decided to go somewhere else and as she unbuttoned her coat, wondered why they hadn't been in before. Sonia's experience of any pub outside London was limited, but she liked what she saw: a blazing long fire, ancient wooden trestle tables and benches on either side and gilt-framed hunting prints on the wall immediately facing her. The woman who served her must be the landlady she decided and there didn't appear to be anyone helping her behind the bar. She liked the atmosphere and for the first time in days she felt the persistent headache beginning to ease. She didn't know the reason for these headaches; she had suffered from them for so long now and had begun to take them for granted, but recently they had become steadily worse. She hadn't told Oliver, knowing what he would say, but she had no intention of making an appointment to see her doctor. She was a healthy woman in her mid-forties and these little aches and pains, in her opinion, were only something to be expected. There was nothing wrong with her. Besides, he would only prescribe some medication which more than likely wouldn't work and any adverse side effects were something she could do without.

The pub was beginning to fill up with very little space left along the bar and with now only a couple of tables free. A popular place, Sonia thought, noticing how calmly the landlady served them all; a non-flappable type of woman, she thought, and then, glancing across towards the door, noticed the man who had just come in. It was his profile she recognised, and at first she thought she must surely be wrong, but he looked remarkably like Oliver's brother. Coincidences liken this do not happen! She had only met Lawrence once and that had been at their mother's funeral years ago, and as he turned slightly she knew she hadn't been mistaken. It *was* Lawrence. And, at precisely the same moment, he turned round and saw her.

'Lawrence!' she called out to him, half-standing to attract his attention, although there was no need; he was already walking towards her.

'Hello, Sonia,' he said, his voice sounding exactly the same, 'what are you doing here?'

'I could ask you the same question.'

'Touché.' a brief smile appearing, but she wasn't fooled. He was not pleased to see her and she wondered why. Lawrence Croft, Oliver's older brother and one she scarcely knew and had only exchanged half a dozen words with. Oliver had never told her much about him; Lawrence had left home when Oliver had still been a schoolboy and she remembered how surprised he had been when Lawrence turned up for the funeral, most of the family believing he had gone overseas. He hadn't kept in touch and this had always puzzled Oliver because he'd said Lawrence and his mother had been close, especially in those years after their parents had divorced.

'Well,' she asked, looking up at him, 'are you going to join me?'

'Of course,' he answered, 'I'll get myself a beer first.'

She watched as he walked back to the bar, reminded as she had been the first time she saw him how very different he was from Oliver. Where Oliver was shorter and stockier, Lawrence must be almost six foot and although his hair was becoming quite grey, he now had what she would call a lived-in sort of face, all of which changed his appearance from how she remembered him. As she looked away from where he was waiting to be served, her attention was drawn to the people at the table next to her.

She wasn't sure whether they had been there when she came into the pub, but perhaps they had, seeing now there was something different about them; they didn't seem like any of the other customers, most of whom were probably residents, or at least worked in the town. These three, two men and a woman, had a cosmopolitan look about them, similar to the people she was used to seeing in London; each of them, in their own way, ultra-smart with a keen awareness about them which she had always felt was unique among city workers. It wasn't only this though; it was the way the woman kept looking over towards her, a quizzical expression on her face.

'Alright, Sonia,' Lawrence said, coming back and sitting down beside her, 'why are you in Meadowbank? Or is it,' he added, 'a big secret?'

'It's no secret,' she answered, turning round to face him, 'I'm here to look up a friend of mine. Someone I've rather lost touch with over the years.' elaborating and having no intention of saying anything more to him. 'And you, Lawrence?'

'I'm working here for the next couple of months and then I'll be moving on.'

'So, where are you living now? Still in Brighton? I remember you telling us you had moved there from London.'

'That's right, yes.'

Why is it, she wondered, but not too concerned, was she getting the distinct impression he was fobbing her off. He was lying, but then, with a mental shrug, was she any different?

'Did you know Catherine had died?' she asked him and, this time, watching his reaction more carefully.

'I heard she had, yes.'

'You knew she lived in Meadowbank, of course?'

'It may, or may not, surprise you, Sonia, but I had no idea she was here, until I read about her death in the local paper.'

'That does surprise me, actually. Surely, when your father married her, you must have known?'

'I was twelve years of age, Sonia, and my mother never told me and, feeling the way I did about him at the time, I didn't ask her, because frankly I didn't want to know.'

'What about you, then,' she asked, although not knowing why she should be showing any interest in a man she hardly knew and the only point of reference being he was Oliver's brother, albeit an absent one, 'did you marry?'

'No, I didn't.' and there it was again; that closed-in look making her think she may have touched on a sensitive nerve; it was clear this was a subject he didn't want to pursue, but a little demon mischievously raising its head made her press on.

'No woman in your life, then, Lawrence?'

'There was once, but not anymore.' he answered and she could tell this time by the way he pressed his lips firmly together she would get nothing further from him. Lawrence was giving out clear signals, obvious to her by the faraway look in his eyes, that he was suffering and, not wishing to be mentally burdened with someone else's personal problems, she had quite enough of her own, she made to change the subject.

'The work you're doing,' she went, 'Oliver never did tell me what you did for a living.'

'Landscape design and I'm involved in the Riverside development across the road, -' he started to explain but was interrupted by his mobile ringing and, taking the phone from his pocket, walked over towards the door to answer it.

He wasn't long and within two or three minutes he had returned, not sitting down this time, but remained standing to drink the remains of his beer: 'I'll have to go, Sonia,' he said, 'I'm needed on site.' and that was all he said, no further explanation, not that she had expected any, but surprised all the same by such a hasty departure. From where she was sitting, she saw him emerge from the pub, but instead of walking across the road, he turned right, back towards the centre of the town. As she remained there, finishing her wine, Sonia went over in her mind everything he had said to her and couldn't help wondering how much of it had been true. So different from Oliver, not only in appearance, but it would seem in other ways also. She would never describe Oliver as a secretive man, but there was no doubt his brother certainly was.

Beginning now to regret her earlier impulse to come to Meadowbank and start what was beginning to seem a pretty hopeless task, she decided she would try the number Arnold Brutton had given her, with a vague idea of arranging to see Emily Craig. At least then she would have met the woman, not knowing how such a meeting could benefit her; today she was following her instincts and not certain whether she would tell Oliver she'd come here and, as for mentioning she had seen Lawrence, she didn't believe Oliver would be all that interested. Continuing to be conscious of the continuing interest of the three at the next table, she dialled Emily Craig's number, letting it ring for several seconds, before giving up. That was that, then, she thought, putting the mobile back into her bag; she may as well head back to London, but first she would call into the chemists in the square for a packet of paracetemals. In her haste to leave that morning she had neglected to bring any with her, although she did realise it was probably unwise to take any too soon after drinking wine.

She had been into the Meadowbank Pharmacy once before, but it had been a couple of years ago and she didn't recognise the woman behind the counter. She was about to pay for the paracetemals when the door of the dispensary opened and Adam Fry, of all people, came out. He didn't notice her at first, but hearing her quick gasp of surprise, looked across the counter towards where she was standing.

'Sonia! My goodness, I never expected to see you in Meadowbank!'

'I'm only passing through.' she managed to say, the feeble explanation being the only thing she could think of; as if anyone passed through Meadowbank.

'It's amazing to see you after all these years. How are you?' and giving no indication he had noticed anything odd about her response.

She told him she was fine, which was far from the truth; this day was turning out to be extraordinary. It was as though she had stepped back in time and was powerless to return to the present; first of all meeting

162

Lawrence after fifteen years and now Adam, whom she hadn't seen for nearly twenty. He hadn't changed all that much, older naturally, but he was still handsome and, as in the past, reminding her of Robert Redford.

'Listen,' he said, 'I was just about to go across to The Market Inn for a bite to eat; would you like to join me, for old time's sake?' he added, the same quizzical smile she remembered so well and even now continued to hurt.

Of course she agreed and, of course she wanted to spend a little time with him, knowing already, even before she had started on the drive back to London, how it would affect her, coupled with the feelings of guilt she would have about deceiving Oliver. Knowing it would only be an innocent chat with an old boyfriend and would never be repeated made no difference.

*

'I wonder what she's doing in Meadowbank.' Carol Cliff remarked, keeping her voice down, not wanting Sonia Croft to hear. Carol was very aware how her strident New York accent sounded to the more sensitive ears of English people; she had been told often enough since arriving in London a number of years ago.

'Who is she?' the man sitting on her left asked.

'Sonia Croft.'

'How do you know?' Carol's other colleague asked, turning his head slightly to look at the woman at the next table.

'Obviously you didn't see the photograph in 'The Courier', Jimmy.' she answered, 'There was a copy lying about in reception shortly after I arrived last Saturday and naturally, being interested to find out what the local rag had to say, I picked it up. Muriel Miller wasn't the only person in the picture. It looked to me as though she must have been attending some function and by a stroke of luck perhaps the paper still had a copy. The only thing was,' Carol went on, 'they hadn't given any of the names, only that of Muriel Miller.'

'So,' Jimmy put in impatiently, 'if it isn't a daft question, how did you find out.'

'I did consider calling in at The Courier office, but decided it extremely unlikely they would be forthcoming, therefore I asked the receptionist at the hotel.'

'Just like that.' Tom remarked, 'You'll be telling us next you know the man she's with.'

'I don't *know* him, Tom,' she corrected him, 'but I know *who* he is.'

'Come on then, Carol, share the results of your exceptional skills at deduction.'

'No need to be sarky, Jimmy. Surely you must have seen him in the bar up at the hotel?'

'Well, yes,' he admitted, 'but that doesn't mean I know anything about him, or his name either, if it comes to that.'

'He's called Bradley Cartwright and he was Muriel Miller's boyfriend.'

'How on earth did you find that out?' Tom asked, looking at her now in admiration.

'Because I asked the barman.'

'You what!'

'You heard.'

'But, what excuse did you give him?'

'I didn't have to. I have never known any barman yet, whether over in the States or in England, who didn't like to chat, especially if they had what they thought to be an interesting snippet of information to pass on.'

'Ted obviously didn't know you were with the press, then.' Jimmy said.

'No, that's true; he should have done from when we were there earlier in the year, but I'm sure he knows now. Anyway,' she continued, 'last Sunday, quite early in the evening and I was waiting for you two guys to join me in the bar, Bradley Cartwright was there, sitting on his own by the window and Inspector Ash came in and went straight over to talk to him. Unfortunately,' she smiled ruefully at them both, 'I wasn't able to hear what they were saying, but I reckoned it wouldn't have been about the weather, so that was when I asked Ted who he was.'

'There's something odd here, though,' Tom said, 'you said his name was Bradley?'

'Yep.'

'But when she called over to him just now, she called him Lawrence.'

'Exactly.' Carol nodded.

'So, who the heck is Lawrence?'

'I would say,' the smile not leaving her face, 'more to the point, who the heck is Bradley!'

'Okay, Carol,' Jimmy said, 'you needn't look so smug. Who's Lawrence then?'

'As you know, I've been in Fleet Street for a while and I remember hearing about a rather spectacular robbery; this was carried out in 1989. Jewellers in New Bond Street. I wasn't involved in the reporting being a mere junior back then, but I read all about it. The brain behind it was a man called Lawrence Croft and he got twelve months for his efforts.'

'Croft?'

'Yes and I'd already got archives to email through a copy of the report because I wanted to re-familiarise myself with the case. It's the same family alright, there's no doubt about that. I expect it caused quite a hoo-ha at the time, mostly because of the business. You see, Oliver Croft owns Croft's Fine Arts which, paradoxically, is also in New Bond Street. I don't think he would have been much pleased to have the reputation of his family name sullied by his crooked brother.'

'Well, well,' Jimmy said, 'so this woman next to us is Lawrence Croft's sister-in-law. Bit of a turn-up, wouldn't you say?'

'As I said a few minutes ago,' Carol remarked, 'why is she here?'

'He seemed surprised to see her.' he commended.

'So was she.' Tom added quickly, 'Fishy.'

'Could be,' Carol nodded, noticing that the man Sonia Croft had called Lawrence was now going over towards the door to take a call on his mobile, 'meeting up with each other may or may not have been a coincidence.'

'I wonder if the police have found out they are one and the same guy.'

'I don't know, Tom, but I would say it is extremely likely that if they haven't by now, they sure as heck soon will!'

'I think we should try to be a bit circumspect here, you know,' he said, 'we're probably not exactly flavour of the month with the police here over that last piece about the possible rigging of Mrs Miller-Croft's accident.'

'I know, I know. You're right of course,' she agreed but with reluctance, 'so, are we agreed for the moment to keep this to ourselves?'

'Okay.'

'And you, Jimmy?' she asked him.

'Okay.'

Chapter Nine

Bradley hadn't been all that pleased to see Sonia and not entirely convinced she had been telling the truth when she had told him she was in Meadowbank to see a friend of hers. If she had been, why wasn't she with her, he wondered, walking along Bridge Street and by the time he had reached the corner where the road turned into the market square, he had convinced himself she had been lying. Although he had only been in her company once before and then only briefly there had been something in her manner which he hadn't taken to. He could think of no rational explanation, except perhaps the answer was quite simple; Sonia just wasn't his type of woman. But, then, who was his type? Not that it mattered, certainly not at the moment he concluded, stopping when he reached the front steps of Meadowbank's police station, bracing himself for the forthcoming interview. He didn't know whether he had been surprised or not to receive the call from Inspector Ash, but couldn't think what else they would want to ask him.

He was no stranger to police interview rooms, although 1989 had been the last time he had been in one, but the one the desk sergeant took him to bore no resemblance to any of them. In here, considerable thought had been put into the general decor of the place: table and four chairs in pale oak; a couple of framed prints on either side of the plate-glass window overlooking the rear of the building and he recognised the beech trees along the side of Winchester Road. Inspector Ash was already there waiting for him and introduced him to the woman seated at the table next to him. Neither of them were in uniform, creating the illusion of an informal meeting, not that he was fooled, neither by the contrived effect of comfort nor the cornflower-blue eyes of the Chief Inspector.

'Thank you for agreeing to call into the Station at such short notice, sir,' she said to him, gesturing for him to take one of the chairs opposite, 'but as we knew you were working in town, we thought it might be more convenient for you.'

'That's alright, Chief Inspector.' Bradley said, equally polite.

'When Inspector Ash talked to you last Sunday, the murder enquiry we were conducting concerned only the death of Miss Miller, however,' she continued, 'there have been a couple of developments since then and we're hoping you will be able to assist us in clearing up a few points which have arisen.'

'If I can, I will of course.'

'Good. Did you read about the shooting of a man at Waterloo Station on Tuesday afternoon?'

'I did, yes, but why do you ask?'

'Because, sir, This was Gary Nicholson and he came from Meadowbank, also we have evidence to support he may have been blackmailing someone –'

'– what's this got to do with Muriel?' Bradley interrupted her.

'Allow me to explain. Gary lived in Bridge Street, about half a mile from the area where your friend's body was found and had passed along that stretch of road possibly at the same time as her killer had been there. Also,' she continued, 'he had been carrying a large amount of cash on Tuesday. He had met, presumably his killer, shortly after five pm, this meeting was caught on a CCTV camera showing him receiving a package similar to the one found on his body, but regrettably for us, but not for his killer, it has been impossible due to the crowded concourse to make out anything about the person he was meeting.'

'I had no idea.' Bradley said, 'The paper didn't give his name.'

'No, it wouldn't have,' she agreed, 'they had to wait until Gary's family had been informed.'

'I see.'

'Before we go any further, sir, and for the record, would you mind telling us where you were on Tuesday afternoon around five?'

'Of course,' Bradley sighed, 'I expect I'm already one of your prime suspects, and now you're tying me in with the murder of this chap, Gary Nicholson.'

'It's a question of elimination, sir,' she pointed out, those deceptively innocent looking eyes focused directly on him, 'so, if perhaps you could confirm where you were at that time, we would be grateful.'

'I was at work, Chief Inspector,' he said, noticing she hadn't made any attempt to contradict or deny what he'd said, not needing to be reminded that this interview was an official one, although neither of them were making any recording of what was being said. Time yet, he thought cynically, 'I would have been in the site office then. Although the light was failing and work had finished for the day, I still had some paperwork to attend to.'

'I see,' she said, 'and you were on your own, Mr Cartwright? Is there anyone who could verify what you've just told me?'

What a doubting Thomas she was!

'The Sales Office was still open,' he said, 'they don't close until six-thirty and it's possible someone would have noticed the light was on in my own office.'

'There may very well have been a light on, Mr Cartwright, but what I'm trying to establish is whether you were actually seen around this time.'

'The answer to that, Chief Inspector, is, I don't know.'

'We'll move on, shall we,' she said, appearing to disregard what he'd said or indeed anything else so far, 'but first of all, have you read any of today's newspapers?'

'No,' he replied tetchily, 'I've been far too busy. As a rule, I don't get around to doing that until later on in the evening.'

'Well, yesterday, we established that Mrs Miller-Croft's accident which ultimately led to her death had been contrived and this was mentioned by the press.'

'What are you saying?' he burst out, 'And what do you mean by contrived, for goodness sake?'

'Mrs Miller-Croft,' she started to explain, 'had a fall in her home on the evening of Saturday, the twenty-first of October, from which she didn't recover, dying in hospital later that night. We now know that she tripped over a length of thread which had been tied across one of the stairs.'

'And you think I was responsible for that as well?'

'I don't *think* anything, sir.' she emphasised. 'I am merely telling you of the latest developments in our enquiry. However, someone deliberately placed that trap and it is our business to find out who it was.'

'Well,' Bradley said quietly, 'it wasn't me.'

'Perhaps, Inspector,' the Chief Inspector said, turning towards Inspector Ash, 'you would like to continue from here?'

'Mr Cartwright,' the Inspector said, leaning slightly forward in his chair, 'were you with Miss Miller at anytime during Saturday, the twenty-first?'

'I was, yes.' and having no inkling from where he was coming.

'Could you tell us, please, at what time you and Miss Miller met each other?'

'We had arranged to meet in The Bridge Inn at six. I was working until then, because normally it would have been much earlier in the afternoon.'

'And you were on the site all afternoon up until you left to walk across to The Bridge?'

'That's right.'

'How long did you both stay there?'

'Just over an hour; Muriel was already there when I arrived, this was about ten past; we had a couple of drinks and then drove up to The Royal Oak where we had dinner in the restaurant as we did most Saturdays when she was spending the weekend in Meadowbank. It was no different from any of our other evenings spent there, in fact.'

'When you met up with Miss Miller did she tell you what she had been doing that afternoon?'

'I don't think so, but is it so important?'

'It could be, sir. You see, the other day, I went along to see the woman who used to clean for Mrs Miller-Croft and she told me that Miss Miller left the house early that afternoon. What we are trying to establish is where she went during the time she left "The Gables" and arrived at The Bridge.'

'I see, at least I believe I can see what you're getting at.'

'You still can't remember whether she mentioned what she had been doing before you arrived?'

'I'm beginning to remember,' he said, 'she said she had driven into

Stockbridge to do some shopping. We used to do this quite often, but as I've said I couldn't get away from the site until later.'

'Mr Cartwright,' Brenda said, after briefly exchanging glances with the Inspector, 'I presume by now you have realised how our investigations have extended, which has meant we have to continue asking as many questions as we can to reach the truth; to find not only the killer of Miss Miller but that of Gary Nicholson and Miss Miller's step-mother, Mrs Miller-Croft.'

'I understand.'

'I am now going to ask you a few questions which may appear to you as irrelevant to this case. In fact, they may well be, but in our profession, we do not like loose ends, or indeed anything which doesn't make sense.'

'Okay,' he said, wondering when and how this was all going to end, 'fire ahead, Chief Inspector.'

'You told Inspector Ash you live in Salisbury, having moved there from Brighton about eight years ago.'

'Yes, that's correct.'

'Originally, sir, did you come from London?'

My God! She was clever, there was no doubt about that, Bradley thought. There was no way she could have guessed that. She had him in the proverbial corner and he knew when he was beaten, meaning he had no choice. He had to come clean.

'I did come from London, yes.' he admitted, selecting his words carefully and trying to remind himself he had nothing to hide; he had served his time. Everyone, after all, is entitled to a life.

'Am I correct in saying, sir,' she said, continuing in the same measured tones she had used since she first started talking to him, 'you changed your name at sometime during 1990?'

'Alright, Chief Inspector. I have no intention of lying to you, but I had, in my opinion, a very good reason for doing this. I changed my name legally, I might add, from Lawrence Croft to Bradley Cartwright. I am sure you will have found out that I served a twelve-month prison service for robbery. I paid the price for being foolish and paid it very heavily. I am not proud of my past, far from it, but I would like to add this; I have never harmed anyone in my entire life. I am not a violent man, Chief Inspector, whether you believe me or not.'

'Thank you for being so frank,' she said when he had finished, 'and do you still maintain you were unaware Miss Miller was part of your family? Her Christian name, for instance, you must have heard it mentioned at some time?'

'I may have done; I don't know, but when I met Muriel it didn't ring any bells in my head and I'll repeat, I had no inkling whatsoever she was related to Catherine Miller-Croft.'

'Alright, sir,' Brenda said, making to stand up, 'I think we can now bring our meeting to a close.'

Neither she nor the Inspector had anything further to say to him and he left the building more than a little light-headed. Had they believed him or not?

*

'What do you make of him, ma'am?' Ian asked her after Bradley had gone.

'A good question.' she said wryly, 'On the face of it, Ian, everything indicates he is guilty, but I don't believe he is, you know. Something continues to elude me in this case and has done from the beginning. While Bradley Cartwright's alibis for the three murders lack any real substance, there is the question of motive. So far, we have been thinking along the lines they had been for gain, except for the death of Gary Nicholson. In fact, his killing is the only one which is making any sort of sense at the moment. But, I'm not so certain now why Catherine Miller-Croft and Muriel Miller were murdered. If Catherine Miller-Croft had not come into the equation, and it had still only been Muriel Miller's death we were investigating, we could possibly have a more solid case against him. We only have his word that he hadn't known the woman with whom he'd been having a relationship was part of his family and had made out a will in his favour. Also, we cannot afford to assume he had been aware all along. No, Ian,' she shook her head, 'we have to consider another reason why the murderer felt the need to take such drastic steps. If, for the moment, we concentrate on what happened to Muriel Miller, we may come up with something more credible than we have done so far.'

'Well,' Ian began tentatively, 'it would appear that, apart from her cousin, Jason, and Bradley Armstrong, nobody else in the family liked her all that much.'

'Yes, you're right, but how intense was this feeling? Was there someone among them who more than disliked her, Ian?' she asked, 'Did he, or she, actually hate her? Not only was her murder premeditated, but it was a violent one.'

'It was, I know. Perhaps, ma'am,' he suggested, 'it was in the form of some sort of revenge over something which happened in the past. They have all known each other for a number of years; whatever it was could have been simmering away, if you understand what I mean?'

'I do, actually.' Brenda agreed, thinking that maybe at last they might be getting somewhere, part of the phrase "a woman scorned" immediately occurring to her, 'We've already discussed the feasibility of a woman committing these crimes, although,' she added, 'she would have needed to have had some experience and knowledge of handling a firearm. I think you've made a valid point, though, saying that any hatred towards Muriel Miller could have occurred some years ago. It looks as though we'll have to back-track, Ian,' she continued, 'find out all we can about each of those people we have interviewed up to now, also, why Christine Mason and her mother hadn't spoken to each other for twenty years. That's a very long time. There must have been a strong reason, although at this stage I'm not necessarily connecting this with Muriel Miller, but then you never know.'

'When I first spoke to Jason Miller he thought it was because of a clash of personalities, meaning, the pair of them just didn't get on, but I did think at the time there must be more to it than that.'

'I would say so. From what you've said, I think it's doubtful whether Jason will have much more to tell us, but what about Christine? We haven't up until now considered her seriously as a suspect. She is, I suppose,' Brenda suggested, thinking back to last Sunday when she had met her it was unlikely she would be all that forthcoming, 'the obvious person to approach, but she may have a very good reason for not wanting the reason for the rift to be known. It is always possible she confided in her husband.' Brenda added.

'Muriel Miller may have known,' Ian said, 'she and Catherine Miller-Croft were quite close, apparently; they had kept in touch and there's the generous gift of the property in Swiss Cottage. What I'm getting at, ma'am is that Muriel may have told Bradley Cartwright.'

'Once again,' she reminded him, 'we don't know how truthful he's been with us. He says Muriel never told him the name of her step-mother and if that was the case, it's unlikely she would have mentioned anything Catherine may have told her. I think, you know,' she went on, 'this might be the time to broaden our thinking. In particular in respect to the complexities of a family which is far removed from what would be considered as normal. Perhaps there is far more to their various backgrounds which could help us unravel it all. If we go back to Catherine Miller-Croft's accident, we don't have many to choose from at the moment. For instance, we know Muriel couldn't have been responsible, unless she returned to the house later that afternoon before she met Bradley Cartwright, but then if she had, she could have bumped into Oliver and Sonia Croft and I'm sure he would have been quick enough to tell me, having no doubt come to the conclusion that either he or his wife must be under suspicion.'

'You think we should start focusing on the Crofts?'

'I believe so, Ian. We do seem to be returning to the question of motive, though, don't we? What reason would they have had for wanting Catherine out of the way, apart from financial gain, which surely rather rules out our revenge theory.'

'And if that is the case, ma'am,' Ian put in, 'by murdering Muriel, they could have thought their inheritance would have been enhanced by what Catherine Miller-Croft had bequeathed to Muriel, although they wouldn't have known about her will in favour of Bradley Cartwright.'

'Neither would they have known about Catherine's other daughter, Emily Craig.'

'A bit of a wasted effort, not to mention the unnecessary risks.'

'You're right, of course,' Brenda agreed, 'and if we are on the point of narrowing down the suspects we have so far, we should be considering whether the Crofts were in this together or not.'

'They could be, I suppose, but somehow if we discard the murder for gain idea, I can't think of any credible reason why both of them would have been sufficiently and equally motivated because of something as personal and deep-rooted as revenge. I know,' Ian went on, 'appearances are deceptive, but I would have thought Oliver Croft would be the more likely and from what you've told me about his wife, she strikes me as rather a colourless character. What's your opinion, ma'am?'

'How does anyone know what makes another person tick, Ian? As far as Sonia Croft is concerned, I wouldn't even hazard a guess. And, you're right, she is colourless, a good description of her, in fact.' she added, 'It could be an act on her part; very much a yes-woman, at least that was the way she appeared to me when I met her. She may not be like that at all; there could be hidden depths there, you know, and I've always believed from the number of people I've met, both professionally and socially, there is a hard streak embedded in the most outwardly docile, which may never surface, unless something sufficiently traumatic triggers it off.'

'A bit like lighting a fuse.'

'Quite. I think it might be a good idea after all, Ian, if you do have another word with Jason Miller. We've already learned the family only met infrequently and with the exception of Muriel, only Jason and the Crofts kept in touch with Catherine Miller-Croft, which brings us full circle; back to that rift between Christine and her mother.'

'I've just thought of someone who may know the reason for that.' Ian said.

'Who?'

'Adam Fry. He and Muriel married in 1986, so the disagreement, or whatever it was, must have happened not long before then. She may have told him.'

'That's a very good point, Ian,' impressed; she hadn't thought of Adam Fry, 'we'll ask him, but it's time we had a break. I've yet to meet him, so it will be a good opportunity for me to walk over to the pharmacy and have a talk with him.'

Before going out for some lunch Brenda returned to her office; she wanted to phone Christine Mason, reckoning she would be at home at lunchtime and dialled the Mason's home number, letting it ring for three or four minutes and was on the verge of giving up, when Christine Mason answered, her voice easily recognisable; the Sloanie vowels sounding more pronounced over the phone.

'Mrs Mason, this is Chief Inspector Masters here, from the Meadowbank constabulary.' she added formally.

'Yes,' she drawled, 'and how can I help you, Chief Inspector? My husband and I told you all we could about the night Muriel was killed and now it would appear we have to endure this latest scandal.'

'I appreciate how difficult it must be for you at this time, Mrs Mason, and apart from attempting to solve this case as speedily as possible, we have no wish to exacerbate the situation. The reason why I'm phoning,' Brenda went on quickly, pre-empting any interruption which would lead nowhere, 'is to ask why you and your mother were not on speaking terms.'

'Really, Chief Inspector! Do you honestly believe this family disagreement to be so important to your enquiry?'

'It could be,' Brenda said, 'and until we're told why you and your mother had this disagreement, we won't be in a position to decide just how important or relevant it is.'

'My mother and I, Chief Inspector,' accompanied by a deep sigh, 'never got on. Even from when I was in my early teens, we would go for days not talking. The situation became infinitely worse, that's all, and one day I simply told her I'd had enough of her attempts to control me and that was that. My mother was a manipulator; she couldn't tolerate anyone who didn't agree with her, to go along with what she expected, or more accurately, demanded! And, as I had already left home by then it wasn't all that terribly difficult to cut her out of my life. And,' pausing long enough to take a deep breath, 'she did have Muriel, after all; dutiful Muriel who danced to her every tune!'

'Were you jealous of your step-sister?'

'Good Lord, no! Why should I have been? Besides, I hardly knew her; she was a lot older than I was and we were never close or all that friendly, we merely tolerated each other, Chief Inspector. I don't know whether that has answered your question, but honestly, it's the best I can do.'

'Mrs Mason,' Brenda said, avoiding any further mention about a family feud which, she felt, was being deliberately covered up, but at the same time, not too disappointed by Christine's spontaneous outburst; a thinly veiled, but vitriolic attack on Muriel Miller, 'how long have you known your brother's wife?'

'Oliver is my *half*-brother.' she emphasised sharply, 'As far as Sonia is concerned, I've known her for simply ages.'

'Was this before she was married?'

'Oh, yes. It was during the time when we were all single and then it seemed she was always around. Our crowd did a lot of clubbing then, wine bars, that sort of thing, you understand. They were good times; no responsibilities and all of us absolutely living for the weekend when we could just enjoy.'

'And Muriel,' Brenda asked, trying to veer her away from nostalgic memories of her youth, 'did you see much of her then?'

'Muriel.' this time an exasperated sigh, 'Oh, she would appear now and again, especially when she wasn't expected and not exactly welcome. She wasn't terribly popular, you realise, although I must admit I never actually heard anyone say so in as many words, but when she was with us, she always managed to put a dampener on everything. Even the champagne didn't taste as good!'

'Why do you think this was?'

'Oh, I don't know. She had been frightfully spoilt. First by her father and then by mother. If Muriel wanted anything, she invariably got it, although sometimes it did back-fire on her.'

'In what way?'

'There were a number of occasions, but nothing to compare with her disastrous marriage.'

'We were aware her marriage to Adam Fry only lasted a couple of years before they separated.' Brenda said, although realising no prompting was needed; Christine Mason was on a roll.

'Poor Adam,' she said, 'he didn't stand an earthly once Muriel got her claws into him. The whole business wouldn't have been so awful if she hadn't done this in full view of Sonia. She practically caught them in bed together! We were frightfully shocked of course.'

Sonia?'

'Yes. You see, Adam was her boyfriend; they'd actually been together for a while, since their university days, but then that was what Muriel was like. She wanted Adam for herself.'

Brenda brought the call to an end shortly afterwards, mentally collating everything Christine Mason had so freely supplied. She had certainly painted an unattractive picture of Muriel, but Brenda wasn't entirely convinced what she'd heard was true, but perhaps more significantly, had she been aware, knowing they were in the middle of a murder enquiry when most of her family were being considered as possible suspects, how she was portraying Sonia Croft. Could this be a clever smokescreen set up especially for her benefit? Could she have been attempting to draw attention away from herself? Brenda continued to run through in her mind the various possibilities, automatically pulling on her coat and leaving the office.

Brian Morrison was behind the bar and gave her a cheerful smile when she walked into The Market Inn: 'Hello, Brenda, this is a pleasant surprise. I take it,' he added, with one of his cheeky grins which instantly reminded her of when they were both at school together; Brian hadn't changed all that much! 'this *is* a social call?'

'It's a social call, Brian. I'm hungry!'

'That's what I like to hear. First of all, what would you like to drink and then I'll ask Melissa to take your food order.'

'I'll have half a lager, please,' watching as he poured it into a glass for her, 'and I already know what I would like to eat; one of Melissa's ploughmans.'

Picking up her glass, Brenda made to move over to one of the tables by the window; the couple who had been sitting there now on their way to the door.

'Thanks, Brian.' the man called out as they left.

'A pleasure, Adam; have a good afternoon.'

It wasn't until the woman who was with him turned round slightly in the open doorway to wait for him that Brenda recognised her. One of life's little ironies she murmured under her breath; she could so easily have missed her, if, instead as she usually did, sent out for a sandwich and stayed in her office where it was virtually impossible to escape interruption, but today she had felt the need to 'switch off' for a while. As that famous Belgium detective would have said, "To renew those little grey cells", but it didn't look as though it would be possible. Why was Sonia Croft in Meadowbank?

'You probably haven't met Adam Fry yet, Brenda; he's recently taken over The Meadowbank Pharmacy.'

'No, I haven't.' she answered absently, her mind only half-concentrating on what he was saying,' but I have heard his name mentioned.' an ambiguous reply she knew, wondering how long it would take for the news that Adam had been married to Muriel Miller to filter through Meadowbank's grapevine. But, more to the point, why after what happened between the pair of them all those years ago, were they still seeing each other. Was their meeting pure chance? And, if it was, the question still remained of why she was here.

'And the woman he was with, Brian,' she asked him, 'have you seen her before?'

'A few times, but not all that often,' he answered, 'except for recently. You know who she is, I expect, Brenda?' giving her an old-fashioned look. Knowing him as well as she did, she knew she wouldn't be able to fool him, not that she wanted to; her job was onerous enough without alienating an old friend. All the same, she was on duty and finding out as much as she could was part of her job after all.

'Yes,' she said, 'she's Mrs Miller-Croft's daughter-in-law. You mentioned she'd been in recently?'

'That's right; she and her husband were in here a week ago last Saturday.'

'What time would this have been, can you remember?'

'It was shortly after two; we had just finished taking orders for lunch, that's why I can remember.'

'And was that the last time you saw Mrs Croft, except for today, of course?'

'That's right.'

'Thank you, Brian,' she said, 'you've been a help.' Not only was he an old friend, he was also a reliable witness, and people like him were invaluable to them.

'Any time, Brenda. I'm as keen as you are to get this town of ours back on an even keel.'

An influx of customers curtailed him saying anything further, but it didn't matter; Brenda was more than satisfied with what he'd told her and, taking her glass with her, moved over to the table. She was about to sit down when she noticed Adam Fry and Sonia Croft outside; they were standing on the pavement directly in front of the window and whatever she was saying, going by the frown on his face, didn't please him. And, then, as soon as she had finished talking, with only the briefest of nods, no shaking of hands, he turned abruptly away from her and walked across the road without a backward glance. Sonia remained where she was for a couple of seconds, watching him as he reached the door of the pharmacy, waiting until he had gone inside and closed the door, before moving away. Not once had she looked through the window of the pub, obviously impervious to any feeling of being watched. Also, Brenda was certain, she hadn't been recognised when for a moment Sonia, only a short distance from the bar, had looked over in her direction. Brenda mentally shrugged off the odd sensation of being invisible; hoping the forthcoming meeting with Adam Fry would prove useful. For the last week, all their hard slogging had achieved relatively little. What did they have? Three murders and possibly one killer? A handful of people who were all connected in some way or another and not a great deal more. About the only positive fact they had established, although any relevance to the enquiry remained to be seen, was that through his own admission Bradley Cartwright had started off in life as Lawrence Croft. The photograph the Met had sent through could have been of a man of that age; average build, dark brown hair and Bradley Cartwright, apart from his hair being grey at the temples, which could only be expected considering when the photograph had been taken, bore a partial resemblance, but it had been sufficient for Brenda to go that one step further and suggest to him he had changed his name sometime in 1990. He hadn't hesitated and by the expression of defeat on his lean and weary looking face, she had immediately taken advantage, although admitting, but not mentioning it to Ian, she hadn't translated that look as one of guilt. Her instinct told her that here was a man who had made a mess of his earlier years and after the prison sentence had wanted to literally wipe the slate clean and she didn't think she was far wrong. But, then, she thought cynically, instincts were no good in a murder enquiry, unless they paid off. And that, she concluded, taking a sip of her lager, remained to be seen.

*

Adam sensed Sonia had still been standing at the edge of the pavement; he could feel her eyes following him as he made his way back to the pharmacy and it was a relief to get inside and close the door behind him, regretting the decision to ask her to join him for a drink. The past, he decided, shrugging off his coat and going into the dispensary, should remain there; well and truly buried and if possible forgotten. Nothing could ever have been gained from trying to re-open old wounds and explaining how much he had always regretted the shabby way he had treated her. He now realised, having seen her again, she hadn't changed all that much. Even before she said anything about what happened between them, he could tell by her expression of passionate intensity, she would never accept any apology from him. It had been quite clear to Adam as she had sat opposite to him in the pub, there was no forgiveness in her make-up and wondering why he had never noticed this before, but then, they had both been young. Not that that was any excuse for the heartless way he had ended their relationship, but there was, he supposed, a small degree of comfort knowing that this could have only been partly true. Those last words she'd uttered, only a few minutes ago, continued to rankle as he re-ran them though his brain: "I don't think you realise, Adam," she had said in that little-girl voice of hers, "just how much you hurt me. Even after all these years I will never forget and you may not believe this, but it was Muriel I blamed, not you. She set out to take you away from me with the full knowledge that you were *my* boyfriend and that was why she did it!"

It hadn't made any difference when he had pointed out that nobody ever owned anyone else; she had been hell-bent in saying what she wanted and he'd had to stand there, in the market square, in full view of any passerby who had been sufficiently interested to overhear, because by then Sonia had begun to raise her voice, and he'd had no choice, but to let her carry on until she came to the end. Even then, when he'd said to her he regretted she had continued to bear such a deep grudge against Muriel, he knew there was nothing he could do about it. That was when he had walked away, hoping he would never see her again.

'Alright, Emily?' he asked, going back into the pharmacy where she had now finished serving a customer.

'Fine, Adam. Quite busy, really,' she added, 'but I'm not complaining.'

'It's the time of the year, I guess,' he said, 'when all the coughs and colds start rearing their heads.' wondering what her reaction would be if he was to tell her he had been talking to a woman who was part of the family she had so recently acquired. Emily had told him about the legacy and he had been glad she had; better than hearing it from any other source, although he hadn't been so honest with her. He hadn't said anything about being married to Muriel. He couldn't explain his reticence, perhaps he considered she had enough to contend with. No doubt, though, she'd soon find out. He had only been in Meadowbank a short time, but already, he had learned how rapidly news, or more accurately gossip, travelled.

'I'm sorry I took a bit longer than I would normally for lunch,' he apologised, 'especially as you haven't had your own break yet.'

'That's alright,' she smiled at him, 'but I'll just nip out now and get a bite to eat.'

As Emily was leaving, the woman who had been at the bar talking to Brian Morrison came in, surprised to see that both women appeared to know each other; Emily stopping to shake hands with her before going out.

'Mr Fry?'

'Yes, that's right.'

'I'm Chief Inspector Brenda Masters,' she said, 'I understand you have already met Inspector Ash?'

'I have, yes,' Adam said, 'first, in The Bridge Inn and then the other day when he came in to ask me a few questions about Muriel Miller.'

'Yes,' she nodded, 'I've read his report. However, Mr Fry, if you can spare the time, there are a few points you may be able to help us on.'

'In between customers, of course I will.' he said.

'That's fine. Would you prefer to talk out here, or would it be better if we go into the dispensary?'

'The dispensary would be best.'

'Mr Fry,' she began, once they were seated at the table in the centre of the room, with the door open to enable him to see if anyone came into the pharmacy, 'as you are aware, we are investigating the murder of Miss Miller and the other two deaths of Gary Nicholson and Mrs Catherine Miller-Croft -'

'- but, I thought Mrs Miller-Croft's death was caused by an accident she had in her home.'

'She did die as a direct result from the accident, sir,' Brenda told him, 'but we now have strong evidence to support her accident had been contrived. She tripped over what had been deliberately placed across her stairs.'

'Who would possibly have done such a thing?'

'You could ask the same question about Miss Miller's death.'

'Yes, I suppose so,' trying to grasp what she'd said; another murder and this one before Muriel's. It all sounded so farfetched and somehow incongruous in a town as small and parochial as Meadowbank.

'However, sir,' she said, 'our investigation continues and so, I regret to say, do our questions. We have to get to the bottom of what has been going on and not only why they happened, but to find the person responsible.'

'Of course.'

'We have been attempting to find out as much as we can about the Miller-Croft family,' she started to explain, 'which means we have to trawl back, even several years, if it is necessary, to discover the relationships between the various members of the family.'

'So, how can I help you, Chief Inspector?'

'We're hoping you can, sir. For instance, the estrangement between Mrs Miller-Croft and her daughter, Christine. Did you know anything about this?'

'Only what Muriel told me. Of course, this was a long time ago, a few months before Muriel and I were married. We had been talking about the plans for the wedding which we had already decided would be a registry office one and I'd asked her which members of her family she would like to invite and I remember how surprised I had been when she said she wasn't all that keen to have any of them there and would prefer the occasion to be just the two of us and a couple of our friends we knew around that time.'

'Not even her step-mother?'

'No, not even her. Mind you, Muriel could be like that; she wasn't what

I would describe a family sort of person.'

'Did you ever meet Mrs Miller-Croft?'

'Surprisingly, I didn't. I suggested visiting her, but Muriel said there would be plenty of time after we were married, but of course, the marriage didn't last long enough. Anyway,' he went on, trying to drag up from his memory what Muriel had said from what now seemed more than a lifetime away, 'I'd already gathered that, although she was fond of her step-mother, she didn't have much affection for any of the others, except perhaps for her cousin, Jason Miller. But her argument was, Chief Inspector,' he explained, 'if she did invite all of them, she couldn't include Christine because she and her step-mother were no longer on speaking terms.'

'Did she explain why this was?'

'She did, but she didn't elaborate all that much, only that it was something to do with money being extracted from her step-mother's bank account and she had accused Christine.'

'Did Muriel believe her?'

'I don't really know; all she said was that she must have done it and she never mentioned it again after that.'

'How well do you know Christine, sir?'

'Fairly well and I have to say, although she could have a rather waspish tongue at times, I never thought of her as a thief. It seemed out of character somehow.'

'Mr Fry,' Brenda said and it could have been the change in her tone, which made him feel she had something more to say, 'I don't know whether you saw me earlier in The Market Inn,-'

'- I did, although I had no idea who you were.' he interrupted, waiting for her to go on.

'No, I don't expect you did. I believe the lady you were with was Sonia Croft who is married to Mrs Miller-Croft's step-son?'

'Yes,' taking a deep breath, preparing to make yet another lengthy explanation, although this one would be considerably more painful, 'it was Sonia alright. I hadn't seen her for years and when she came into the pharmacy it was a complete surprise to me. You may as well know this, Chief Inspector,' Adam continued, 'but I have known Sonia since our university days and for a number of years after that we remained together; she was my regular girlfriend, in fact.'

'I see, and yet you married Muriel Miller.'

'Yes, that's right. It was what one would probably describe as a whirlwind romance. Not to put too fine a point on it, Chief Inspector, immediately I met Muriel I was smitten. I am not proud of the way I quite literally ditched Sonia, not proud at all, but then I've had plenty of time to regret that foolish episode in my life.'

'Thank you for being so frank, sir,' Brenda said, 'I appreciate that. As you say, it was all a long time ago.'

'True.'

Chapter Ten

'What's wrong, Sonia?'

'What do you mean? There's nothing wrong with me; I'm fine.'

'You've been acting strangely for the last couple of weeks now,' Oliver said, peering at her above the top of his spectacles, 'abstracted, as though your mind was miles away. In fact,' he continued, 'there have been times when you haven't heard a word I've been saying, I don't believe you even knew I had been talking.'

'Oh, surely I haven't been as bad as that, Oliver, but if I have, I expect it's all this horrible business about Muriel and now hearing about Catherine's death has only made things worse somehow. I'm finding it very distressing.'

'Hmmph.' rustling his newspaper in exasperation and making a pretence of reading it. She didn't fool him for a single second. Sonia was a poor liar, always had been; her way of avoiding the truth was to ignore the subject, trusting as he had always thought, it would evaporate into thin air. Either her memory was diminishing or she was going out of her way to mislead him. She couldn't be grieving over Muriel's death; she had disliked her intensely. Oliver was under no illusions about his marriage and, although she never mentioned Adam, he had always realised she had married him on the rebound, remembering back to the night in Annabel's when Muriel met Adam for the first time and from that moment completely monopolised him. Oliver hadn't needed Christine, who had been with them at the time, to tell him how devastated Sonia was, nor anyone else either. To those other friends of theirs in the club it must have been all too clear by the bereft expression on Sonia's face. They had all felt sorry for her, he had as well, and strangely, no-one had blamed Adam when shortly afterwards he and Sonia had split up; Muriel, already unpopular, was the wrong-doer.

'By the way,' he asked her, abandoning the newspaper, 'where were you this lunchtime? I tried to phone you on your mobile.'

'I was probably driving, Oliver; it would have been switched off.'

'You must have been driving for some time then because I tried two or three times.'

'Why were you trying to get hold of me?' she asked, and she was at it again; avoiding a direct explanation and it wasn't difficult for him to understand why; she didn't want him to know where she had been and he knew from experience he would be wasting his breath trying to get her to tell him. As far as she was concerned, the subject was closed.

'It doesn't matter now,' he said, 'but Vera had a spare ticket for "Mama Mia" and thought you may have liked it.'

'Of course I would, Oliver. How kind of Vera.'

'Well,' he explained and not without a certain satisfaction that in some respects he was getting his own back on her, 'as it was for this evening's performance and I couldn't get in touch with you, I suggested she offered it to one of her friends which, as it happens, she was able to do.'

'That's a shame, dear.'

'It is, isn't it.' further irritated by her matter of fact manner, 'I'm going out for an hour, Sonia,' he said abruptly, standing up and pushing his chair back from the kitchen table where they'd been sitting since finishing their meal, 'Along to the local. I don't suppose you'll want to come.' guessing in advance it was unlikely; the Hare & Hound not being one of her most favourite of pubs.

'Do you know, Oliver,' she answered, 'I believe I will, just this once. It will be a change and I might just be able to tolerate the gay landlord.' she added.

The Hare & Hound was only a short walk from their house in Thomas Street and, being a Friday night, was packed with many of the customers spilling out on to the narrow pavement in front of the building.

'It looks as if it's going to be standing room only.' Oliver said, raising his voice above the noise; shrieks of spontaneous laughter competing with Tom Jones telling them all he thought he'd better dance now, as Oliver, with Sonia closely behind him, pushed his way through the crowd blocking the open doorway.

'Good evening, my dears.' Greg, the landlord, greeted them when they finally reached the bar.

'Good evening, Greg.' Oliver said, noticing the look of annoyance appearing on Sonia's face. Why did she have to make her dislike of the man so obvious? Oliver liked to think of himself as being entirely unbiased by a person's particular persuasions, besides, he had always found Greg to be an affable kind of fellow, he had nothing against him. 'You've a good crowd in here tonight.'

'It's always the same at the weekends; the darlings like to unwind after a hard week in the office, don't you know?'

'It's only understandable, I suppose,' Oliver agreed, realising he was really no different, although his weekend didn't start until the Sunday, Saturday being one of his busier days.

'What would you like to drink?' Greg asked him, 'And your lady wife, of course?'

'I'll have a Heineken, Greg and, Sonia,' he asked, turning round to her, 'a white wine?'

'Please.'

'A wine and a Heinekin coming up!'

'Is this too noisy for you?' he asked her when Greg's attention had been caught by a demanding group standing next to them, all clamouring for refills.

'Rather.' and he could tell she was making an effort to enjoy herself and no doubt by now regretting her decision to come with him.

'You have to admit, though,' he commented, 'they are a cheerful bunch.'

'Do you know, Oliver,' she said, after taking a sip of her wine, 'I think I'll only have this one and then I'll go back home. To be honest, all this noise has given me quite a headache.'

'Just as you wish, Sonia. You'll be alright, won't you, walking back on your own?'

'Of course I will. Fortunately, Thomas Street is well-lit; we're lucky in that respect, Oliver. It isn't like some parts of London where a woman isn't safe out there after dark.'

Why was it, Oliver wondered, he was getting the distinct impression she was coming out with what really were inconsequential statements, ones which had been uttered a hundred times before and had long lost any meaning. He knew as well as she did that the area in which they lived was relatively crime-free; why else had he chosen to buy their house in Thomas Street, only metres away from the centre of Mayfair?

He'd had every intention of only having one more beer, but the arrival of a neighbour he hadn't seen for a number of months and insisted on buying him another one made him change his mind. Feeling in the need of some convivial company without any questionable undertones, he didn't need a great deal of persuading, not looking forward to going back home to be confronted with more of the same.

Dick Trent was good company; he'd known him since they'd moved into Thomas Street more than ten years ago. He never talked about money, pensions, even politics and Oliver appreciated that. Dick owned a small art gallery in The Strand and they spent a good hour comparing notes and by the time he was turning the key in his front door it was well after ten. There were no lights from upstairs, only the one they had left on in the lounge as they always did when they went out in the evening, which could mean anything or nothing; Sonia may have gone to bed and already be asleep, or she was watching television waiting, with a martyred expression, for his return.

As soon as he stepped into the hall, he had the uncanny feeling of the house being empty, but if anyone had asked him why, he would never have been able to explain. The place just felt empty; therefore, it was no great surprise to find when he went into both the lounge and the kitchen she wasn't in either. Upstairs was the same. He had the house to himself. This had never happened before in all the years they had been married. Sonia was not a night bird; she had always been at home when he came in. Always. She hadn't left any message for him, although she had been back to the house; the kitchen light had been on and he remembered switching it off before they left. Not exactly worried, but becoming concerned, he dialled her mobile number, but it was still switched off. He had never known a woman who was so casually unaware of why she had a mobile phone in the first place, not yet sure whether her absence could be classed as an emergency. As he went through the automatic motions of filling the coffee pot, taking, as he always did, two mugs from the top shelf of the cupboard above the work top, he was rapidly coming to the conclusion those earlier thoughts of his had been right. She *was* acting strangely, but on glancing up at the clock, watching as the hands reached ten forty-five, and with a sinking feeling at the bottom of his stomach, this behaviour of hers was fast approaching the bizarre. Where the hell was she? She wouldn't have gone to another pub; that would have been totally out of character and all her friends were married with families; she would hardly have called on them unannounced and then he recalled how he'd been unable to contact her at lunchtime and her far from satisfactory explanation; in fact, she had adroitly avoided any explanation. While the coffee was percolating, he walked through the kitchen to their integral garage, which he should have done before. Her car wasn't in there. Had she left him, then? This was the first thought which entered his head. Was there another man in her life? Another Adam? But, trying to keep a grip on reality, if there had been, surely she would have had the decency to come out with it. Wouldn't she? Suddenly, he didn't know his wife at all.

Oliver waited until midnight before phoning the police, ringing their number in Mayfair. He could tell straight away by the desk sergeant's tone of voice he wasn't interested. Another domestic, he would be thinking. Another wife deciding she'd had enough. But, it wasn't until Oliver gave him his surname, his attitude changed and within seconds he had been put through to one of their inspectors.

∗

Brenda took the call from Mike Harper at ten the following morning as she was about to tackle the back-log of paperwork which had been accumulating since the beginning of the Muriel Miller enquiry.

'Why is it, I wonder,' she said to him, 'my instincts tell me this call isn't merely to ask me how I am.'

'My word,' he chuckled, 'you're on form this morning and you are quite right, of course, but something rather strange has turned up.'

'And?' she prompted, her pulse quickening in anticipation. Was this what they had been waiting for at last? She hoped so; they had been going over and over the same ground and still unable to make any sort of headway.

'Oliver Croft's wife seems to have disappeared.'

'Now, this is something I did not expect, Mike.'

'That's why I thought it strange. She may, of course, turn up at any time and normally we wouldn't be taking such a keen interest in a report which is only in its initial stages.'

'Presumably her husband reported her as missing?'

'Yes, that's right. Apparently, they were both having a drink in the Hare & Hound, close to where they live in Thomas Street, but then you've been there, haven't you?'

'Last Saturday and I remember noticing the pub and, as you've said, it's not far from their house, only about a five minutes' walk at the most.'

'Right, well, being a Friday night the place was packed and too noisy for her so she decided to go back home after only one drink. This was around eight-thirty. He stayed on for a while, chatting with one of their neighbours, and didn't get home until after ten only to find she wasn't there.'

'And had she been home?'

'He said she must have been because her car had gone from the garage.'

'Do you know whether she took anything with her, Mike?'

'Well,' he answered, 'he'd been a bit vague about that; didn't know whether she had or not.'

'So, what time did he phone the police, presumably this would have been the Mayfair Station?'

'That's right,' he agreed, 'he'd waited until midnight, hoping she may turn up and the desk sergeant, being pretty well switched on, was reminded of the latest development in the Muriel Miller case when he heard him say his name was Croft.'

'As you say, Mike, it does sound strange. Perhaps they had a row and he's not admitting it. And, you've only got his word for it that she wasn't in the house when he got back there, haven't you?'

'Exactly, so all in all, it doesn't place Oliver Croft in a very good position. They've been asking around the neighbourhood, but nobody remembers seeing her last night, either when she returned or when she drove off.'

'It's anyone's guess, then,' Brenda said, 'where she could have gone.'

'I know. You've met her, Brenda; what sort of woman is she?'

'Difficult to say,' she said, remembering back to last week when Oliver Croft had introduced them, 'but my first impression was that she seemed fairly nondescript. Pretty, in a sort of washed-out way, at least that was what I thought then, but now, well, I'm not so certain that's such an accurate description.' and going on to tell him about seeing Sonia yesterday in Meadowbank with Adam Fry, who had recently taken over the pharmacy in the market square, adding he had been married to Muriel Miller and according to Christine Mason, Adam had once been Sonia's boyfriend.

'All this happened almost twenty years ago, Mike.'

'You say they were together; where was this?'

'In The Market Inn, around lunchtime.'

'Why was she in Meadowbank; did this appear like a chance meeting?'

'Hard to tell,' she answered, 'but Adam Fry didn't look too happy when he returned to the pharmacy which is across the road from the pub and, presumably, she collected her car and drove back to London.'

'Puzzling.'

'Very.'

'And she did return to London; the landlord of the Hare & Hound has confirmed Sonia Croft was with her husband last night.'

'Incidentally, Mike,' Brenda said, 'we've located Lawrence Croft.'

'Have you, now?'

'Yes,' recognising the smile in his voice, 'we questioned Bradley

Cartwright yesterday and he freely admitted he had changed his name from Lawrence Croft in 1990.'

'Well, that's solved that problem.'

'It's the only one we *have* solved on this case, Mike.'

'Don't get disheartened, Brenda; you'll get there, believe me, I know how frustrating all this sorting and sifting can be. I expect you feel you're struggling through a quagmire.'

'That's exactly how I have felt all week, but perhaps once the whereabouts of Sonia Croft are known, we'll have something more positive on which to work.'

'All the more reason for you to have a break, then. Any chance of seeing you this weekend?'

'I'd love to, you know that.'

'The old guilt thing?'

'Silly, isn't it? But, I don't see why not. It isn't as if Ian Ash won't be able to get hold of me if anything crucial should turn up.'

'Great, so when do you think you'll get away?'

'By four this afternoon, I would say. I really must clear my desk before Monday.'

'Do you want to drive straight home, or would you like us to meet up for a drink first?'

'I'll drive straight to your place; I'll probably want to freshen up first.'

'That's no problem, so I'll expect you around five-thirty or so.'

'I'll be there, Mike.' thinking it may be a good idea to try and see Oliver Croft some time tomorrow and find out, first-hand, what he had to say about his missing wife, knowing Mike would understand and had probably already reached the same conclusion.

*

'So, Jessica, how did your morning go?'

'Well -' hesitating, a look of concern in those expressive eyes of hers, '- I don't know how you're going to take this, Mum.'

'So long as it's nothing to do with you, love, I think I'll be able to handle it, whatever it might be.'

She had arranged to meet Jessica during her lunch break, Jessica having volunteered to drive up to "The Gables" and to be there when the valuers arrived. Arnold Brutton had recommended the firm which had in the past been used by not only Catherine but several of his other clients.

'It looks as though a number of the contents are no longer there. As you know,' Jessica went on, 'the last valuation had been carried out five years ago and their check this morning fell short of that one.'

'Perhaps Catherine sold these pieces.'

'She could have done; that's what they said, but it goes a bit further than that, actually.'

'Yes?'

'There were two guys there this morning,' she said, 'one of them was a specialist in paintings and he told me six of them were definitely forgeries.'

'Forgeries!'

'Yes, that's right. The canvases at some time had been removed and replaced with, as he said, quite excellent replicas, but he was quite positive.'

'What on earth have we got ourselves into here, Jessica,' Emily sighed, 'we are well and truly saddled with this – this legacy which, quite honestly, I never wanted. What are we meant to do now? Report it as theft or accept it and say nothing?'

'I don't think we can ignore this, you know.' Jessica said, 'It wouldn't have been so serious perhaps if it hadn't been for those paintings, but –'

'You're absolutely right, of course.' She sighed again; in fact, practically since arriving in this town she had been doing rather a lot of sighing, 'Once again, we don't have any choice, do we?'

'I don't think so.'

'Are the valuers going to give us a copy of their new inventory?'

'Yes, they've promised to email it through to you later this afternoon.'

'Alright, Jessica. Look, I'll have to get back to the pharmacy soon; shall we order a sandwich?'

'Good idea.'

'Apart from that little shock,' Emily said, once they had ordered, 'did the rest of your morning go okay?'

'I suppose so, except for members of the press hanging about outside "The Gables" when I arrived.'

'What!'

'There were three of them, one of them a photographer. He was taking photographs of the house. Don't ask me what he expected to achieve.'

'Of course,' another sigh, 'they are probably trying to expand on what has already been printed.'

'To be expected though.' Jessica reminded her.

'I know. Did they say anything to you?'

'One of them did. She was American and super-confident. I didn't like her, Mum; she wanted to know what I had to do with the family.'

'What did you tell her?'

'Well, there wasn't a great I could tell her, was there? So, I just said I'd been asked by the owner to assist the valuers. I couldn't think of anything better than that, especially as their van was already parked by the kerb.'

'Do you think they believed you?'

'I think the photographer and the other guy did, but not her. She even went as far as to ask me my name and this is where you would have been really proud of me,' Jessica grinned, reminding her of when she was a cheeky ten year-old, 'I asked her what business it was of hers.'

'And how did she take that?'

'Not very well, actually. Anyway, by the time she had recovered I had walked past them and closed the gates behind me. Fortunately,' she added, 'by the time I left they'd gone.'

'I guess this sort of thing is inevitable.' Emily said, 'But, they really are grasping at straws, aren't they? They're trying to make a story out of something which, up to now, hasn't got a great deal of substance. What a job!'

'They're a pain in the proverbial.'

'Perhaps they are.' she agreed, 'There's something I meant to mention to you yesterday, Jessica when I got home from work, but it slipped my mind.'

'Yes?'

'Do you remember the report in the local paper about Muriel Miller's death when they included a photograph of Catherine's family?'

'Yes. Why?'

'Because yesterday, a woman came into the pharmacy who looked remarkably like one of them.'

'Really?'

'She knew Adam; mind you, the pair of them seemed surprised to see each other. I thought at the time they must have been old friends. Anyway, they went off to lunch together. It was strange though; he called her Sonia which of course didn't mean anything to me; a pity the paper hadn't included the names with their photograph, but it has made me wonder all the same.'

'A small world.'

'Do you know, Jessica, I'm beginning to get like everyone else in this town; far too interested in other people's business.'

'But, then, Mum, the Miller-Crofts, when you think about it, *are* our business.'

'Touché.'

They had finished their sandwich before mentioning the discrepancies in the valuation, Emily having up to then made a feeble effort to put the problem to the back of her mind.

'What are we going to do, Mum?' Jessica, in her forthright and practical way asked.

'Well,' Emily answered, 'first of all I'll give Mr Brutton a ring. It may always be possible that Catherine had sold them and if she had I'm sure he would have handled this for her.'

'And the forgeries?' Jessica prompted gently.

'I don't think I should mention them to him. At least, not at first. You really believe we should go to the police, don't you?'

'We have to.'

'I know. And, I will, Jessica, but later today, after work. I'll walk across there and talk to someone. Incidentally, Adam had a visit from Chief Inspector Masters yesterday; it was just as I was leaving for lunch.'

'The plot thickens.'

*

'It's good to have you home again, darling. I've missed you this week.'

'It's great to *be* back!' Carol Cliff emphasised, leaning across the table to kiss him passionately on the lips, 'Meadowbank sure isn't my sort of place, Rocky. I'd shrivel up and die if I had to live there!'

'As bad as that, eh?'

'As bad as that, my darling husband. You have no idea what the people are like! If you should as much as sneeze, word would be around the place that you had Asian flu or something equally as contagious.'

'You're a city girl, Carol.' he reminded her.

'I know I am and that's why living in London suits me just fine.'

They were in one of their favourite Chinese restaurants in China Town, Carol having spent most of the afternoon in the office. She'd gone there as soon as she'd arrived back in London and hadn't been home yet. Rocky had been at work all day; Saturdays invariably hectic with everyone running this way and that, trying to make sure the paper would be 'put to bed' on time. She'd phoned him earlier and it had been his idea they should make a night of it, meeting up in the Suk Woon restaurant. Suk Woon, herself, resplendent in an embroidered scarlet cheongsam, had greeted them at the door, leading them to the table in one of the alcoves.

Carol hadn't been joking when she'd told him how she had found this last week in Meadowbank. She couldn't remember ever having felt so stifled and when she had driven through the market square that morning she had been reminded of Hank Marvin when he had sung that he'd never known a town that didn't look better looking back, because those words aptly described exactly how she had felt, taking her last glimpse of Meadowbank in her rear view mirror as she'd joined the Winchester Road and headed towards the motorway.

'Mind you, Rocky,' she said after they had given their order, 'going back to those folk in Meadowbank and their insatiable appetite for gossip and their inability to keep their voices at a reasonable level, unknown to them a great deal of what they had to say was far better than reading up on their local history.'

'In what way?'

'Hey, there!' she laughed, 'You don't really expect me to tell you, do you? I'm sorry, I shouldn't have said anything, I suppose, but -'

'- but,' he interrupted, 'you're on a high this evening, aren't you? You're up to something, Carol. Surely, you don't imagine I would stoop so low as to pinch anything from my wife. This murder case is your baby; I realise that.'

'I know, darling; it's just that I'm so used to watching my back, but we do work for rival newspapers after all, even if you are my husband.'

'So,' he was teasing her now, 'when do you plan to 'spill the beans'?'

'Tomorrow.'

'Well,' he grinned, 'that isn't so long to wait.'

'All I will say,' she said, 'there are going to be quite a few people more than a little surprised when they read my latest piece.'

'Including the Meadowbank constabulary?'

'How perceptive you are, darling. And naturally enough I'm not exactly their best friend, especially with their Chief Inspector.'

'What's he like, then?'

'It's a she,' Carol explained, 'an attractive blonde and too clever by half.'

'It sounds as though you may have met your match.'

'Now you come to mention it,' she admitted, 'it's like a game of chess, so let's hope it won't end up as checkmate.'

They were half-way through their meal, both having done full justice to the dishes of beef in black bean sauce, sweet and sour pork, chicken in a lemon sauce and bowls of Cantonese rice all presented to them with a professional flourish by one of Suk Woon's sons, when Carol, her attention caught by the arrival of two more customers, looked across the restaurant to see the very woman she had been telling Rocky about only minutes earlier.

'I don't believe it!' she gasped.

'What?'

'You'll never guess who's just come in to the restaurant, Rocky! Talk about coincidences.'

'I don't want to turn round and stare, so you'd better enlighten me.'

'Meadowbank's Chief Inspector. What the heck is she doing in London?'

'It is meant to be a free country, darling,' he pointed out to her, 'she obviously must leave Meadowbank sometimes. Perhaps like us, she's having a night out on the town.' Besides,' he went on and she knew he was making fun of her, no doubt trying to cheer her up, 'to you, Meadowbank may seem as though it's on another planet, but it isn't much more than an hour away on the motorway.'

'I know that. I'm being ridiculous, paranoid even, Rocky and I'll try to snap out of it. They're sitting down now, over to your left; I don't think she'll notice if you glanced in her direction.'

She watched him as he did as she suggested, wishing, and not for the first time, she could be more laid-back. He had this ability, which she doubted whether she would ever manage, of being able to completely switch off from the work mode. Right from the beginning, in the early days, she had always admired his sheer professionalism. He was also a brilliant journalist and had a gift with words which she knew she could never match.

'You're right, Carol; she's a good looking woman.' he remarked, turning back to face her, 'I happen to know who she's with by the way.'

'Really?'

'Yes, I've met him a couple of times, but not for a while now. He's Mike Harper from New Scotland Yard.'

'Her boyfriend?'

'I would say so, that is, if the way he's looking at her is anything to go by.'

'Well, well,' Carol murmured, 'the woman is human after all.'

'Now, darling,' pretending to rebuke her, 'don't be catty; it doesn't suit you.'

'Sorry.'

'You're not sorry at all!'

*

Brenda woke early the following morning and not wanting to disturb Mike, she gently pushed back the duvet and, pulling on one of his towelling dressing gowns, padded barefoot through to the kitchen. She loved this time of the day, especially when she was here, spending these precious times with Mike and already, after only a matter of months, feeling comfortably familiar in his apartment and now, looking out across towards Regent's Park, watching as the mist began to dissipate and within seconds becoming a hazy film above the grass, Meadowbank felt another world away. Yes, she decided, it was time to make a break away from there and vowed as soon as this case was wrapped up she would make inroads.

'Hi.' he said softly, coming up behind and placing his arms around her.

'Hi.'

'Happy?'

'Very.' turning round to kiss him.

'What would you like to do today?'

'A pub lunch, I think; a traditional Sunday roast.'

'The Moon?'

'That sounds good to me, but I feel I should try and get in touch with Oliver Croft, you know, Mike. You don't mind?'

'Of course I don't,' he smiled, 'although you hadn't said anything last night, I rather thought you would want to.'

'I need to find out how he's reacting to this disappearance of his wife.'

'I understand. So,' he asked, 'do you want to see him this morning or later on?'

'Oh, this morning would be best, I think.'

She waited until after nine before phoning Oliver Croft and although he didn't sound over-keen to hear from her, he didn't attempt to put any obstacles in the way, adding, albeit caustically, he had no intention of going anywhere that morning.

It was perhaps fortuitous she was able to take a quick glance at the headlines in a couple of the newspapers before she left for Thomas Street. At least she thought, skimming down Carol Cliff's Sunday column, she would be prepared for the inevitable backlash she could expect from Oliver Croft when she met him. She had certainly excelled herself this time and stifling a groan Brenda read through to the end before passing the paper over to Mike.

"LAWRENCE CROFT IS ALIVE AND WELL," it began, "Lawrence Croft, the former notorious jewel thief, who succeeded for over a decade to evade the authorities until his arrest in 1989, is living in the south of England, having, since his release, taken on a new identity.

For legal reasons, this newspaper is unable to reveal the name he is now using, but interestingly, it has come to light he was in a close relationship with Muriel Miller, whose body was found last week on waste ground in Meadowbank, the Hampshire market town which is currently the centre of a triple murder enquiry. As reported on Friday, the enquiry now includes, not only the fatal shooting of one of the town's residents, Gary Nicholson, but the suspicious circumstances surrounding the death of Catherine Miller-Croft a week earlier. Mrs Miller-Croft was married to the art dealer, Trevor Croft, who was Lawrence Croft's father. The reappearance of Lawrence Croft after an absence of a number of years will be adding a further twist to these intricately woven series of events within the Miller-Croft family, leaving many of the residents of Meadowbank wondering what is going to happen next."

'My word,' Mike said, 'she certainly knows how to get to the nub of the matter, doesn't she?'

'She's shrewd, Mike; there's no doubt about that, also cunning. She knows exactly how far to go as well. Mind you,' she went on, 'to certain people in Meadowbank, she may as well have spelt out the name of

Bradley Cartwright. And doesn't she know it!'

'How do you think she was able to get hold of this?' he asked, pointing to the article.

'By being on the spot and at the right time. When you think about it, Mike, and given the extent of the gossiping which has been going on, it may not have been all that difficult. Bradley Cartwright has been staying at The Royal Oak for some months and I know Carol Cliff and two of her colleagues were there all week. Also, it's just possible she remembered the Lawrence Croft business all those years ago. She's bright enough, that's for sure, but the damage is done now; it's in black and white.'

'True. It doesn't bode too well for your meeting with the brother though.'

'Not really,' she smiled at him, but not all that concerned about Oliver Croft's reaction. She was well used to his type; she was more worried about how she was going to contend with having to face an irate Bill Simms, as she surely would be.

Oliver Croft took several minutes to open the front door, but she definitely wasn't prepared for his dishevelled appearance. The man looked ill and had obviously not slept much since his wife had gone.

'Good morning, Chief Inspector,' he said, gesturing as he had that first time for her to come into the hall, 'I make no apologies,' he added, 'for the way I must appear, but I am a very worried man.'

'I'm sure you are, sir,' she said, but at the same time finding it difficult to raise any real sympathy for him. She couldn't explain why she should be feeling like this, but somehow she got the impression his distress wasn't genuine; there was something contrived about his whole manner, even the way he was shuffling across the parquet floor towards the dining room, didn't ring true, more like the actions of a man considerably older than his forty-odd years, 'but I was in London this weekend,' she went on to explain, 'and I thought it would be a good idea to have a word with you.'

'What can I say?' motioning her to one of the chairs, 'Sonia has gone. I have absolutely no idea where, and neither do I know why. What's happened is a complete mystery to me, Chief Inspector.'

'I've been given a copy of the report you made to the police on Friday night, sir,' Brenda said, making an attempt to skirt round his melancholy which would take her nowhere, 'and it's my understanding it was only, at the most, a couple of hours from when your wife left The Hare & Hound and to when you returned home. Is that correct?'

'Yes,' he answered, drawing the word out, as if lacking the energy to make any sort of elaboration.

'What I would like to ask you,' she went on, 'what was your impression that evening of her frame of mind?'

'Her frame of mind?'

'Yes, what sort of mood was she in? Did she appear worried or depressed in any way?'

'Can't say she did. She did seem somewhat pre-occupied, but then she'd been like for several days now, ever since this blasted business over Muriel started.'

'I see. When I spoke to her last Saturday, it's true she did sound distressed by Miss Miller's death.'

'Did she, Chief Inspector? I can't remember.'

'How close were they; your wife and Miss Miller?' she asked, deciding to let that comment pass.

'Not close at all, as it happens; they were poles apart, Chief Inspector. Poles apart,' he repeated, 'in fact, they had nothing in common.'

'Mr Croft,' Brenda asked, 'were you aware your wife was in Meadowbank on Friday?'

'In Meadowbank? Are you sure?'

'Quite sure, sir,' she said, 'I saw her myself; having a drink in The Market Inn, around one o'clock.'

'So, that's where she was.' he muttered under his breath and this time the look of bewilderment on his face did look genuine.

'I take it you didn't know about this?' she prompted.

'No, I didn't. I had tried to phone her, a couple of times, but her mobile wasn't switched on.'

'And,' Brenda asked him, 'when you saw her later, did you mention this to her?'

'I did, but she was quite vague; didn't give me a straight answer. Mind you,' he continued, 'Sonia can be like that, so I wasn't unduly concerned.'

'When you describe your wife as sounding vague, sir,' Brenda asked, trying to understand the woman's personality, 'just how vague exactly. In other words, and I know you felt this began at the time of Miss Miller's death, but in what form did this vagueness actually take?'

'Hard to say, Chief Inspector. It was as though her mind was somewhere else entirely. I would start to say something to her and half-way through the first couple of sentences I realised she hadn't heard a word I'd said.'

'Were you worried about this?'

'Not really.'

'If I can return to Friday evening when you were both in the Hare & Hound, you say she didn't stay long.'

'That's right; she didn't. She complained about the place being too noisy for her and that she had a headache and would go back home after she'd finished her wine.'

'And was the pub noisy, sir; I mean unreasonably so?'

'It was busy, of course, and the music was fairly loud, but I wouldn't have said it was exactly ear-shattering.'

'Does your wife suffer from headaches as a normal rule, sir?'

'She never used to, that's true, but recently she has been.'

'Why do you think this was?'

'I have no idea, Chief Inspector. It wasn't as though she's been complaining; in fact, I rather suspect she didn't want me to know. Suffer in silence and all that sort of thing, if you know what I mean?'

'Mrs Croft wasn't on her own when I saw her on Friday.' Brenda said at last, deciding it was time to change the subject. The headache could have been an excuse, but on the other hand, there could have been a more serious medical problem which was causing them.

'So, who was she with then? One of her women friends, I expect, not that she knows anyone living in Meadowbank.'

'She was with a man called Adam Fry.'

'Adam! Adam Fry!' he repeated, 'After all this time! I don't understand; what's he doing in Meadowbank?'

'He has recently taken over the Meadowbank Pharmacy.'

'Of course I knew he was a chemist, but Meadowbank – of all places!'

'How well do you know him, sir?'

'We weren't close friends, you understand, but at one time he used to be around the same pubs as the rest of us.'

'This was before you were married?'

'Before *any* of us were, Chief Inspector. He and Sonia had been friends during their university days.'

'We are aware he was married to Miss Miller.'

'Ah,' he sighed, 'I thought you might have heard. The marriage didn't last, though; not more than a couple of years.'

'Do you know whether your wife kept in touch with him?'

'I would say that was extremely unlikely.'

'And yet,' Brenda pointed out, 'they did meet on Friday.'

'I have to accept what you're telling me, of course,' he said, 'but whether it was a chance meeting or not is surely anyone's guess.'

'That's true, but if they hadn't made arrangements to see each other, we have then to ask why she was in Meadowbank. You've already mentioned she had no friends living there.'

'She hadn't and quite frankly, Chief Inspector, I cannot come up with one single reason why she should have been there.'

'I understand you were unable to tell the officer you talked to on Friday night whether your wife took anything with her; a travel bag, perhaps, or a change of clothes.'

'Why should this be so important? She's gone!'

'It could turn out to be quite relevant, sir,' she explained, 'because, if she had packed a bag, it could have meant she had every intention of either spending some time away from home or had taken the decision not to return. Either way,' she continued, 'I would consider it somewhat unusual for a woman not to have taken even essential toiletries. Presumably, you have checked to see whether they were still here?'

'Of course I have,' he replied, 'and everything is exactly where it usually is, even her toothbrush.'

'If,' Brenda said, 'we are for the moment to work off the premise she left of her own accord, we should be asking whether this decision was a spontaneous one or she had already planned it earlier.

'Surely that's impossible to find out, Chief Inspector. Only Sonia can answer that one.'

'First of all, sir, what was her manner like towards you earlier in the day, when you left for work, I mean.'

'She was asleep when I left the house.'

'And was this normal?'

'Quite normal.'

'Let us go on to when you returned home from work then. Whose decision was it to go along to the Hare & Hound?'

'It was mine; I often have a drink in there after our evening meal.'

'And was your wife in the habit of accompanying you?'

'Hardly ever.'

'But she did on Friday; did that surprise you?'

'Now you come to mention it,' he said, 'it did actually.'

'Why was that?'

'Because Sonia wasn't all that keen on the pub, preferring the ones in the West End and on Friday night, more or less as soon as we'd arrived, she was talking about going back home.'

'Did she give you any reason for her change of mind?'

'Only about the noise. She only had the one drink, a white wine, and then she walked back to the house.'

'I don't need to remind you, Mr Croft,' Brenda started to explain, 'but your wife has only been gone for two days and in normal circumstances, this wouldn't be treated, officially that is, as a missing person case, but because of our current investigations we have no option but to view this matter as serious and one which we need to look into as a matter of urgency.'

'You think something's happened to her, don't you?'

'I don't think anything at this stage, sir; it's too early. Apart from your wife's disappearance, there are a couple of anomalies here which we should be concentrating on. The first one being to find out why she visited Meadowbank on Friday, also where else she went, apart from The Market Inn. This is something we can look into by asking a few questions back in Meadowbank. Meanwhile, the call you made to your local police station in Mayfair will be receiving attention and they will be liaising closely with us.'

'And the press, Chief Inspector?'

'Yes?'

'I've read that piece this morning about Lawrence.'

'I wondered whether you had, sir.'

'Even if I hadn't,' he said dryly, 'I would have learned soon enough, I'm sure. And now, once word leaks out about Sonia, my God! They are going to have a field day!'

'Unfortunately, sir,' she said, 'this is something we are powerless to prevent. If and when, as you say, word does leak out, apart from putting a formal block on any coverage which, incidentally, we wouldn't be able to do, we have no choice. We can't prevent the publication of such reports and providing the content doesn't contravene the libel laws, neither can we prevent people from reading the newspapers.'

Chapter Eleven

'I think we might be in for a storm, Phil.'

'Why should you think that?'

'Just look at that sky over there.' Joyce Nicholson said, pointing out towards the fields at the back of the farm buildings and as far as the quarry.

'That's no storm, Joyce,' he said, coming over to stand beside her at the kitchen window, 'they're crows and have been gathering since first light this morning.'

'Oh!'

'Nothing for you to concern yourself about,' he said, patting her gently on the shoulder, 'the quarry has been their breeding ground for a number of years now; probably something has disturbed them, but let's get through today, shall we?' doing his best to veer her mind away from how, possibly the very same crows had been hovering above the body of the woman who was murdered.

They both had quite enough to worry about without thinking of what may or may not be happening in and around the old quarry. Soon, they would be leaving to drive into Meadowbank to attend their son's funeral; this day was not going to be an easy one. It had been a harrowing week since they'd heard about Gary's death, each day being taken up by dealing and emotionally coping with the various formalities, plus the added stress of frequent visits by the police which had only served as a constant reminder of what had happened to the lad; all of which meant neither of them had had the time, or the energy either, to sit down and quietly talk about Gary and try, somehow, to come to terms with his death. So far, Joyce had been coping well, although he knew she had scarcely slept since Tuesday. He'd heard her downstairs pottering about in the kitchen way after midnight, but he hadn't said anything to her the following morning, realising it was probably her way of dealing with the situation.

It was a real comfort to see so many familiar faces in the church; many of whom he and Joyce had known for years, ever since they had moved into Bridge Farm when they were first married. The service was a short one and, miraculously, when it was over he was able to find his voice, relieved it sounded to him the same as usual, when they'd filed out of the church and he was able to thank those who had attended the service. He had booked a table across the square at The Salmon's Rest; a simple lunch, although if he was being honest, Phil would have admitted he would have much preferred one of Melissa's ploughmans washed down by a couple of pints. He had spotted Brian Morrison at the back of the church when they had arrived, but he'd gone by the time they came out; no doubt to get back to The Market Inn in time to open at eleven-thirty, but he appreciated the kind gesture of him being here this morning.

Brenda saw the mourners emerging from Saint Stephen's from her office window. She already knew Gary Nicholson's funeral was being held today and not all that surprised to see such a big turnout. They couldn't all have known him though, she thought, recalling he had not been exactly the sociable type, but perhaps most of those people out there had attended out of sympathy for Phil and his wife. She knew how cynical she would sound if she were ever to voice her opinion, but nevertheless, she was fairly sure it were true.

She had arrived back in Meadowbank shortly before nine, having made an early start from London. The weekend away had helped; she felt refreshed, at least this was before she was collared by Bill Simms in one of his more briskly officious moods as soon as she had walked up the front steps of the Station. She was hoping to meet up with Ian first thing, but the summons to 'The Warrior's' office promptly curtailed that plan.

'I don't want to make a great issue of this, Brenda,' he said, tapping a forefinger at the folded newspaper on the desk in front of him, 'but, I consider these poorly veiled aspersions towards the Miller-Crofts as being unfortunately miss-timed as well as distasteful. I'm sure they won't be too pleased to be reminded *publicly* they have an ex-jailbird in their family! How on earth did the intrepid Miss Cliff discover Lawrence Croft had changed his name?'

'As to that, sir,' Brenda answered, having waited patiently for him to reach the end of his spiel, 'I don't know. Inspector Ash and I only learned on Friday when we both interviewed Bradley Cartwright. This was immediately after we had asked him whether he had changed his name, although we had nothing positive to support our theory, only that the dates Lawrence Croft and Bradley Cartwright moved from London to Brighton coincided and we had been unable to trace anything about Bradley Cartwright's past, further back than that time.' and going on to explain that because he had been on intimate terms with Muriel Miller and had been with her on the night she had been murdered, plus she had bequeathed him her entire estate, made him one of their prime suspects.'

'So, Brenda,' he asked, 'do you think he's our man?'

'I don't believe he is, sir, although there's no doubt he may have had sufficient motive, also with the fatal shooting of Gary Nicholson, but somehow now with the suspicious circumstances surrounding the death of Mrs Miller-Croft, something doesn't jell.'

'Too pat, eh?'

'Yes, sir.'

'I see. Well, I won't put any pressure on you. You don't need me to tell you this is a hard case and, above all, we want to get it right.'

'There has been a further development, sir.' Brenda went on quickly, anticipating in advance what his reaction would be, 'but Oliver Croft telephoned his local police station in Mayfair late on Friday night to report his wife as missing and this,' she added, 'as I explained to him when I saw him at his home yesterday, given the likely Miller-Croft connection, we have no option but to treat as serious, but at the same time not ruling out that Mrs Croft could very well return at anytime. For the present, I considered it best to try and keep these enquiries as low-key as possible.'

'Because of the press?'

'Yes.'

'Well, I hope you can, Brenda.'

'Mrs Croft was in Meadowbank on Friday, sir,' she told him, 'in fact, I saw her myself, although I didn't talk to her.'

'So when did her husband last see her?'

'When he returned from work on Friday, sir. She was back home by then. They went along to their local for a drink that evening, but she didn't stay long, complaining she had a headache and was going back home, but when he returned later she wasn't there.'

'Strange behaviour, but then, Brenda, as we know well enough, one never does get the full story.'

'I know, sir. What we'll try to do this morning is find out why she came here. When I saw her she was having a drink with Adam Fry -'

'- that's the man who was married to Muriel Miller?'

'Yes, that's right. I had a word with him later and he told me he was surprised to see her when she walked into his pharmacy. She used to be his girlfriend in the days before he knew Muriel Miller. He was quite frank, as a matter of fact, saying that the romance with Muriel Miller had been a whirlwind one and he wasn't proud for – to use his words – ditching Sonia the way he had.'

'Did you believe him?'

'Yes, I did. I'd already had this confirmed by Christine Mason when I spoke to her. She didn't have a good word to say for Muriel, although I'm not too sure whether this animosity towards the woman wasn't out of jealousy. It would seem that Catherine Miller-Croft favoured her step-daughter, but going back to Sonia Croft, sir,' Brenda went on, 'I feel there is something askew here. As you mentioned, her behaviour is strange and her disappearance at this juncture could be significant. What I mean is this happened within hours of meeting her ex-boyfriend. I know it was almost twenty years ago, but -'

'- a woman scorned?'

'Could be, sir, but we do need to find her.'

By the time Brenda came out of Bill Simms' office it was well after eleven and as she walked through the main office there was no sign of Ian, although he had left a message on her desk to say he was meeting Emily Craig up at "The Gables" as the valuers had discovered a number of discrepancies in respect to the contents of the house.

The mourners who had attended Gary Nicholson's funeral had now dispersed, Phil and his wife, she noticed, walking with half a dozen others across the square in the direction of The Salmon's Rest. The end of yet another sad episode in this case, Brenda sighed, turning away from the window and picking up her coat from the chair where she'd left it before going into Bill Simm's office. But, as she had said to him, they had to find Sonia Croft, unable to shrug off a strong feeling of foreboding, remembering back to Friday when she'd seen her outside The Market Inn and interpreting the expression on her face as Adam had left her: it had been one of abject misery and how she had remained standing there, at the edge of the pavement, watching him until he had gone inside, before walking away. Had that meeting acted as a sort of catalyst? Had seeing him again, after so long, triggered off something which had been lying dormant in her mind? Perhaps these were questions which would never be answered. But, difficult though it was, she had to try and retrace the woman's steps from when she arrived in Meadowbank up and until the time she met Adam Fry, but at the same time not ruling out she may have met someone else before going back to London. The main puzzle remained; why had she decided to come to Meadowbank if it hadn't been to see Adam Fry? Adam had told her that Sonia had called into the pharmacy and that was when he first saw her. Had the pharmacy been the first place she'd been to or had she gone somewhere else first? Well, Brenda decided, she had to start somewhere, remembering also how, when Adam had gone, Sonia had turned to the left as though, perhaps, she was returning to where she'd parked her car. It had been after two by then; too late to find anywhere to eat. This is where my so-called woman's intuition should come to the fore she thought, leaving the office and closing the door behind her. The drive from where the Crofts lived in London would have taken her at least an hour and a half; perhaps by this time she had felt in the need of a coffee. She could have gone up to The Royal Oak, but unless she'd had a reason for going to the hotel it was out of her way; it was more likely she would have found a place in the town. There was the Bridge Cafe, but then, there was also The Bridge Inn. Talk about tossing a coin, she thought, nodding to the desk sergeant on her way out of the building and deciding she'd try there first.

*

Emily hadn't been able to contact Arnold Brutton until Sunday afternoon and, apologising for disturbing his weekend, told him about the variation in the two valuations. He had sounded noticeably concerned, especially when she had read out the description of those items which were no longer in the house, which puzzled her at first until he explained that each one of them: a fine-boned eighteenth-century teapot and matching cups and saucers; a silver-backed hair brush and hand-mirror; three embroidered miniatures; an ivory cameo brooch; a solitaire diamond ring; an eighteen-carat gold wedding ring and an emerald pendant on a silver chain, had all belonged to Catherine's mother, Evelyn Singleton.

'The lady in the painting.'

'That's quite correct, Mrs Craig and, if I may say so, you bear an uncanny resemblance to the lady. I met her once, many years ago; I was only a boy then, but I can still remember her. How sad she would have been about those precious pieces which, incidentally, had been in the Singleton family for years, also this dreadful business, once again involving the family. Very sad.' he repeated.

'From what you've said, Mr Brutton,' Emily put in, 'it's clear to me that Mrs Miller-Croft would not have sold them.'

'Never, Mrs Craig. I'm positive about that. She probably never wore her mother's jewellery; in fact, as far as I'm aware, I don't think she ever did, but the fact that it all belonged to her family I believe and just knowing they were with her was sufficient for her; a comfort even, if you understand?'

'I believe I do, Mr Brutton.' although not really sharing his views. Emily had found since Adrian died, that everything they had bought together over the years, only served to remind her of having lost him. It had been hard enough coming to terms within herself that he was no longer here, without the constant and visible evidence of how happy they had been, but perhaps if she, like Catherine, had come from a similar background, where families expected possessions to be handed down through the generations, she would feel differently.

'What do you intend to do now, Mrs Craig?'

'Well,' she began, taking a deep breath, 'my first instinct was to do nothing. A rather negative attitude, I know, but mainly this was because I thought the family had quite sufficient to contend with at the moment and learning about this would only have added to their distress. But –'

'- but,' he interrupted gently, 'you've had second thoughts?'

'Yes, I have. You see, Mr Brutton, something else has been taken which could be considered as far more serious.'

'Yes?'

'One of the valuers, a specialist in paintings, in particular the Old Masters, was quick to discover six of the paintings had been forged.'

'Dear me, this is quite shocking. And you're right, of course, Mrs Craig. This is a very serious matter indeed and should be reported.'

'I hoped you would agree with me,' she said, grateful to have his support, 'but I wanted to make sure first that those missing items hadn't been sold by Mrs Miller-Croft, before I made the report to the police.'

'I'm glad you did. It's true that on the occasions when Mrs Miller-Croft made any purchases and on the rare occasion sold any, she always came to Bruttons, as her father did, in fact.'

Before ringing off, Emily promised to keep in touch and to let him know of any further developments, should they occur, and thinking as she replaced the receiver it was too much to hope there wouldn't be any.

Now, waiting for Inspector Ash to arrive and standing at the window of Catherine's sitting room, she wished she was anywhere but here, in what to her seemed overwhelmingly depressing.

*

Isobel Gallier was unfastening the shutters as Brenda drew up outside The Bridge. The resigned expression on her face reminding her of the last time she'd called in to talk to her, but Brenda was well used to such a reception which, while not exactly hostile, certainly couldn't be described as welcoming.

'Good morning, Mrs Gallier.' she said, following her inside.

'Good morning, Chief Inspector. I wondered how long it would be before I could expect a visit from you. Mind you,' she went on, as though regretting her initial coolness, 'I know you must have your work cut out at the moment and I certainly don't envy you your job. At least,' she added, going round to the other side of the bar, 'those reporters from London have gone.'

'Believe me, Mrs Gallier, I am as pleased as you are; they can create an unpleasant intrusion, not to mention acting as a constant reminder to people of what's been happening recently.'

'Don't I know it! And, now the latest news about poor Mrs Miller-Croft. It is all very hard to take in, I can tell you. Anyway, Chief Inspector, how can I help you, but first can I get you a drink?'

'I'll have a coffee, please. I'm not sure whether you will be able to help me or not, Mrs Gallier, but we're trying to retrace the steps of a woman who was in Meadowbank on Friday.'

'Yes?' at the same time preparing the coffee, but Brenda waited until she had finished and had passed the cup across the bar towards her before continuing.

'Have you ever met Sonia Croft, Mrs Gallier,' Brenda asked, 'she's married to Mrs Miller-Croft's step-son.'

I suppose you could say I've met her,' Isobel said, a slight frown creasing her forehead, 'but at the time I didn't know who she was.'

'When was this?'

'On Friday, as a matter of fact. She came in around midday and ordered a glass of wine; it wasn't until she had gone that one of my regulars told me her name. I don't need to tell you, Chief Inspector, there isn't a great deal which goes on in this town that the older generation don't know about, although I have to say, their information isn't always one hundred per cent accurate.'

'And was she on her own?'

'She came in on her own, but was joined by the landscape designer; he's working on the Riverside development across the road and often comes in here at lunchtime.'

'Bradley Cartwright?'

'Yes, that's right; he's been in Meadowbank for a couple of months now.'

'Do you think they had arranged to meet, Mrs Gallier?'

'I'm sure they hadn't. In fact, I don't believe he noticed her at first because he walked straight up to the bar as soon as he came in. She was the one who called over to him. It was funny, though,' she added quickly, 'she called him Lawrence, not Bradley, but perhaps he has two Christian names.'

'I see.' Brenda nodded, wishing all the people they interviewed could be so forthcoming, 'And did you have many other customers? I know you said it was only midday, perhaps a bit too early for most of them.'

'There were quite a few; it's often like that on a Friday for some reason, but I think people are beginning to unwind for the weekend. Anyway,' she explained, 'my usual regulars were here, also three of the reporters I was talking about a minute ago; they were here as well.'

So, Brenda thought, that's how they heard and no doubt the too clever by half Carol Cliff, having done her homework on the Miller-Croft family, had quickly put the proverbial two and two together. That female was definitely in the wrong profession; she should be in the criminal investigation department!

'How would you describe their attitude towards each other, Mrs Gallier? For instance, would you say, Mr Cartwright was pleased to see her?'

'I don't think he was, now you come to mention it, but he took his drink over to where she was sitting and they chatted for about ten minutes before he was interrupted by his mobile and then he left soon after he had finished the call. Mrs Croft went about five minutes later.'

'How did she appear to you?'

'Hard to say, really, although if anything, a little distracted; as though she had something on her mind.'

'Well, thank you, Mrs Gallier and you have been helpful.'

'I'm not going to ask why you should be asking questions about Mrs Croft, Chief Inspector, but I sincerely hope it doesn't mean any more unpleasant shocks.'

'I'm afraid I can't give you any reassurance, as much as I would like to, but all I will say is we are doing our utmost to clear up this investigation as rapidly as we can and at the same time try to avoid more unwanted press coverage.'

Back in the car, Brenda was about to reverse in the entrance to The Bridge's car park when she noticed what at first appeared to be a dark cloud further along the road and beyond Phil Nicholson's farm and then realising it was too low in the sky, also that now and again, straining her eyes to focus more clearly, it would break up before reforming. The feeling of foreboding she had experienced earlier that morning returned and, switching on the ignition, she pulled away from the kerb and continued along Bridge Street, past the farm and having the road to herself, reached the old quarry on the left-hand side. There were hundreds of them; a thick dark menacing clump of blackness hovering above the quarry, with even more crows flying up from the base to join the mass above. Leaving the car on the road, Brenda walked across the rough ground until she reached the edge of the quarry and looked down.

*

Ian Ash was leaving Mavis Coleman's house, having gone back to talk to her after he'd seen Emily, when his mobile rang.

'Ian,' Brenda's voice, crackling with static, 'I'm at the old quarry. I've already phoned the Station, there should be a team along within a matter of minutes, but this is bad.'

'Yes, ma'am.' a tiny quiver of unease at the back of his neck. Brenda sounded as calm and controlled as usual, but he sensed whatever she had discovered was going to be pretty grim.

'There's a car down there, Ian,' she said, 'and it's Sonia Croft's.'

'How do you think that happened, ma'am; did it go over the edge?' remembering there was a rough track at the far end which the trucks had used years ago when the quarry was in full operation.

'I would say so; it must have rolled over several times. In fact, it's a wonder it didn't burst into flames.'

'And is she inside the vehicle?'

'I can't see all that well, but someone is.'

'Alright, ma'am; I'll be along there as soon as I can.'

Ian arrived at exactly the same time as the recovery vehicle and the team of officers with their barrier tape and tarpaulin required for cordoning off the whole area, followed by the pathologist and his assistant. The well-honed and much-practiced routine didn't take long to complete and by the time the first curious onlookers from Meadowbank came along, having seen the fleet of vehicles emerging from the yard at the back of the Station and making their way across Market Square and into Bridge Street, there was no way anyone could possibly get near enough to the quarry to peer down into the chiselled-out sides of the stone to see what was happening on the quarry floor.

'I was hoping to have a word with you earlier this morning, Ian,' Brenda said, standing beside him inside the tape, 'but I was called into Bill Simms' office.'

'I knew that,' he said, 'they told me at the desk; I think we have quite a lot to catch up with, ma'am.'

'We do, in particular I didn't tell you I had a call from New Scotland Yard on Saturday to say that Oliver Croft's wife had disappeared from their home late on Friday. I managed to see him yesterday and he appeared to be quite distraught. As I mentioned to you before we finished on Friday, I actually saw her in Meadowbank with Adam Fry, and now it seems she also met up with Bradley Cartwright shortly before then. I only learned this a short while ago from Isobel Gallier; Sonia Croft had gone in there for a drink and, and, according to Isobel, she was certain their meeting hadn't been planned. Little did we know,' she added wryly, 'when we talked to him, he had been in her company only minutes earlier. You'll be interested to hear,' she added, 'that Isobel heard her refer to Bradley as Lawrence.'

'So much for all his efforts to change his identity.'

'I know, Ian. Anyway, I feel, particularly with this latest development, we may very well be coming to the end of this rather messy case.'

'I hope so, ma'am.'

'Excuse me, Chief Inspector,' the pathologist, Dave Burrows, said walking over to them, slightly out of breath from walking up the steep track from the quarry base, 'but we're going to bring the body up now and then we'll hoist up the car.'

'Right, Dave. I don't see much point in us both staying on here; we'll make our way back to the Station and wait for your report.'

'Of course,' he nodded, 'a couple of hours should do it okay.'

'Have you any idea how long she's been down there?'

'Apart from and mind you this is very much off the cuff, I would say at least since last night, quite late I think.'

'I'm surprised the petrol tank didn't blow up.'

'Normally it would have,' he agreed, 'but there's a fair amount of water at the bottom, more than a foot of it; that could be a possible explanation.'

'In that case,' Ian put in, 'the noise of the impact wouldn't have been all that great.' thinking of the close proximity to Bridge Farm and how Phil Nicholson or anyone else up there may not have heard anything.

'I should say so,' Dave said, 'nasty business. Well,' he continued briskly, 'I must get back. I'll be in touch later, Chief Inspector.'

'Thanks, Dave.'

'I wonder how long it will be before the press get to hear.' Ian commented as they returned to their cars.

'I would say as far as the local press is concerned not all that long, but I understand the journalists from London have already left Meadowbank, but you can be sure they'll be back. With a vengeance and you know what this will mean, don't you?'

'A press conference.'

'Yes; not that they ever achieve much and I'm sure this one, which is inevitable once Bill Simms gets hold of the news, will be no different from all the others.'

'Shall I get a sandwich for us on the way back, ma'am; I'm feeling a bit peckish.'

'That's a good idea.' she agreed, 'Why is it, Ian, I wonder when we become embroiled in a case of this magnitude, we are inclined to neglect the simple act of re-fuelling? I suggest we call into The Bridge Cafe; there won't be much happening until we get Dave's report and then, once again, it's going to be a very long day for us both.'

The Bridge Cafe, always a popular place at lunchtimes, was fairly packed, but Molly, who had worked for them for more years than Ian could remember, found them a table in the corner away from the front window which he thought was probably better than having to look out and see the vehicles coming back from the quarry. Instead of a sandwich they ordered cheese omelettes with a bowl of their home-made chips and Brenda relayed to him everything she had been able to glean about Sonia Croft's disappearance, following on from when she had returned to London on Friday afternoon to the time she had left The Hare & Hound, and going on to tell about the interview she'd had with Oliver Croft the previous morning. And now, Ian thought resignedly, it would appear the woman had decided to take her own life, but realising there was nothing to be gained by conjecturing until they had Dave's report and to find out exactly how she had died.

'This is not a straightforward enquiry, Ian,' she said, 'we started off with one murder, namely the death of Muriel Miller followed within a matter of days by the shooting of Gary Nicholson and then discovering that Catherine Miller-Croft had also been murdered. I have always felt up to now that these killings were carried out by the same person and, so far, nothing has occurred to make me change my mind. And now,' she went on, 'even before we've heard the exact details of how Sonia Croft, assuming of course, it is Sonia Croft in that smashed up car, met her death, you're telling me about the discrepancies in the latest valuation form "The Gables". As Bill Simms would say, "What on earth is going on?".'

'The reason I decided to call in and see Mavis Coleman,' Ian started to explain, 'at the risk of her passing on some more titbits to her husband and it subsequently going around the town, was because I considered her to be the only person who could throw any light on those faked paintings.'

'And was she?'

'She was, as it happens. Quite enlightening, in fact, because she told me she had seen Muriel on more than one occasion carrying paintings out to her car.'

'Well, that *is* interesting.'

'I know and, not unsurprisingly, it had been a Saturday each time and she told Mavis she was taking them into Salisbury for cleaning.'

'A logical explanation.'

'I thought so and, naturally enough Mavis believed her.'

'Indeed and why not;' Brenda said, 'after all, Muriel was Catherine's step-daughter. And then, presumably after a certain length of time, Muriel would have brought them back.'

'Yes, and no doubt she did have Catherine Miller-Croft's agreement to do this. Muriel Miller hasn't come out of all this exactly squeaky-clean, has she, ma'am?'

'No, she hasn't. Did you ask Mavis Coleman about those missing items?'

'No, I considered it best not to, because if word did leak out about the pictures that would be quite enough for the present.'

'I believe you were right. If Muriel had taken them, I think she would have made sure not to have been seen by either Catherine or Mavis.'

'Mrs Craig told me this morning she'd checked with Arnold Brutton before calling into the Station.' Telling her that all of those missing pieces had belonged to the Singleton family for several years and saying how Arnold Brutton had stressed that Catherine would never have parted with them. 'I've a copy of the first valuation here,' he added, passing it across the table, 'as you can see, ma'am, there are several circled in pencil.'

'And these are the ones that are no longer there.' she said, scanning through the list, 'Most of it is jewellery, I notice.'

'Yes.'

'Which, as I'm sure has already occurred to you, Ian, does tend to bring us back once again to Bradley Cartwright?'

'Given his background,' Ian said, 'I think it would be quite feasible for him to know who to contact in order to offload them.'

'That is if Muriel didn't want to keep them for herself, of course.'

'True.'

''But, Ian, the paintings are another matter. Whoever had done the work on the forgeries, must have been sufficiently skilled, so would Muriel have been likely to have known such a person?'

'I expect Bradley Cartwright would.'

'Exactly. Unless the originals have been sent overseas, it may be possible to locate them. And,' she continued, 'as far as the jewellery and the other missing items are concerned, I think we should apply for a search warrant.'

'For the Swiss Cottage property?'

'Yes; it might just pay off, you know. We only need to find one piece in the house; it would be enough to support this part of the investigation.'

'Although if we did, it wouldn't necessarily implicate Bradley Cartwright.'

'I realise that, but one step at a time, Ian. We'll get there.'

He couldn't help but admire her confidence. At that precise moment he felt mentally bogged down with a hotchpotch of imponderables, remembering words of an old nursery rhyme: ".... if ifs and ands were pots and pans ....", If Muriel Miller had been a thief and if her boyfriend had been her accomplice, had he, becoming greedy knowing he was going to inherit, decided to murder her? If Bradley had known Muriel's step-mother was Catherine Miller-Croft, had he planned the double murder? And where did Sonia Croft fit into this conundrum, Ian wondered.

*

'There's a lot of activity out there, Isobel.' Bradley remarked, 'Have you any idea what's going on?'

'I don't know, Bradley,' she answered, pouring his lager, 'but this town is becoming more and more like downtown New York!'

'Have you ever been there, then?' he asked her.

'You may be surprised to learn that I have been to New York; a long time ago, mind you, but I can remember all too well with the amount of yellow cabs and the heavy police presence, how very noisy it was.'

'I don't think you've anything to worry about here; Meadowbank has a long way to go before it's as frenetic as that.'

'Perhaps,' she shrugged, 'but you've only been here for a few months, Bradley and, honestly, for over a year now there has been one tragedy after another. And as to the unusual amount of vehicles in Bridge Street during the last hour, well, I only hope we're not in for some more bad news. It isn't good for the town, you know; especially for the youngsters. Goodness me, they're familiar enough these days with their lurid DVDs where violence is the norm without it happening on their doorsteps.'

They were, at that moment, interrupted by the heavy trundling of wheels from the road, the natural light in the bar dimming as the vehicle passed the window.

'What in goodness sake,' Isobel asked, craning her neck to see above the heads of those standing in front of her at the bar, 'is that?'

'It's a recovery truck, Isobel,' one of her regulars called out, having had the added curiosity to walk over towards the window, 'and judging by the crushed state of the car on the back, someone has had a very nasty accident. It has to be a complete write-off!'

'The car's not from around here.' his drinking companion commented.

'How do you know that, Jack?'

'I don't recognise the number plate, that's why, at least what's left of it. Also,' he added with the characteristic confidence of one who knows all about the town and area he has lived in for over fifty years, 'I've not seen any cars of that make in and around Meadowbank.'

'Are they always like this?' Bradley asked her, but keeping his voice down.

'Oh, yes,' she smiled wanly, 'always, and the thing is, although they are very often way off-beam, there are times when they're spot on.'

'He's right about the car being a write-off, though,' Bradley said, 'it's a mess. Must have been some accident.'

'Something else for our local police to sort out; as if they haven't enough already to contend with.'

The momentary excitement over, and a number of her customers finding they were thirsty, crowded up to the bar to replenish their glasses, meaning Isobel was kept occupied for the following ten minutes, but in many respects glad to have something to do, recognising all too well that whatever had happened out there would be the main topic of conversation until they had thoroughly exhausted the topic and something else had come along to feed their insatiable appetite for gossip because, she concluded, that's what it was tantamount to. She was no doubt being uncharitable, but unless they had known and liked the person unfortunate enough to have suffered misfortune, it wasn't as if they were truly sympathetic, not much different from those youngsters she had mentioned to Bradley Cartwright only minutes ago. To many of her regulars, most of them long-retired, life these days must seem like one long soap opera!

Chapter Twelve

A white-faced Oliver Croft arrived in Meadowbank around five in the afternoon and formally identified the body of the woman pulled from the wreckage as his wife. Hardened though she was by the shocked reactions of people in a similar situation, Brenda thought it would be some time before she would forget Oliver Croft's stricken expression as he stared down at the dead woman and how, for a couple of seconds, he closed his eyes before looking up and nodding silently in Brenda's direction.

Ian stepped forward and without saying anything took Oliver Croft's arm and led him out of the mortuary and into the corridor, with Brenda following close behind them.

'If you would take Mr Croft along to the interview room, Inspector,' she said to him, 'I'll arrange for some tea to be brought in.'

'Why? Why? Why did she do it?' Oliver Croft kept repeating, his words barely audible, 'It couldn't possibly have been an accident, could it?'

'No, sir,' she answered, 'it wasn't and as to why, we will do our best to try and find out.' and reaching the door of the interview room, Brenda carried on along the corridor towards the front desk, reaching it at the same time as the main doors opened and Adam Fry walked into reception.

'Chief Inspector,' he said as soon as he saw her, 'could I have word with you; something rather disturbing has happened and I think you should know. I've only just gone through my mail today and there was a letter from Sonia.'

'Alright, Mr Fry,' she said, 'we'll use my office, but first I must have a brief word with Inspector Ash.' she added, and asking him to wait for her, she walked quickly back to the interview room.

'Tea's on its way, Ian,' she said to him quietly, not wanting Oliver Croft to overhear her, 'but Adam Fry has just arrived; apparently he received a letter from Sonia Croft. I haven't read it yet, but this could be the suicide note.'

Brenda read the letter twice before she said anything, placing the single sheet of notepaper, with the incongruous heading and logo of The Royal Oak printed along the top of it, on her desk, smoothing the paper where it had become slightly creased; all of these actions to allow her time to collate what had been written. It looked very much as though Sonia had returned to Meadowbank on the Friday night, perhaps booked herself into the hotel and none of them had known during those hours when the feelers were out to find her that she had been here, literally under their noses all the time. Although the letter to Adam could never be described as a love letter in the truest sense, while it could be taken as a suicide note, written she felt, recalling the nuances of many of the words and phrases, by a woman deeply troubled and overwhelmed by a terrible bitterness. Brenda could only guess the depth of Sonia Croft's feelings as she had started to write, but no more than that. How could anyone really see into the mind of a person so deeply disturbed when they were driven to take the ultimate action of ending their life? Impossible, she concluded.

'We will need to keep this of course, sir, for evidence,' she said to Adam, 'but if you would like a copy -'

'- no thank you, Chief Inspector,' he interrupted, 'I don't want to see it again. One of my customers told me about the accident, but I had absolutely no idea. Didn't even know how it happened, but as soon as I read that -' pointing to the letter, 'well, I had a premonition it could have been Sonia. Also,' he went on slowly, 'although I knew when we were talking on Friday she still continued to bear a grudge against Muriel, it never crossed my mind for one minute it had taken such a strong hold. To do something as drastic as what she did surely must be the actions of a mad woman.'

'I don't know about mad, certifiably mad, I mean,' Brenda said, 'but definitely mentally unbalanced, but then that's something which may well be discovered later.'

'She really believed she wouldn't be suspected for those murders, didn't she?'

'I think so. There still remains a missing link as far as we're concerned in this triple murder case, sir, which is that of Gary Nicholson. Whoever shot him had more than a reasonable knowledge of firearms, but perhaps this is something you may be able to help us on.'

'I believe I can,' he said quickly, 'you see, Chief Inspector, Sonia had a rather unorthodox upbringing. Her parents, both of them lawyers, were in their forties when she was born and she was actually brought up by her mother's younger brother and his wife and he was, according to what Sonia told me when we first met, a gunsmith. He had a business, quite a successful one it would seem, in one of those streets leading off from the Strand close to The Arches. Sonia used to help him in the shop on Saturdays and during her school holidays; this was before she went to university. Also, he was a keen marksman and belonged to a firearms club and would often take her along with him; highly irregular, of course, but that's what she said.'

'So,' Brenda said, feeling at last that various segments of their investigation were beginning to neatly slot into place, 'it is feasible he would have taught her how to handle a gun?'

'I'm fairly sure he did, Chief Inspector.'

After Adam had gone, she remained at her desk and read the letter again. The gist of the contents was, if you discard what Sonia had to say about Oliver being a poor replacement and how she had been incapable of giving him the love she had offered so freely to Adam, her first and only real sweetheart, and how when she had seen him on Friday she had read the cold rejection in his eyes which made her decide she no longer wished to carry on living, and concentrated instead on the core of her message; namely that she had planned to dispose of Catherine for two reasons. The first one being, guessing Catherine would be leaving the bulk of her estate to Muriel and the fact Muriel had no dependants, Oliver would duly inherit. The second reason was that she was convinced Muriel would be blamed, whether she was dead or not. Murdering Muriel, in Sonia's view had been necessary, also shooting the greedy young man who should have known better. Crazy deductions, Brenda murmured under her breath; absolutely crazy. Perhaps Adam had been right. Perhaps Sonia Croft had been mad. At what point, Brenda wondered, getting up from her desk, does an unbalanced mind become a mad one.

*

Sonia Croft's suicide made the nine o'clock news, but missed the London Evening Standard, although the following day's nationals made up for this by, in most cases, giving it front-page coverage, mainly because of what had become in recent weeks the unfolding and, to the more sensational-seeking public, scandal of the Miller-Croft family; the remaining members of whom reacted in their own predictable way. Christine, in particular, voicing her chagrin of not hearing directly from Oliver. It made no difference when Godfrey, tactfully pointed out, not wanting to exacerbate her further, that very likely Oliver was in a state of shock.

'In a state of shock! Do you really think so?'

'Well, yes, I do; he must be, Christine.'

'All I can say,' she went on, 'even if he is, we are his family, his closest family, after all. All he had to do was pick up the phone, dial our number and tell us. It would have been much better than hearing about Sonia by a newsreader who might just as well have been reporting something as mediocre and mundane as the weather! She even had a smile on her face as she prettily informed the viewers.'

There was nothing to be gained by appealing to her better nature, the more charitable one, Godfrey decided. It had always been the same with Christine; as far as certain members of her family were concerned she had little or no time for them, so why should this recent tragedy be different from any of the others? He should, he supposed, give Oliver a ring, commiserate with him, but knowing he wouldn't find it easy. What do you say to a man whose wife had made such a monumental decision to end her life? And what a way to do it, he thought, inwardly shuddering. Poor Sonia, a woman he had always thought to be quietly, albeit somewhat complacently, content with being a suburban housewife. She had never struck him as the dramatic type, given to making statements, far less voicing her opinion.

'Also, Godfrey,' Christine broke into his thoughts, 'have you considered the girls? What on earth are they going to think when they hear that their aunt, whom I'm sure they were fond of, has committed suicide?'

'They may not hear, being away at school all week. We can tell them when they come home on Friday.'

'You are an out and out ostrich, Godfrey! Not all the girls are weekly boarders, as you well know, and those who aren't will be bound to hear and will be full of it when they get back to school tomorrow morning. And what about the head mistress? I'm sure, like almost everyone else in the country, she'd have been listening to the nine o'clock news. It won't make one iota of difference that their surname is Mason. The Miller-Croft family have, for the last week or so, been dominating the newspapers and this latest – event,' stumbling over the word, '- this latest disaster,' she corrected herself, 'is only going to make matters a hundred times worse. Do you know, Godfrey, Sonia, no matter what sort of trauma she was suffering, has piled even more disgrace on to our family.'

'What do you want me to do, Christine?' sighing in exasperation. It didn't help either to realise she was absolutely right; his daughters should be told and as tactfully as possible, aware he was shirking his responsibilities as a parent.

'Oh, nothing, Godfrey. I'll give the head mistress a ring myself; she'll be able to tell them when they're both together tomorrow which, of course, isn't possible over the phone.'

Christine was halfway out to the hall when the phone rang. From where he was sitting at the kitchen table with a half-drunk glass of wine in front of him which no longer held any appeal, he heard her quickening her step as she reached the phone and picked up the receiver. Only minutes later she was back; for once an unreadable expression on her face, as she sat down and leant forward to refill her own glass.

'Yes?' unable to bear the suspense any longer.

'That was Lawrence.' she said at last, taking a sip of her wine, 'He's coming round, Godfrey; in fact, he should be here in about five or ten minutes. He was phoning from the pub on the corner and he'd heard about Sonia earlier today.'

'Lawrence. After all this time.'

'I know.'

'How did he sound?'

'Hard to say,' she answered, all her previous indignation gone, 'devastated, I suppose.'

'But why, Christine; he scarcely knew her.'

'That's true, but apparently he saw her on Friday in Meadowbank.'

'What was he doing there?'

'He didn't explain, only to say he's working there and has been for the last few months and on Friday Sonia had walked into the pub where he usually goes at lunchtime.'

'But why phone us? Surely Oliver would be the one he should be talking to?'

'He said he'd tried to call him, but there was no answer. Anyway,' she added, standing up again, 'before he arrives, I must phone the school; it's getting late.'

Christine was still on the phone when the front door bell rang, meaning he had no alternative but to answer it and wondering whether he would recognise a man he had only met once before, at his mother's funeral fifteen years ago, the same year Christine and he were married and being surprised at the time by a rare display of filial support for Oliver. This family he had married into, Godfrey thought as he opened the front door, took some understanding.

*

The search warrant for Number fourteen, The Mews, Swiss Cottage; the property Muriel Miller had been given by Catherine, arrived first thing on Tuesday morning and the investigative team from the Met, together with Ian Ash, pulled up outside shortly after eleven. It didn't take them long to work their way through the two-storey house, systematically sifting through the entire contents. Within a matter of minutes, they found the jewellery which matched those pieces detailed on the original valuation from "The Gables", with the added proof of both rings being engraved in the names of E and H Singleton, leaving them in no doubt they had belonged to Evelyn, Catherine's mother and her father, Harold Singleton, also the date of their marriage: 1st June, Nineteen twenty-four.

'And they were in one of the drawers of the dressing-table?' Brenda asked when Ian, wasting no time, had called her.

'That's right, ma'am; she hadn't even made any attempt to conceal them.'

'Probably didn't think there was any need to, Ian.'

'There's something else which has turned up.'

'Yes?'

'We very nearly missed it, but we found a small notebook; it wasn't in her desk, but tucked in between a row of cookery books in the kitchen.'

'Secretive.'

'Well, yes. There weren't many entries, although a couple did jump out at me.'

'Go on, Ian.' and he recognised the impatience in her voice, not that he was prevaricating on purpose, far from it, but the possible significance of what he'd seen had struck him as so incongruous, he was still finding it difficult to formulate in his mind what it could actually mean.

'Sorry,' he apologised, 'but she had written in James Thornton's name and telephone number.'

'Godfrey Mason's partner?'

'Yes,' he said, 'it would be too much of a coincidence for it not to be.'

'I would say so, Ian. Anything else?'

'There was, yes,' he explained, 'it was as though she had compiled her own sort of code, but not all that difficult to work out, because she'd repeated his name, or I should say his initials, at the back of the book and next to this she'd listed those paintings which had been faked, along with dates, the first being in May last year, together with amounts of money which she had totalled and deducted fifty per cent.'

'James Thornton's cut.'

'Could have been, ma'am.'

'Well,' Brenda said, 'this certainly throws a different light on things. Also,' she went on, 'if Muriel Miller was in with James Thornton, it does take the suspicion away from Bradley Cartwright. By the way,' she added, 'do I take it that he hasn't been to the house since her death?'

'He told me when I spoke to him earlier today that he hadn't. I got the impression he was putting off that moment. I think her death has hit him quite hard and now, coupled with what has happened to Sonia Croft, especially as he saw her on Friday, he sounded even more so.'

'No doubt he's starting to wonder what kind of woman Muriel Miller had been.' Brenda suggested, 'However, I think we should press on now we've reached this stage of the proceedings.'

'Another search warrant?'

'Probably, Ian. We should be asking ourselves whether Godfrey Mason was also involved, but certainly a further visit to their office is essential. We'll be able to obtain the authority to view their accounts, but it's a bit too soon for that, and when we do we'll find out how financially sound they are; matching their incoming revenue with their clients' accounts and whether they've had any unexplained deposits since last year. At the moment we haven't a great deal to go on, but merely by your presence it would be a start and might, if nothing else, make at least two people nervous.'

'Godfrey Mason and James Thornton?'

'Exactly.'

'I'll go along to their office, then?'

'If you would, Ian,' she agreed, 'I suggest you take it step by step though. Until we get the necessary authority, I wouldn't mention their accounts, but focus instead on the relationship between Muriel Miller and James Thornton. By the way,' she paused for a second, 'you said there was a telephone number alongside his name in the notebook?'

'Yes.'

'I've a note here of their office number, if you'll just wait a minute and I'll read it out to you and then you can see if it's the same. At least that way, you'll know without much doubt whether he is the same James Thornton. Your biggest problem, Ian, is going to be whether Godfrey Mason was in on this deal or not.'

'I know.'

'Also, from what you've been saying, Ian,' she went on, 'the money she'd been receiving for the sale of these original paintings must have been banked somewhere and we know from what we've already seen from her current and deposit accounts with Barclays, there was nothing untoward there, quite straightforward, in fact.'

'An overseas account, perhaps?'

'More than likely, I would say.'

'I've been through the contents of her desk here,' he explained, 'and apart from the Barclay bank statements, they're the only ones.'

'Once again, secretive.' she commented.

'It seems to be very much guesswork from here, doesn't it, ma'am?'

'That's true,' Brenda agreed, 'I'll try to put out a few feelers this afternoon. See what comes up. Without permission we haven't got the authority, but I know someone in New Scotland Yard who will have.'

*

It was well after two when James Thornton arrived back in the office, the business lunch with a couple of clients lasting longer than he'd anticipated, resulting in him missing the call which Belinda had taken from an Inspector Ash of, apparently, the Meadowbank Constabulary, who wanted to see him.

'Surely it's Godfrey he wants to see, Belinda?'

'No, he said your name, James.'

'Well, all I can say is, I can't think why. So, when is he planning to call into the office?' he asked her and as he spoke he felt the first tiny stab of unease.

'Three o'clock. That's alright, isn't it; I've checked your diary and you haven't any other appointments for the day.'

'No, that's alright,' he sighed, resisting the urge to abruptly retrace his steps and leave the building, but, of course, he had no choice and, picking up the handful of mail which had been delivered earlier, he reluctantly continued down the hallway to his own office.

Up until now James had had a good run, which he'd put down to a well-developed sense of self-preservation and never doing anything to jeopardise the finely balanced lifestyle he had gone to great lengths to build up over the years, but hearing Meadowbank mentioned had triggered off certain memories: Meadowbank; the town where Catherine Miller-Croft had lived, coupled with the name Croft, reminding him of when he had first heard of the family.

It had been well over ten years ago and he had been working for his old firm, Petersons, the restorers and valuers, in Baker Street. They had recently purchased by auction on Oliver Croft's behalf a marble Napoleon-the-third mantle-clock and a pair of matching candelabras; Croft's Fine Arts, as he was told at the time, being one of Petersons' most prestigious clients. By this time, James was already earning a lucrative additional income, along with a colleague whose criminal leanings were on a par with his own, until unfortunately for him making a monumental misjudgement, which had resulted in instant dismissal from Petersons. After that, James decided he would continue to operate on his own. Fortunately, the colleague had made no mention of him, although this narrow escape did make him more circumspect, but the undeniable fact remained; there were rich pickings out there and he wanted a share of them.

James didn't think about the Crofts again, although he had learned while still working for Petersons, that Oliver Croft's step-mother owned an impressive art collection, the main part of which she had inherited from her father, Harold Singleton, and from time to time he did wonder how he could possibly view the collection and see for himself exactly what she did have, but these were only idle thoughts and eventually he dismissed them as no more than that. When, by a strange quirk of fate after striking up a friendship with Godfrey shortly before they went into partnership, he learned that Godfrey's wife was Catherine Miller-Croft's daughter, he thought there might just be a chance to introduce himself to the woman, but this idea was soon dashed when Godfrey had gone on to say Christine hadn't spoken to her mother for years and, as far as he was concerned, he had never even met her. And, then, over a year ago, all that changed when Godfrey mentioned Muriel Miller to him.

When James suggested they have a drink in The Ship & Shovell after work that day, Godfrey was quick to agree, which slightly surprised him, Godfrey being a stickler for routine and as it wasn't a Friday, their usual way of winding down at the end of the week, he thought it probably had something to do with his concern about their current hiccup with a decidedly shaky cash flow. Certainly Godfrey, normally a pretty stoic sort of person and not easily ruffled, had appeared pre-occupied for the last couple of days as though he had something on his mind, but James waited until they had bought their drinks and taken them over to one of the tables by the window overlooking Craven Passage, before saying anything to him.

'I can see by your expression, James,' he'd said, pre-empting him, 'you're wondering about my eagerness to drown my sorrows.'

'Not as bad as that, I hope.' he answered, not sure whether he was being serious or not. Sometimes he found it difficult to fathom out his partner's dry sense of humour. They really were like chalk and cheese, James thought, raising his glass and looking across at him wondering whether he was going to elaborate although knowing by this time Godfrey Mason was not easily given to taking anyone into his confidence.

'Perhaps not;' he said, 'that was an exaggeration, but I heard something last night which disturbed me and which has, quite honestly, placed me in a bit of a dilemma.'

'Yes?'

'Well,' he started to explain, taking another sip of his beer, 'as I mentioned to you earlier in the week, Christine has taken the girls up to Norfolk for a few days and I took it into my head to pay a visit to her mother last evening -'

'- but, why?'

'I had this ridiculous notion of asking her for a loan, to tide us over for the next couple of months, but I really should have known better.'

'She refused?'

'She most certainly did.' tight-lipped and making to pick up his glass again, 'She is one formidable woman, James.'

'So, what's the problem, then? You did your best and she refused, is that so important?'

'That's not what's worrying me. She proceeded to tell me why she and Christine had stopped communicating. Mind you, by the time she had finished, I wished she hadn't.'

'Why?'

'Because she told me some story about how, having obviously convinced herself Christine had somehow managed to extract money from her bank account. This was before Christine and I met and, reluctant though I was to talk to Catherine about her, she was insistent and I had to hear her out.'

'And you don't believe Christine did this?'

'No, I don't. And the more I think about it all, the more unlikely I believe it could be. I tried to stop the woman's flow, venom more like, by saying how much I disliked talking about Christine behind her back in that way when she wasn't in a position to defend herself.'

'And what did she have to say about that?'

'Not much, actually, but enough. She said Christine had always denied writing out those cheques and as there was no-one else, it had to have been her.'

'There must have been some-one else, then.'

'Oh, there was.'

'Who?'

'Muriel.'

'Muriel?'

'Sorry, I'm not making myself very clear, but I'm still pretty upset about the whole incident and dearly wish I hadn't gone there. Muriel,' he went on, 'is her step-daughter and, not to put too fine a point on it, James, she's not all that likeable, but it would seem over the last few years she has been keeping in regular contact with Catherine, spending weekends with her, in fact. I suppose, naturally enough, both Christine and Oliver came to the conclusion this was for one reason only.'

'I see; hoping Catherine would be generous to her in her will, I suppose.'

'That's exactly what they do think and they could be right. I can't say I like her all that much, I always thought she was a bit of a schemer. Muriel was the daughter of Catherine's first husband, Howard Miller, and from what I've been able to glean, which isn't a great deal, apart from having been thoroughly spoilt, Catherine has always made a point of favouring her, with the result Christine felt somewhat ostracised. So much so, in fact, she left home fairly early and didn't visit her mother very often, mainly I think, because Muriel was always there.

'And was Muriel there around the time of this business with the cheques?'

'She was, yes. And I wish now I had remembered that when I was talking to Catherine last night, but it didn't occur to me until I got home. Muriel was working for Barclays Bank in Regent Street, still is as far as I know, and at that time commuting to and from London. Mind you,' he shrugged, 'I don't expect it would have made any difference if I had mentioned this to Catherine; as far as she is concerned, Muriel is perfect. It would have been a total waste of effort to even try. No, James, she was adamant; Christine was the guilty one and I don't believe, now having met the woman, anything will shift that idea.'

'If Muriel had been at home, it wouldn't have been all that difficult to gain access to her cheque book, I suppose.'

'No, I don't suppose it would. I don't like to cast aspersions at anyone, but what I don't like is the unfairness of it all.'

'And naturally you haven't had time to say anything to Christine?'

'No, I haven't. She won't be back until the end of the week, but I can't tell her.'

'Why not; it would prove to her you were on her side.'

'I can't James, for the simple reason I would have to explain why I went to Catherine in the first place. She would be furious if she knew. Furious. It's just something I will have to live with, I guess. Anyway, James it's been a help being able to talk to you about it. Thanks.'

What James had heard had helped him also. The seed had been sown. And, if Godfrey was right in the thumb-nail description he had given him of Muriel Miller, this could be the very opening he needed.

It had been surprisingly easy to meet up with her and luck was certainly on his side from the moment he walked into the Regent Street branch of Barclays the following afternoon only minutes before they closed and the first consultant's desk with the name tag informing anyone who didn't already know that the woman seated there was Muriel Miller. His luck continued to hold. By exercising his charm which had never failed him before, James introduced himself, mentioning he was in partnership with Godfrey. She hadn't been all that impressed by this, but the speculating look in those grey-green eyes encouraged him to continue. Even he, with all his past experiences and conquests, was surprised when she actually agreed to have a drink with him when she finished work and from there on in, they were in business. It didn't take him long to realise they were two of a kind; both of them fuelled and stimulated by excitement and avarice. Their relationship, a purely platonic one, continued right up until the moment he heard about her murder a week ago. She had, over the last twelve months, systematically supplied him with selected pictures from Catherine's collection which he duly passed on to his contacts to be replaced by excellent copies, Muriel taking them back with her to Meadowbank.

And now, James thought as he waited for Inspector Ash to arrive, was this going to prove to be the moment of reckoning? Had the police, in what he had believed to be a foolproof system, found a fatal flaw? And, he sighed, if they had, what the hell was he going to do about it?

*

Brenda called a press conference for two o'clock at the insistence of

Bill Simms. Not unsurprisingly, Carol Cliff was present, including, Brenda noticed, several journalists from the other nationals, including locally the "Winchester Chronicle" and Meadowbank's "Courier". The sheer professional eagerness of the 'big boys' could have been intimidating, but she was well accustomed to what was likely to be a fierce confrontation with members of the press, all eager to hear something new. Well, she thought, taking a deep breath before addressing them, she certainly had that for them this time and bracing herself for the inevitable bombardment of questions, knowing in advance who would be the first.

'Ladies and Gentlemen,' she began, 'the purpose for calling the conference today is to inform you officially that the murders of Catherine Miller-Croft, Muriel Miller and Gary Nicholson have now been solved.'

'And the culprit, Chief Inspector?' Carol Cliff on cue stridently called out.

'If you will allow me to continue, Miss Cliff.' although realising the woman was totally impervious to the slightest degree of a reprimand, 'The perpetrator of these three crimes cannot be brought to task. We have conclusive proof they were carried out by a woman called Sonia Croft whom, as you are no doubt aware, died as a result of a car accident, her body having been found yesterday afternoon.'

For a fraction of a second there was a stunned silence in the room, for once, even Carol Cliff was speechless and Brenda looked round at them all, gauging their various reactions to what to them must have been totally unexpected.

'Chief Inspector,' the journalist from "The Daily Telegraph" was the first to raise his hand, followed immediately by the rest of them, 'did the deceased leave a suicide note?'

'She did, yes. This was in the form of a personal letter.' Brenda added, anticipating the barrage of questions which would follow, with Carol Cliff, judging by the heightened colour in her cheeks, appearing very much like the leader of the media 'pack'

'This letter, Chief Inspector,' she asked, not taking the time with the customary courtesy of raising her hand to await her turn, 'was it addressed to the husband?'

'Did she explain why she committed all three crimes?'

'Why did she choose Meadowbank?' this naturally enough from the "Courier's" journalist.

'Had Sonia Croft left her home in London, Chief Inspector?'

'Is there any truth in the rumour she was having an affair?'

'Had her meeting on Friday with her brother-in-law, Lawrence Croft, any bearing on her decision?'

'Alright,' Brenda interrupted the flow, 'first of all,' she began, 'we are not in a position to give you the name of the recipient of the letter; that will be the decision of the coroner at the inquest in due course and yes, she did give her reasons for the three murders, again this will, if considered appropriate, be mentioned at the inquest. And,' Brenda looked across at the young man from the "Winchester Chronicle", 'as far as any rumours are concerned, they cannot constitute as evidence in any enquiry and have therefore to be discarded. Finally,' deciding it was time to bring the conference to a close and, judging by the disgruntled expressions on their faces, knew from experience she would have to be firm, missing the support she had come to rely on from Ian, 'I would like to put you right on one point, Miss Cliff; it is our clear understanding that the meeting between Sonia Croft and her brother-in-law was purely one of chance, it had not been pre-arranged.'

'But you do agree, Chief Inspector,' Carol Cliff interjected rapidly, 'he is now using a different name.'

'Once again, Miss Cliff, I must correct you. He is not *using* a different name; he has changed his name legally which is quite in order and, in our opinion, has no relevance to this enquiry and therefore does not warrant any specific mention by the press.'

At last, Brenda was able to bring the meeting to an end, only too aware of the general air of disappointment as the journalists filed out of the room. She knew, apart from telling them about Sonia Croft's written confession, which no doubt they would elaborate on as far as they were able to, she had not answered most of their questions, but then how could she? Their part of the murder enquiry was complete; the remainder of any newsworthy pickings would have to be gleaned at the time of the enquiry and, as events had been occurring so rapidly over the last few days, she hadn't even been able to tell them when that would be. She needed now to concentrate on this latest development, namely, the theft of a substantial part of Catherine Miller-Croft's art collection; that's where Ian and her own energies had to be focused and only until it had been finally and conclusively resolved would she be able to wind up the whole business. Dealing with the press, as she had come to realise, was an element of policing which had to be endured and not one with which Brenda had ever felt comfortable. Each time and, fortunately over the years, there hadn't been all that many, she had felt ridiculously at a disadvantage; a bit like a cat and mouse game and it took no guesses who was the mouse! These switched-on men and women knew very well she had more information to hand out to them, also why she'd had to be so cautious. On the other hand, she also knew whatever morsel she passed on would be stretched and elaborated on to such a degree if she did read what appeared in their papers the following morning, would bear little true relationship to what she had actually conveyed to them.

It didn't do her somewhat jaundiced view any good to see, seconds before she reached her own office, the slight figure of Carol Cliff breaking away from the others and walking quickly towards her.

'Chief Inspector?'

'Yes, Miss Cliff.'

'I'll come straight to the point.' she said without the pretence of any preamble, but then that wasn't Carol Cliff's way and Brenda by this time had come not to expect anything else from her.

'Yes.' Brenda repeated.

'I didn't mention this at the press conference back there,' she began, 'because quite honestly, I didn't want the others to hear, but what is happening about the discrepancies of various contents in the house once belonging to Mrs Miller-Croft?'

'What exactly do you mean by discrepancies, Miss Cliff?'

'I happen to know that an inventory was made last week and it seems it doesn't tally with the last one.'

'I don't know where and how you gather your information,' Brenda said, 'but has it ever occurred to you that you could be totally off-beam?'

'In this case, Chief Inspector, I don't think I am. I'm a journalist, remember, and it is my job to find out as much as I possibly can to feed the readership of my paper. It's my understanding that a number of paintings from "The Gables" have been replaced by forgeries.'

She was lying, of course, Brenda thought, wondering and not for the first time, just how far these people were prepared to go to find their scoop, although it was always possible Carol Cliff had been, somehow through her own particular devious way, able to find out almost as much as they had so far.

'What basis do you have for making such a statement and, before you answer, I will remind you that you are talking to a member of the police force, Miss Cliff. I'll also remind you that if you have any information which could help us in our present investigation it is your public duty to inform us.'

'Gee! I know all that! So, it's true, then,' she continued, completely undaunted, 'forgeries have been made?'

'No comment, Miss Cliff.'

'Okay,' she shrugged, 'so you're not prepared to give my paper exclusivity?'

'We do not bargain, Miss Cliff, but what I will say is this; if you continue to suggest you have information which should be reported and decide to withhold, we will have no alternative but to formally question you.'

'Okay,' she repeated, 'I take your point. Last week, I happened to overhear a conversation between one of the valuers and the daughter of the new owner of "The Gables", when he told her about the paintings.'

'Where were you when you heard this?'

'Oh, in the grounds, one of the windows was open.'

'You were actually on the premises?'

'That's what I said, Chief Inspector.'

'You do realise that is private property?'

'Oh, sure, but then the gates were open, so being curious, I walked up the drive.'

'I see.' but not really seeing at all. Was there no end to this woman's confident impertinence? She had, apparently, been at "The Gables" at the same time as the valuers and had casually walked up the drive and conveniently found an open window from where she had heard what was said to Jessica Craig.

'Well, Miss Cliff, this is all very interesting, but I have nothing more to say to you. In fact, on the face of it, you were trespassing and it's always possible the owner could lodge an official complaint.'

'I guess that's always possible,' another shrug, 'but how could she; she didn't see me?'

'I don't know what you intend doing with this piece of information,' Brenda said, 'but if you go ahead and print something as insubstantial as what you've just told me, you would eventually have to admit how you came by it in the first place.'

'Chief Inspector,' she put in, 'I have spoken to the woman who cleaned for Mrs Miller-Croft and she has already confirmed that she saw Muriel Miller taking a number of paintings away from the house. Surely that would add credence to my article?'

'I'm sure it would, Miss Cliff, but I wouldn't advise it.' moving away. Enough had been said, Brenda thought, continuing along the corridor to her office; the woman was a menace but there was no way she was going to add any frills to what she had been able to find out.

The phone on her desk was ringing as she went in. Relieved to be back in the sanctuary of her office she picked up the receiver.

'Brenda; it's Mike.'

'Hello, Mike, it's good to hear your voice.'

'Having a harrowing day, or is that an unnecessary question?'

'Put it like this, I've had better. For instance,' trying to sound more cheerful than she felt, 'a press conference, followed by a one-to-one with

Miss Cliff.'

'Oh, dear. Anyway, Brenda,' he said, 'I've received some feedback for you about an off-shore bank account in Muriel Miller's name.'

'Yes?

'Predictably, our first guess paid off; she opened an account with a bank in Zurich on the first of June last year and since then there have been regular deposit transfers of fifteen thousand pounds, the last one being made on the fourteenth of October.'

'It fits in with those dates she'd written in the notebook. Any idea where they were from, Mike?' and holding her breath. This could be exactly what they wanted.

'Unfortunately, no, but given time we will, Brenda.'

'How many deposits were there altogether?'

'Six.'

'So,' making a rapid mental calculation, 'fifty per cent would be ninety thousand which tallies exactly with the final total she made.'

'Pretty conclusive evidence, wouldn't you say?'

'I would say so; thanks Mike. Hopefully this will go a long way to wrapping up the case.'

'He's going to find it difficult to wriggle out of that one.'

Chapter Thirteen

Ian's mobile rang as he approached the main entrance to the offices of Mason & Thornton.

'Ian,' Brenda's voice reached him without too much interference in spite of the noise from The Strand and then immediately exacerbated by a police siren, followed by an ambulance, as both vehicles weaved their way in and out of the traffic, 'have you spoken to James Thornton yet?'

'No, ma'am; I'm outside the building at this moment.'

'That's good. I have something which should give you considerably more to go on, but I'll warn you, it's not going to make your meeting as straightforward as we had previously thought.'

She proceeded to tell him in as few words which were necessary to get the salient points over of what she had learned from New Scotland Yard. As he finally switched off the mobile, he realised from what Brenda had said, she hadn't been exaggerating and hoped, as he mentally prepared himself for what could turn out to be one of the trickiest interviews of his career to-date, he would be able to handle the situation, regretting he hadn't had more time to prepare, even if only in outline, a revised strategy to the questions he'd planned earlier.

Mason & Thornton's offices were on the second floor and, to allow himself more time to think about the forthcoming meeting, he walked up the stairs rather than taking the lift, not that it made much difference as all too soon he was there.

'Mr Thornton is expecting you, Inspector;' the receptionist greeted him, 'his office is the last door on the right-hand side along the corridor.'

He had no pre-conceived idea of what James Thornton would be like, having had little experience of dealing with guys who worked in the centre of London and occupying prestigious office suites, but the man who stood up from behind an over-sized and paper-free desk was certainly not what he had been expecting; he didn't resemble any proto-type Ian had envisaged. Although wearing the traditional dark grey business suit, expensively tailored he was certain, there any resemblance to a typical city gent ended. Ian wasn't quite sure why this was, but perhaps, formerly shaking hands with him, it was the hair. No conventional short back and sides for him or even neatly cropped, but styled slightly longer than the average male he'd seen in London that day, also he'd had it highlighted and, in Ian's opinion, his whole appearance was verging on the effete, also more than a little off-putting, especially considering James Thornton was in the business of advising people how best to invest their money. Ian knew one thing; even if he was ever in the unlikely position to need financial advice, he wouldn't choose him.

'Inspector Ash,' James Thornton said, gesturing for him to take a seat, 'how can I help you? I was certain when Belinda told me you'd phoned asking to speak to me there must have been a mistake.'

'There was no mistake, sir.' deciding the best way of handling this meeting was to keep it as simple and straightforward as possible. In that way James Thornton may be more forthcoming.

'I hope there hasn't been, Inspector. I'm an extremely busy man with a heavy and demanding workload.'

'How well did you know the late-Muriel Miller?' Ian asked; following a more direct approach and watching the man's reaction closely, but there was no change in those slightly hooded pale eyes and, except for an infinitesimal lifting of one eyebrow, the bland expression on the plump features remained the same.

'Not frightfully well, actually.' and taking his time to answer.

'Were you friends, sir?'

'I suppose you could say so. I trust I'm not one of your suspects for her murder, Inspector.'

'I'm not here in respect to what happened to Miss Miller. That part of our investigation has now been resolved.'

'Oh, I see. Well, why are you here, then?'

'I'll come to that in a moment, sir,' Ian said, 'but first I would like to hear more of your friendship with Miss Miller.'

'There's not a great deal more to tell you. We met a year ago, but only saw each other a handful of times.'

'Did she ever mention her step-mother to you?'

'No, why would she have?'

'You had no idea she was related to the late-Mrs Miller-Croft?'

'Not until I read about it in the papers; last week sometime I believe it was.'

'You will also have learned in that case the extent of Mrs Miller-Croft's wealth; this was also mentioned by the press.'

'Yes, I read that and I must admit it came to me as a complete surprise. I had no idea.' he added.

'Over several months, sir,' Ian started to explain, 'there have been a number of thefts from Mrs Miller-Croft's home, including several paintings, which had later been returned to the property, the original canvases having been replaced by fakes. We have strong evidence to prove that Muriel Miller carried out these thefts, but it is our understanding she had an accomplice. In other words, she would not have had the necessary expertise to make the forgeries; this would have taken someone with that ability.'

'My God! And you think *I* was that person?' he emphasised, the colour heightening on his face, 'An outrageous assumption! Outrageous!'

'However, sir,' Ian went on, ignoring the outburst, 'initially, the thefts were reported by the new owner of Mrs Miller-Croft's property and while realising they were carried out by the deceased, namely Muriel Miller, it would normally be the owner's prerogative whether to continue to press charges, but due to the seriousness of the forgeries, this cannot be possible and the matter will now be transferred from the Meadowbank Constabulary to New Scotland Yard.'

'Of course I understand all of that,' he protested, 'but what has this got to do with me?'

'We believe it may have quite a lot to do with you, sir.'

'You don't say.' his voice heavy with sarcasm.

'On going through Miss Miller's personal papers,' Ian said, mentally distancing himself from such open belligerence, 'we found a notebook in which she had written your name, together with the telephone number of this office.' and pausing intentionally, not all that surprised at his immediate response.

'And, Inspector, why shouldn't she have made a note of my name and, if it comes to that, my telephone number? Surely you're not reading anything sinister into what should be considered perfectly normal.'

'I don't know about sinister,' Ian put in, keeping his tone of voice level, wanting to gauge as much as he could from how James Thornton would further react to what he had to say next, 'but Miss Miller had made an attempt to conceal the notebook, also the rest of the notes she had written down were in a code –'

' – code!' he didn't exactly splutter, but to Ian's sensitive hearing, it certainly closely resembled one.

'Yes,' he nodded, 'and fortunately for us, not too difficult to decipher.'

'Do go on, Inspector.'

'Details of the paintings which had been removed from Mrs Miller-Croft's property, and tying in with the listing we had from the valuers, had been jotted down, together with relevant dates of amounts of cash received. She had totalled these, deducting fifty-per cent. From this information, sir, it wasn't unreasonable to deduce the fifty-fifty split would have been shared between herself and her accomplice. Before you say anything further,' Ian warned him, sure that another verbal explosion was imminent, 'it has been officially confirmed that transfers equivalent to half the total figure were made to Miss Miller's overseas bank account.'

'I have heard quite enough! As I've just said what has all – all this *stuff* got to do with me? Alright, she'd written my name in this notebook of hers, but that's no proof of any involvement I may have had with such an amateur piece of subterfuge.'

'It's true we have no proof of your involvement, sir,' he told him, 'but the very fact your name had been mentioned is sufficient for us to treat this as part of our enquiry in attempting to discover who had assisted Miss Miller, but whether you were involved or not isn't the only factor here, sir.'

'What do you mean?'

'We are talking about large sums of money and the actual forgeries were, we understand, executed by experts, not dismissing the transport and distribution of the originals, meaning there must have been more than two people involved.'

'So, I can expect to hear from New Scotland Yard?'

'I would think that extremely likely; as will anyone who was associated with the deceased. Also,' Ian continued, 'the possibility of larger implications, not only concerning those forgeries we've been discussing, will have to be considered.'

Ian believed enough had been said; as he'd told James Thornton, the enquiry would now be passed over to New Scotland Yard for them to handle and not sorry to be leaving his office, although he couldn't help experiencing some disappointment in now not being in a position to proceed further in a case which had every appearance of turning out considerably more complex than either Brenda Masters and he had thought right from that first moment when the body of Muriel Miller had been identified by her cousin.

'Excuse me, Inspector,' the receptionist called out to him as he was crossing the main office towards the door, 'but Mr Mason would like a quick word with you, if you wouldn't mind.'

For the second time he walked back up the corridor, stopping as she had told him at the first door with a small gilt plaque bearing Godfrey Mason's name.

'I'm sorry to take up your time, Inspector Ash, but when Belinda told me you were in the office I thought it would be a good chance to speak to you.'

Godfrey Mason was totally different from his partner; a tall thin frame, glasses and light brown hair, greying at the temples and cut ultra-short. There was nothing in the least flamboyant about him, Ian thought, wondering how such two different types could possibly work amicably together.

'That's alright, sir.'

'Sit down, won't you? Would you like some coffee?' pointing to a coffee pot on the top of the bookcase. 'I drink a lot of it,' he added, 'too much, according to my wife.'

For once, Ian accepted a cup and waited for him to explain. A reversal of roles he thought, taking a sip of the coffee which was good; usually it was the police who wanted to see members of the public, not the other way round.

'It's about my brother-in-law, Oliver Croft, Inspector. My wife and I are a bit worried about him. We've been trying to get in touch with him since last night, but he's not answering his mobile and he doesn't appear to be at home. Of course, we fully appreciate how devastated he must be about his wife and as I already knew you and the Chief Inspector were handling the case I thought you might know where he is.'

'He's very likely still in Meadowbank, sir. He arrived yesterday afternoon and you're right, he was distraught. There will be a number of formalities for him to attend to while he's there and as to why he's not answering his mobile, perhaps he doesn't feel up to taking any calls.'

'I suppose so.'

'I'll phone Meadowbank for you now, if you like, and see if anyone at the Station has seen him today.'

'I'd be grateful if you would, Inspector. It never occurred to me that he would be there. It's been such a shock; these last few days have been something of a nightmare for all of us.'

The desk sergeant was able to quickly confirm that Oliver Croft had been into the Station around midday and was planning to return to London later in the afternoon. Reassured, Godfrey thanked him and, surprisingly didn't show any curiosity of why he should have made an appointment to see his partner. Either he wasn't the inquisitive type or at the moment his mind was too preoccupied with what had been happening in the family.

The receptionist was on the phone as he passed her desk and he heard quite clearly everything she was saying, the words following him as he reached the door: 'I've made the reservation for five twenty-five tomorrow, James .... yes, that's right, it's the first Eurostar in the morning .... yes, you have to check in at least an hour before departure ....

*

Events moved rapidly. Officers from New Scotland Yard were waiting at St Pancras Station the following morning and intercepted James Thornton as he checked in for the five twenty-five Eurostar to Paris Nord and immediately took him into custody for formal questioning. Further evidence against him had come in some hours before; the most significant being the fact that he held an account in the same Zurich bank as Muriel Miller and, apart from an extremely healthy balance, deposits of thirty thousand pounds, followed by transfers of half that amount being made since June last year, all of which neatly matched those deposits in Muriel Miller's account. Also, a background search revealed that prior to going into partnership with Godfrey Mason, he had worked with Peterson's, the restorers and valuers in Baker Street and an interview with the managing director revealed that, although they never had any actual proof, only suspicions, the Board were much relieved when he finally left the firm.

'So, Ian,' Brenda said, after Mike had phoned through to give her the outcome, 'that's that.'

'A bit of an anti-climax.' Ian remarked.

'Yes, it always is in a situation like this when you have to hand over an incomplete case. Fortunately, it doesn't happen all that often, but I know what you mean alright.'

'You did say someone would slip up, didn't you ma'am?'

'I know,' she smiled, 'they very often do and James Thornton was no exception. If, instead of asking the receptionist to make that reservation he had made it himself, he might have made it to Paris and, presumably by now be on his way to Switzerland.'

'That's true.'

'Incidentally, Ian,' she said, 'I've requested a transfer; to London.' she added.

'Really? We'll all miss you at the Station, ma'am.'

'Thank you, Ian. It wasn't an easy decision to make, but I believe it's time I made a change.'

*

Meanwhile, that evening in The Market Inn, Stanley Coleman had become something of a celebrity, on the strength of which he consumed more than his usual quota of The Market Inn's Best Bitter and had to be escorted home to face a far from pleased Mavis who, by this time, regretted ever telling him anything about what had been going on at "The Gables".

'My goodness, Brian,' Melissa said, after the last of their customers had reluctantly gone, 'what a business. And to think that Miss Miller actually stole from her step-mother. That's really terrible.'

'I know, love,' he agreed, 'some people are never content, are they? With all their money they're still not satisfied.'

'What do you think will happen now with "The Gables"?'

'Well,' he grinned, 'according to the oracle, and his 'prophecies' have been spot-on recently, the property is on the market.'

'Just as well,' she nodded, 'I don't think Mrs Craig and her daughter would have been all that happy living up there. I wonder if they'll stay in Meadowbank.'

'I hope so,' he answered, 'and now all this business is cleared up and everything gets back to some semblance of normality, perhaps they'll be able to settle down in this old town of ours.'

Other titles by Margaret Alty:

Tangled Web – ISBN: 978 1 84549 422 3

Jenny – ISBN: 978 1 84549 442 1

Camouflage – ISBN: 978 1 84549 478 0

The Last Orange – ISBN: 978 1 84549 560 2

A Meadowbank Mystery

Murder in Meadowbank –ISBN: 978 1 84549 494 7

Double Act –ISBN: 978 1 84549 537 4

Murder After Hours –ISBN: 978 1 84549 579 4

All published by arima Publishing.

www.ingramcontent.com/pod-product-compliance
Lightning Source LLC
Chambersburg PA
CBHW051634260626

47170CB00004B/1179